THE *Best Medicine*

THE *Best* *Medicine*

ANNE MARIE RODGERS

Guideposts

New York, New York

www.guideposts.com
(800) 932-2145
Guideposts Books & Inspirational Media

Cover design and illustration by Lookout Design, Inc.
Interior design by Lorie Pagnozzi
Typeset by Aptara

Printed and bound in the United States of America
10 9 8 7 6 5 4 3 2 1

In loving memory of Lynn Rishell Henthorn.
You were a Spirit-filled beacon of light during your brief life.
How brilliantly you must shine now!

My flesh and my heart may fail,
but God is the strength of my heart
and my portion forever.

~ Psalm 73:26 (NIV)

The Best Medicine by Anne Marie Rodgers

Acknowledgments

With deepest thanks to Jacqueline Y. Duffey, RN, BSN, for her assistance with information regarding hospital practices and for saving me from being clueless about the nursing profession.

Chapter One

"AND FINISH WITH A DEEP, CLEANSING BREATH."
Candace Crenshaw demonstrated, inhaling deeply
and then slowly releasing her breath as thirty faces
watched her with intense concentration. "It's important to remember to fill your lungs at the beginning and end of each
contraction. This will provide both you and your baby with additional oxygen."

As a registered nurse who worked in the Birthing Unit at
Hope Haven Hospital, Candace taught a Labor and Delivery
class every week. The first meeting of her latest session was being
held on a Thursday evening in the hospital's conference room.
Tables had been pushed to the sides of the room to accommodate fifteen pregnant women and their labor coaches.

Candace continued. "I'm going to send around a handout
reviewing the first two breathing patterns. Please take some time
to practice them for a few minutes each day in the upcoming
week. Now, ladies, we are going to take a five-minute break.

Afterward, I'd like you to unroll your mats and sit down. Labor coaches, you'll be moving behind them."

Immediately, there was a low buzz of conversation. Several women made a beeline for the door, no doubt heading for the restroom. Candace smiled as she stepped away from the podium where her notes lay. She picked up the attendance roster and began moving around the room trying to match names with faces. She would be seeing many of these ladies over the next few months when they delivered their babies, and she liked to be able to greet them by name when the time came and they arrived in the Birthing Unit.

"Hello, Candace! Do you remember me?"

Candace looked up from the roster. A small woman with short dark hair stood before her. She looked familiar. Candace did a mental scan, trying to place a name with the face. "Robin King! Is that you?" Candace moved toward the woman with her arms out, and the two women exchanged a warm hug. Then Candace pulled back to look at Robin more closely. "You're all grown up. How are you?"

"I'm great," the young woman said, beaming. "It's Robin Overing now, though. This is my husband, Andrew. Honey, this is Candace Fuller—ah, Candace Crenshaw. She was my babysitter way back when."

"We lived in the same neighborhood," Candace told Andrew as she shook his hand. He was a pleasant-looking man who appeared to be in his midtwenties. "It's nice to meet you."

"My pleasure," Andrew said. "I imagine I'll mean that even more sincerely when Robin goes into labor, and we'll need your help to get this baby born."

They all laughed.

"Your hair is shorter," Robin said, studying Candace. "I remember you always had it in a ponytail, and I bugged my mother incessantly to let me grow mine long like yours." She turned to Andrew. "Candace was my idol. I loved it when she came to babysit."

Candace chuckled, lifting a hand to touch the wavy brown hair that brushed her jaw. *Hard to believe it was once so long.* "How many years has it been since we last saw each other?"

"At least ten. I was in high school when you came back to town with your husband. You were pregnant."

"Brooke is eleven now," Candace said.

Robin was still smiling. "It's so wonderful to reconnect! How's your mom? Where is she living now? I've tried to talk my folks into moving into something smaller and easier to take care of, but so far, they refuse to consider it."

"My mother lives with us now," Candace told her. She cleared her throat. "I don't know if you heard, but my husband passed away very unexpectedly. Mom has been my rock since his death."

"My mom told me." Robin put a hand on Candace's arm, her eyes welling with tears. "I was so sorry to hear about his passing. I can't imagine how you kept on going."

Candace forced a smile, refusing to let the lump in her throat prevent her from speaking. "It wasn't—still isn't—easy," she admitted, swallowing. "But I have the children, and they need me."

There was a moment of awkward silence. Candace filled it by asking, "When are you due?"

"August twenty-ninth," Robin told her. "We can't wait. Neither can my parents. This is their first grandchild." Her smile dimmed for a moment, and her eyes had a faraway look. But then she blinked and grinned.

"Oh, I bet your mother is over the moon," Candace said, wondering whether she had just imagined Robin's fleeting expression. "Please tell your folks I said hello." Glancing at her watch, she said, "I'd better mingle a bit more before our break ends. It's so great to see you again, Robin; and it was lovely meeting you, Andrew."

The young man nodded. "Likewise," he said with a smile.

The following afternoon, Candace finished work promptly at three. As she walked to her car, she realized she was smiling.

The sun was shining, and it had been a good day. She was even getting off work on time—and wasn't that a minor miracle? She had assisted with the birth of twins only a short while ago, but the labor had gone unbelievably well. The mother hadn't even needed a cesarean section. The babies were healthy and both parents were ecstatic. Candace herself was brimming with a rare sense of euphoria. So many multiple births were fraught with problems that it was a good day when one went really well.

Humming a folk rock tune by her favorite contemporary Christian band, Candace started her car and drove south to Rishell Elementary School where her eleven-year-old daughter, Brooke, was a fifth-grader. She'd barely had time to park when she heard the last bell ring. Moments later, Brooke came walking toward the car.

The child's shoulders were slumped, and her head was down. Candace's heart sank. It had been such a good day, but it didn't look as though Brooke could say the same.

"Hi, honey," Candace called through the open passenger window. "How was school today?"

Brooke looked up. There were tears streaming down her face, and she began to run. *She's such a little thing*, Candace thought, her heart aching as she watched her unhappy child approach. Like Candace had been while growing up, Brooke was small for her age. But Candace didn't think she had ever been as thin as Brooke.

Brooke opened the car door and plopped down into the passenger seat, then flung herself into her mother's open arms.

"What's wrong, sweetheart?" Candace asked.

Brooke just shook her head, her face buried against her mother. Elementary school kids could be cruel, and the last thing Brooke needed was to be teased. "Bad day, honey?"

Brooke nodded. Her head was bowed and her long, blonde curls hid her face. But Candace knew her daughter was still crying as tears fell to her denim skirt.

Candace waited a moment, but Brooke didn't speak. A rush of fear shot through Candace. *Calm down*, she thought. *Just because she isn't talking right now doesn't mean she'll again revert to not talking at all.* But it was difficult to ignore. After Dean's death, Brooke hadn't spoken for two months, despite counseling and all the patience and attention Candace had been able to muster during those awful days. Still Candace got a jittery feeling in the pit of her stomach when there was even a hint that Brooke might be headed back to one of those episodes.

"I'm sorry you're unhappy," she told her daughter. Brooke would speak when she was ready, Candace reassured herself. "If there's anything I can do, I'll be happy to help."

"C-Carla's cat d-died," Brooke stuttered. She began to sob. "His name was Mr. Whiskers. I used to pet him when I slept over."

"Carla's kitty died? What happened?" Though Candace was relieved to hear her daughter speak, she hid her dismay. Brooke couldn't even watch nature programs where predators hunted smaller game. Since her father's passing, death was a very difficult topic for her.

"He was seventeen years old, and he didn't wake up this morning," Brooke told her. "Carla didn't come to school until after lunch, but she told me about him after school."

Candace took one hand off the steering wheel and gently patted her daughter's knee. "It's hard to lose a pet, especially when you've had one as long as Carla had Mr. Whiskers. Seventeen is pretty old for a kitty."

"That's what she said." Brooke swiped tears off her cheek. "Mom, why do you think God let Daddy die before he was old? Why did He let Mr. Whiskers live so long?"

Oh boy. Candace wished she could ask Brooke's counselor for advice. "I don't know if that's how we should think of it," she told her daughter, shoving the fact that she'd had similar thoughts to the back of her mind. "Bad things happen in life sometimes. God helps us get through those times."

Brooke was silent, and Candace wondered what her daughter was thinking. But she forced herself not to pepper her child with questions. *Don't push it,* she reminded herself, thinking of what Brooke's counselor had said. "Would you like to send Carla a card?" she asked.

Slowly, Brooke nodded. "When we get home, will you help me make one?"

"Of course."

"Can we use your special stamps and embossing powder and watercolors?"

Candace smiled, as she registered the returning normalcy in Brooke's cajoling tone. "We'll pull out all the stops. I think I might even have a stamp that says With Sympathy."

"You also have three kitty stamps," Brooke reminded her.

"It'll be the prettiest card Carla has ever seen." She glanced over and winked at her daughter.

With a final sniff and swipe of her nose, Brooke sat back in her seat and smiled.

The weekend passed uneventfully as Brooke was preoccupied with making the card. On Monday, Candace went to the staff lounge and got her packed lunch from her locker. She then walked to her mailbox and pulled out several in-house notices and one sealed envelope with the hospital's return address and logo in the corner. *It's not payday*, she thought, wondering what the letter could be. As she opened the envelope, she noticed that there appeared to be one in every staff mail cubby.

She withdrew the letter as she walked toward the lounge door. Moments later, however, she sank into a chair and reread the short statement with a feeling of shock.

As you know, Hope Haven Hospital has been facing ongoing serious financial difficulties for several years. Unfortunately, this budget crisis has significantly worsened during the recent economic downturn. Pending an unforeseen source of funds, the board of directors has reluctantly agreed upon a plan to close the hospital by the end of the year. . . ."

She read the letter for a third time, trying to absorb the words. Her chest grew tight. What would she do? What would the community do?

A nurse came into the lounge then, and Candace rose, quickly stuffing the letter into its envelope. She couldn't stand to see other people's faces as they received the bad news. She left the lounge and headed downstairs to the first floor, retreating to the small courtyard outside the chapel for her lunch break.

As she barged through the door, she halted, squinting against the bright noonday light. The north-central Illinois weather was sunny and mild in May. A brilliantly plumaged cardinal warbled a musical solo in the scrawny paperbark maple tree that shaded the weather-beaten picnic tables.

The front lawn and entrance to Hope Haven Hospital were beautifully landscaped with perennials and flowering shrubs, but it appeared that little thought had been given to the cramped picnic area where members of the staff ate lunch on pleasant days like this one. Loose gray stone covered the ground beneath the three picnic tables and single wooden bench, while a waist-high privet hedge divided the space from the adjacent visitor parking lot.

The sky was a beautiful blue, and the warmth of the sun, a pleasant bonus. Unfortunately, it couldn't melt the icy dread that had formed in Candace's stomach.

Just then, the door opened, and a tall, slim woman wearing blue scrubs stepped outside. "Hello," she said. She attempted to smile, but it faded before it had fully formed. "Did you get this yet?" she asked, holding up her copy of the letter.

Candace nodded. "Just now."

"This is just terrible." The woman looked vaguely familiar, although Candace didn't know her name.

A light breeze stirred tendrils of Candace's brown, chin-length bob; and she reached up to tuck a strand behind her ear. She wasn't exactly in the mood for company, but good manners won out. "I'm Candace Crenshaw. Would you like to join me?"

"Thank you. I'm Elena Rodriguez from Intensive Care." Elena looked about a decade older than Candace's thirty-seven years. Although she currently had a grim expression, there were laugh lines at the corners of her eyes. Her thick dark hair was pulled back with a sturdy clip, and there didn't appear to be a hint of silver in it. "You're in the Birthing Unit, right?"

Candace managed a weak smile and nodded.

Elena glanced down at the letter again. "I can't believe the hospital might close. I've been here for sixteen years, and I thought I'd work here until I retired."

"I know what you mean. I've been here for ten."

Just then, the door opened again and a tall man with dark hair touched with gray, also wearing scrubs, surveyed the courtyard. He smiled pleasantly at the two women and nodded, though his smile quickly faded as his thoughts seemed to return to the letter he clutched in his hand. Elena said, "Hello, James. Would you like to join us?"

"Thanks, Elena." James settled himself at their picnic table.

"Candace Crenshaw, this is James Bell."

As Candace reached over to offer her hand to James, she asked, "I've seen you around the hospital before, but I'm afraid I'm not very observant. What department are you in?"

"I'm a nurse in General Surgery," James told her. "Been there for almost twenty years now."

Just then, the door flew open with enough force to send it banging against the wall. A slender, older nurse started outside, letter in hand. She stopped short when she saw the three already seated in the courtyard.

"Hello, Anabelle," Elena said. "Come, join us."

The other woman shook her head. "I'm sorry," she said with a distressed expression. "I didn't mean to bother you."

"It's all right," Elena assured her. "Do you know Candace and James?"

James waved Anabelle over. "Anabelle and I go to the same church. We've known each other for years."

Anabelle managed a smile. "It's true," she said. "But I refuse to say *exactly* how many years."

Everyone chuckled, though the laughter died quickly.

Candace extended a hand. "I'm Candace Crenshaw from the Birthing Unit."

"Anabelle Scott," the older woman said. "From Cardiac Care."

"Please join us," Candace said, patting the bench beside her.

Anabelle shook her head again. "My lunch break is just about over. I need to get back. But when I went to the staff lounge to pick up my mail, I found *this*," she said, shaking the letter. "It made me so upset that I had to come out here and calm myself down before I went back to work."

"I felt the same way," Candace told her.

James added, "This means local people would have to travel greater distances, especially for emergency care."

Anabelle paced back and forth over the gravel. "This is terrible. This would affect the entire community."

"Does the community even *know* that its hospital might close?" Elena exclaimed.

"They will after today," James pointed out. "There's no way this could be kept quiet, especially if several hundred people are suddenly looking for jobs in health care."

Candace felt as if someone had punched her in the stomach. Judging from the look on James's face, he felt much the same. She imagined he was the primary financial support for his family, just as she was. "There has to be something that can be done," Candace said.

"I imagine the board is desperately trying to find an answer." James rubbed the back of his neck. "But if they're sending this letter to all employees, that tells me they're at the end of their rope."

"This feels like a bad dream." Candace could feel the beginning of a headache forming, and she pressed her fingers to her temples.

"Unfortunately," Elena said, sighing, "we're not dreaming."

Chapter Two

WHEN HER LUNCH BREAK ENDED, CANDACE WALKED to the large elevator on the first floor, rode it to the third floor, and headed for the staff lounge to stash her lunch sack in her locker. As she walked out the door, she received a page to return to the Birthing Unit.

What could be wrong? There hadn't been any ladies close to delivery an hour ago. Maybe she had received a new admission.

Quickly, she took the stairs to the second floor. Cardiac Care, Peds, Oncology and Intensive Care were also located on the second floor, and a large central nurses' station stood at the intersection where the two hallways of the cross-shaped building converged.

She saw Marge Matthews on the computer at the nurses' station. Marge—a full-figured woman with curly brown hair in which several strands of silver glinted—was the day shift nurse supervisor of the Cardiac Care Unit.

"Hi, Marge," Candace said. "I got a page from the nurses' station. Do you know what it's about?"

Marge glanced up. "Riley paged you," she said. Riley Hohmann was the supervisor of the Birthing Unit during the day. "I think you have a visitor. I got the impression it was personal."

Candace hurried down the hallway looking for her supervisor. Riley was in a private birthing suite massaging the back of a woman in labor. When Candace opened the door, Riley said, "Oh, good. There's a lady here to see you. She's waiting in the lounge."

"Who is it?" Candace asked.

Riley shook her head. "Sorry, I can't remember her name. She said she's in one of your prenatal classes."

"Thanks." Candace closed the door and doubled back toward the nurses' station and second floor visitors' lounge. Who could be asking for her? Had one of her moms-to-be gone into labor early? Surely not, or Riley would have known about it.

In the lounge, Candace instantly recognized the small, dark-haired woman and the taller man with reddish chestnut hair, his right arm protectively draped around her. The Overings looked scared to death.

"Robin! Andrew! Hello. What brings you in today?" Candace saw that Robin's eyes were swollen and red. "What's wrong?" she asked.

"Oh, Candace," Robin said. "I received terrible news this morning." She stopped, shaking her head as tears rolled down her cheeks. Her husband gripped her tighter, his expression bleak.

"What's the matter?" Candace's heart clenched as she antici-pated the worst news any pregnant woman could receive. Had something happened to Robin's baby?

"At my appointment this morning, I asked the doctor to check my left breast because I thought I had felt a lump in the shower. He said it probably was an enlarged milk duct, but just to be safe, he scheduled some tests. I'm so afraid it might be cancer."

Candace was deeply concerned, though she did her best to hide it from the young couple. She embraced the pregnant woman and squeezed the hand of her anxious husband. "Let's not borrow trouble," she said. "What tests are they conducting, and when are you scheduled to have them?"

"She already had blood drawn and a mammogram done," Andrew said. "Next she has an ultrasound at three o'clock today, and a fine-needle biopsy right after."

Candace didn't hesitate. "Would you like me to come with you? I get off at three, and I could meet you in Diagnostic Imaging if you like. That's where both procedures will be performed."

Robin's eyes widened and she appeared to sag with relief. "Really? You'd do that? I'd feel so much better if there was a familiar face beside me. The needle biopsy sounds scary."

"It won't be so bad," Candace promised her. "I'll come up-stairs and find you as soon as I can, all right?"

"Thank you," she whispered.

Candace called her mother after leaving the lounge.

"Hello?" Mom sounded breathless when she answered the phone, and Candace remembered she sometimes did aerobics with a DVD in the afternoon.

"Hi, Mom."

"Hi, honey. What's up?"

"I won't be leaving on time today." Candace explained that she wanted to accompany one of her patients for some testing. "Do you mind picking up the kids?" As she normally did, Candace had intended to pick Brooke up from school herself. Candace felt strongly that it was important to not take her mother's presence for granted. And it gave her special time with her daughter as she heard the details of Brooke's day. *The good details and bad*, she thought, recalling the Mr. Whiskers incident from Friday.

Candace's mother Janet Fuller had retired and moved in to help after Dean's unexpected death, and Candace was more grateful than she could ever express. Consequently, she tried to ensure that her mother wasn't always imposed upon. Howie attended preschool a few hours a week and would be starting kindergarten in the fall; but until then, Mom watched him every day Candace worked. She swore she didn't mind, and Candace believed she was sincere; but she was still leery of letting her mother take on too much.

"Of course I don't mind," her mother said. "Do you think you'll be home for dinner?"

"I hope so. I don't expect this will take long."

"All right. We'll see you then. Love you."

"Love you too, Mom. Thanks." *Thank You, Lord*, Candace prayed, *for my mother. What a blessing she is to me in so many ways.*

The afternoon passed quickly. There were two women in labor in rooms across the hall from one another, and a planned cesarean section was on the schedule. Candace had been assigned to one of the laboring mothers that morning, and everyone was delighted when the labor progressed quickly. The baby was born healthy and alert, shortly after one o'clock.

Upon finishing her shift at three, Candace headed for the third floor. She took a moment to wash and change into fresh scrubs before crossing the hall to the Radiology and Diagnostic Imaging suite. Andrew was seated in the small waiting area. He leapt to his feet the moment he saw Candace, his hair sticking out in all directions as if he'd run his hands through it repeatedly.

"Thanks for coming," Andrew said, shaking her hand with such fervent gratitude that she feared for her bones. "Robin will feel so much better with you by her side."

"You're welcome," she said. "Do you know where she is?"

He shook his head. "They took her back. All they said was that they would do the biopsy immediately after the ultrasound."

Candace nodded. "How about if I go see how she's doing and let you know? Then I'll stay with her."

The young man's eyes looked moist. "You're an angel," he said in a choked voice. "I can't thank you enough."

Candace smiled. "It's what I'd like someone to do for me in the same situation. I'll be back in a few minutes."

She left Andrew in the waiting area and walked to Radiology where a staff member directed Candace to Robin's room. She opened the door and peeked in.

"Candace!" Robin exclaimed. "I'm so glad to see you!"

Candace patted her hand. "I was happy that my shift ended on time. What's happened here so far?"

"The ultrasound is over, but the technician couldn't tell me anything about what she saw." Robin made a wry face. "I'm waiting for a doctor to review the results, and then they'll take me for the biopsy."

Candace nodded. "Let me bring Andrew up to speed. I'll be right back."

It took her only a moment to update Andrew. When she returned, she was directed to another room where the radiologist would discuss the results of the ultrasound, mammogram, and blood work. When the doctor entered, he shook hands with them. "I am Dr. Hashimi," he said in lightly accented English.

Although she knew of him, Candace had never been introduced to Dr. Omar Hashimi, a slim, handsome man with striking dark eyes and a warm smile. She introduced herself, and he nodded when she explained who she was and why she was with Robin. "This is a very good thing," he told her. Then he turned to Robin. His dark eyes were sober. "I am very sorry to give you bad news. The lump you felt has distinct characteristics of malignancy."

Robin drew in a sharp breath as Candace put her arm around the young woman.

"I suspect the results of the biopsy will confirm this," the radiologist continued. "The fact that you caught it early gives us every reason to expect a positive outcome."

Candace felt Robin's shoulders shake as her friend began to cry, and she tightened her grip. Her own throat felt as if she had swallowed a rock, but she nudged Robin and said, "Did you hear what he said? If this is malignant, there's every reason to believe you'll beat it."

Dr. Hashimi went on to explain what was involved in performing a biopsy. "I will call you personally with the results," he told her. "If it is malignant, we will help you schedule an appointment with the oncologist to develop a treatment plan." He gently answered a few other questions and then shook hands with them again before leaving the room.

Robin immediately turned to Candace, tears streaming down her face. "What am I going to do?" she cried. "Will Andrew have to raise our baby alone?" Her sobs grew even more wrenching.

Candace put her arms around her young friend. She suddenly remembered hugging and comforting Robin in very much the same way after she'd fallen off her bike and skinned her knee. If only this were as easy to fix. She rubbed Robin's back and then pulled back to look at her. "Breast cancer is very curable these days, especially in the early stages. And you heard what Dr. Hashimi said—he has every reason to believe it will be gone soon."

"But what will they do?"

"I imagine the first thing to do is schedule the surgery to remove the lump, and then maybe there will be other treatment to follow."

"I can't have surgery or chemo now! It would do terrible things to the baby, wouldn't it?"

"*Shh-shh-shh*," Candace said. She fully embraced Robin, her heart aching as the pregnant woman began to sob again. "The doctors would never do anything that might harm your baby." She took Robin's shoulders in her hands, pulling back to look deep into her eyes. "This hospital is called *Hope* Haven for a good reason," Candace said with a small smile.

"It's hard to feel positive," Robin mumbled, leaning her head against Candace's shoulder.

"I know." Candace took the younger woman's hands in hers. "Are you ready to go out and tell Andrew what you've learned?"

Robin's lip quivered. "Will you explain it to him?"

"Of course." She rose and put an arm around Robin's shoulders as they left the room and made their way back to the waiting area.

Anabelle Scott had certainly had better days. She'd worked at Hope Haven for over thirty years, but this was the first time she had ever worried about losing her job. And on top of that, she was filled with worry for her daughter Kirstie, who was finishing moving into her own apartment this evening.

Her spirits were low as she pushed through the heavy side door near the first-floor elevators that opened to the physician and staff parking lots. Her brand-new, silver Ford Fusion was parked at the far end of the lot. As she walked briskly toward the car, Anabelle reflected bleakly that her timing couldn't have been worse: just six weeks ago, she had traded in her trusty ten-year-old Ford Escort, which had been paid off. While she had bought the new car—a dealer's demo model with a few thousand miles on it—at a reduced price, it still meant an extra monthly payment she wouldn't have taken on if she'd known she might lose her job.

"Hey, Anabelle, wait up."

She turned around to see Nellie Harvey, her oldest friend at Hope Haven, whom she'd met at orientation. Nellie stopped at Anabelle's side. "So what did you think of the letter?" she asked in a rush.

Nellie was a registered dietician and head of the hospital's dietary staff, a position of importance belied by her fluttery mannerisms and trilling voice. Today, strands of her fine, wispy hair had slipped free of the knot pinned at the back of her head and blew about in the light breeze. With blonde highlights covering the liberal streaks of silver, Nellie looked younger than her fifty-six years. Her wide gray eyes normally sparkled with good humor, but today they imparted serious concern.

"I was pretty shaken up," Anabelle admitted with a sigh. "I've heard so many stories about Hope Haven's grim financial picture that I'd become immune to them. *Boy Who Cried Wolf* and all that."

Nellie nodded. "Same here. I can't believe there's a chance the hospital might close."

Anabelle's shoulders sagged as she exhaled. "I think there's way more than a chance, Nell. It takes a staggering amount of money to keep even a small hospital like this running."

"Excuse me." A young woman with brilliant red hair stopped them, her blue eyes intense. "I'm Valera Kincaid with the *Deerford Dispatch*. I've heard the hospital may be closing. Do you know anything about that?"

Anabelle and Nellie exchanged worried glances. "What have you heard?" Nellie asked the reporter.

Flipping back through her small notebook, the young woman paused. "Rumor has it that the hospital is going to be sold to Prairie Health Corporation. Prairie Health is a large organization that takes over small failing hospitals."

"We're familiar with Prairie Health," Anabelle said, knowing her tone wasn't complimentary. "The company has a reputation for streamlining, for sending a lot of services to their main hospital in Peoria."

"But," the reporter continued, "I haven't been able to verify the hospital will be sold. Is there anything you can tell me?"

Nellie looked at Anabelle and said, "This isn't going to be a secret for long, and I think the community needs to know what's going on."

Nellie had a point, Anabelle had to concede. With a sigh, she told the reporter, "Every employee received a letter about it today."

The reporter's eyes widened. "May I read it? Maybe jot down a few notes?"

"Here," Nellie said, handing the woman the envelope she'd slipped into the side pocket of her handbag.

The reporter scanned the contents, then handed it back to Anabelle and scribbled furiously for a moment. "How are the employees feeling about this? Are you worried about your jobs?"

"We're, of course, very worried about personal issues like our incomes and finding new jobs," Anabelle told Valera, "but we're most concerned that there won't be a significant local medical facility in Deerford. The people of this town need their own hospital."

"Perhaps they're preparing us for the worst so that another option might not seem so horrible," Nellie theorized.

Valera was taking notes as fast as she could. "Thank you, this is great information," she enthused. "May I use your names?"

Anabelle and Nellie looked at each other again. "I don't see why not," Anabelle said. *In for a penny, in for a pound,* she thought.

Everything we said is nothing less than the truth. The two women shared their names and occupations at the reporter's prompting. Then Anabelle gestured over Valera's shoulder. "Here come some more folks if you want to get more reactions."

The young woman wheeled around. "Thanks," she said as she dashed off. "Be sure to check the paper tomorrow!"

Chapter Three

*J*AMES BELL SQUARED HIS SHOULDERS BEFORE HE opened the kitchen door and walked into his home after work. There was little he dreaded more than being the bearer of bad news. Fern, his wife of twenty years, had been diagnosed with multiple sclerosis seven years ago; and stress invariably caused her symptoms to flare up.

James recalled the day Dr. Andrews in Chicago had broken the news. The physician had been the latest in a long line of doctors they had seen in an effort to find out exactly what was wrong with Fern. She didn't have lupus. She didn't have Lyme disease. She didn't have a B_{12} deficiency . . . but no one was sure exactly what she did have. Her symptoms included extreme fatigue, impaired coordination and vision trouble, but only sometimes. Other times, many of her symptoms seemed to disappear.

Finally, they had been referred to a highly regarded specialist in Chicago. After Dr. Andrews had reviewed earlier test results and put Fern through yet another round, James had been prepared for the same thing they'd heard several times before: "Your wife *doesn't* have . . ."

Instead, the doctor had sighed, came around the end of his desk and placed a chair in front of Fern. "You have multiple sclerosis, Mrs. Bell." He'd gone on to discuss the specifics, pointing out newly formed lesions from her most recent MRI, the definitive clue to the elusive diagnosis.

Seven years later, they were still learning new things about the disease. But one thing James knew for sure was that the prospect of losing his job was *not* going to be helpful in keeping Fern's illness in check.

Fern sat in a rocking chair near the hearth in their cozy kitchen, her Maine coon cat, Sapphire, in her lap. They made quite a picture. His tiny wife wore a dark blue dress which accentuated the cat's striking silvery fur.

Fern's pretty brown eyes lit up when she saw him and she smiled; Sapphire lifted her head and meowed once, then laid her head back down and closed her eyes as if the effort had exhausted her.

Gideon, his elder son, sat at the claw-footed oak table with his laptop in front of him. Sometimes, James felt looking at Gid was like looking at himself at age fourteen. They shared the same wavy chestnut hair and blue eyes, though James had to admit he was definitely sprouting more and more silver of late.

"Hey, Dad," Gideon said.

James clapped the boy on the shoulder. "Hey, yourself. How was school?"

"Great. Got an A on my algebra test. And *yes*, I finished my history paper." He made a show of carefully putting away his books. "The soccer coach asked me to consider trying out for the soccer team this fall. Do you think I should?"

"That's pretty neat that he's recruiting you. But you should only consider soccer if you think you would enjoy it."

Gideon frowned. "I'm not sure I would. I like soccer and all, but it would take up a lot of my time."

"Don't rush your decision. You have the whole summer to think about it," James counseled. He patted Gideon's shoulder once. "Way to go, son."

As Gideon closed his laptop and left the room, James moved to Fern's side and leaned down to kiss her, stroking Sapphire as the cat arched against his palm. "Hello," he said. "How was your day?"

He could see she knew what he meant. "I've had better," she said quietly.

"New symptoms?"

Fern shook her head. "Just really exhausted all day. I'd much rather read than sit in front of the television, but my vision's too blurry right now."

James winced. "I'm sorry. Maybe it will clear up in a few days."

"Maybe." Fern usually tried to maintain a cheerful façade, but today she seemed lethargic and depressed. "How was your day?"

James busied himself getting a glass from the cupboard and added ice cubes and chilled water from the dispenser on the refrigerator. He grabbed one of the chairs from the table and set it near Fern's, then seated himself. "My day started out fine, and I made some very pleasant friends at lunch. But I'm afraid I have bad news."

"Oh no. What's wrong?" Fern visibly braced herself.

"We got a letter from the hospital board." James went on to share the contents of the letter with her, detailing his coworkers' reactions.

"What are we going to do?" Tears slowly rolled down Fern's pale cheeks. "I'm so sorry I can't work. It isn't fair that the burden of supporting us falls entirely on you."

"Hey." James rose from his chair. He picked Sapphire up from Fern's lap and set her on the floor. The cat went to the corner where her food and water was kept to get a drink, dipping her paw in the water first to stir it up. James knew Maine coons liked water, but the routine always made him grin.

He tugged Fern to her feet and took her place in the chair, pulling her down onto his lap. "The world isn't fair. Stuff happens. But we're a team, right?"

Fern nodded. "Yes, but—"

"Yes, but nothing." James kissed her cheek. "Remember those vows? 'For better or for worse, in sickness and in health'? This isn't a contest, and there are no scales to balance. This is just us, Team Bell, rolling along together with a little support from the Man Upstairs."

The barest hint of a smile curved Fern's lips. "Team Bell, *hmm*?"

James nodded, smiling. "Yes. And teams work together, so let's talk about our options here."

Fern nodded. "Okay. The pity party's over. Options—seems to me there are only two. Either you stay and hope for the best; or you start looking for another job, just in case the closing does come to pass."

"I suppose it's time to update and polish my résumé," James said.

"I can help with that," Fern offered. She was still able to use their computer on her better days. James had adjusted the font size so she could read more easily.

"Great." James did his best to sound cheerful and positive, even though his heart ached at the thought of leaving Hope Haven. Then again, he would only be leaving if he were forced to.

Sapphire returned and walked across the room to her toy basket. She stared into the basket for a moment, then carefully selected a plastic ball with a small jingle bell inside. She carried it back to Fern, then jumped up to her mistress's lap, dropping the ball and looking expectantly between Fern and the ball.

Fern began to laugh, a sweet, high lilt that warmed James's heart. "You're not going to let us mope, are you?" she asked the cat. Then she picked up the ball and flung it across the room. Sapphire shot off like a bullet, retrieved it, and returned to drop it in Fern's lap.

The sound of footsteps stomping down the steps reverberated through the house, distracting James from the cat's antics. Seconds later, the commotion burst into the kitchen and skidded to a stop in front of them, brown hair flying wildly. It was their second son, Nelson. His arms were raised, hands in fists as he mimed celebrating a victory. "I'm the man! I'm the man!"

"All right, I'll bite," James said, chuckling. "Why are you the man?"

The seventh grader grinned, his blue eyes sparkling. His expression so resembled his mother's that James was amused. "I finished my science fair project, and it turned out great."

"What topic did you end up researching?"

"I investigated the difference between music and noise—when is a sound considered music, and when is it just noise?"

"That's a good topic. What made you decide on that?"

Nelson grinned. "Mom's always telling me to turn down that noise I call music. So I thought I'd see which it really is."

James laughed, and Fern smiled. "And what did you find out?"

"That the noise *is* music! I measured waveform, amplitude and wavelength of common noises and compared them to well-known melodies to see how they differed."

James grinned, shaking his head, awed by his younger son's sky-high intelligence score.

Nelson grinned. "I have to enter it in the fair tomorrow. I'm hoping to win." Then he frowned, mimicking exaggerated disgust when he realized his parents were cuddled together in the rocker. "*Blech*! Yuck! Are you two kissing *again*?" he demanded.

"We weren't, but thanks for the idea," James told his son, a twinkle in his eye. He pressed a kiss to Fern's cheek and then lifted her and set her back in the rocker as he turned to Nelson. "So where's this science project? I want to see just how great it is."

"So that's what the letter said." Elena rose from the dinner table and began to clear the dishes. Over dinner, she had shared the unwelcome news about the possibility of the hospital's closing with her husband Cesar, their twenty-six-year-old son, Rafael, and Rafael's daughter Isabel who would be five years old in August.

"So what are you going to do, Mama?" Rafael asked. As he stood, he picked up his plate and Isabel's, and his black eyes met her own across the table. "Do you think you can find another job around here? There are going to be an awful lot of nurses looking for work."

"I'm not looking for another job yet." Elena carried a plate of strawberry-filled dessert enchiladas and some small dishes to the table. "I'm sure we can figure out a way to keep the hospital open."

"Who's 'we'?" Cesar asked. He ran a hand through his short dark hair. "Do you have any idea how much money is needed to run a hospital? How are you going to come up with such a sum?"

"I don't know yet. But there must be a way." Elena's eyes shone with conviction. "I'm going to pray about it. I have faith that if I do—"

Cesar heaved a sigh and rolled his dark eyes. "We know, we know. Your prayers will be answered."

Elena's own eyes flashed with ire. "You don't have to be sarcastic," she informed him.

Their conversation was interrupted by Isabel. "Oh, Buela, you made your special enchiladas! May I have one? I ate all my broccoli, remember?"

Elena laughed. Her granddaughter, with her father's dark curls and sparkling black eyes, was a shining light that brightened both her grandparents' lives beyond measure. "I surely do, my busy-Izzy." She placed an enchilada on Isabel's plate.

"Dessert," Isabel crowed. "Daddy, I get dessert!"

Her father smiled. "Yes, and I'd like to see your good table manners while you eat it."

As the little girl dug into her sweet treat and Elena served the others, Rafael glanced up at his mother. Monday evening was his band's rehearsal night. "Mama, Izzy has a little school project after dinner."

"Homework?" Elena asked. "Isn't that a little excessive for preschool?"

Rafael chuckled. "It's just a fun little art project."

"I have to color five bricks," Isabel announced.

"Color five bricks?" echoed Elena. "How on earth can you lift one brick, much less five?"

Isabel howled with laughter, pointing to some papers sticking out of the top of her backpack, which hung on the front closet doorknob. "Paper bricks, Buela."

"The class is making a picture of a house on their classroom wall," Rafael explained. "It's going to be 'built' with the bricks."

"I see," said Elena.

Rafael glanced at his watch and stood. He had wolfed down his dessert so fast that Elena was certain he couldn't have tasted it. "I'd better get going." He bent to kiss his daughter's cheek. "'Night, *mi bonita*," he murmured. "I'll see you in the morning." He had been calling Isabel his "pretty one" in Spanish since the day she was born, Elena recalled.

"Come kiss me when you get home, Daddy," ordered the little girl.

Elena watched them with a smile, enjoying the clear affection between the pair. Isabel's mother, Sarah, had vanished without a word shortly after Isabel's birth, leaving Rafael to raise his daughter alone. While Elena didn't know all the details, she was pretty sure that drug addiction had been at least part of Sarah's problem.

Still, how a woman could walk away from her baby . . . Stop, Elena. She wasn't going to judge, Elena reminded herself. But, oh, living that conviction sometimes took a great deal of willpower!

Rafael smiled and tugged on Isabel's long ponytail. "I always kiss you good night," he assured her.

Elena helped Izzy get into bed every Monday night and on some weekends, although Rafael was a devoted father and cared for the child himself as much as possible.

"Good night," Elena murmured as Rafael kissed her brow.

"'Night, Dad. See you in the morning, Mama. Thanks again." Her son never took his parents' assistance for granted.

"Good night," Cesar replied. He had finished his dessert and rose to place his dishes in the sink. "I want to check the weather," he said to Elena, going to the computer desk in the living room.

"Buela, I'm done with my enchilada. Can I color my bricks now?" Isabel asked.

Elena nodded. "Take your dishes to the sink, please."

The little girl did as she was told before turning to the closet to get her homework.

While Elena cleared the table and loaded the dishwasher, her thoughts returned to the disturbing events of the day. *Lord*, she prayed silently, *give me inspiration. There has to be a way to keep Hope Haven from closing. I'm placing this in Your hands.*

"Buela, look at my bricks," Isabel said, interrupting Elena's prayer as she tapped her crayon on her paper. "Did I make them pretty?"

"They're beautiful," Elena said, filling her voice with admiration. "You did a very nice job. Now. Guess what time it is?"

"Bath time," Isabel said. She hopped down from her chair and skipped to the hallway of the small ranch-style house. "I wanna run the water!"

"I'll be there in a moment," Elena called after the child. "Do not turn that water on until I get there!" She smiled at the crayons still scattered across the table. Isabel tended to forget the cleanup part of her activities. Usually, Elena asked her to help; but tonight, she absently began to gather up the crayons and paper as she thought about the hospital. There had to be some way to get the employees involved in saving Hope Haven.

In Candace Crenshaw's spacious, four-bedroom home, the bustle of dinner and homework was over. Howie had taken his bath. His stories and prayers were done, and he had been put to bed. Brooke had gotten into the shower while Candace was reading to Howie.

Candace walked down the half flight of stairs from the bedrooms to the main level where the kitchen, dining room, and living room were located. Then she walked down a second half flight to the family room. Entering the room, she quietly took a seat on the couch and smiled at her mother. "Howie's in bed looking at a book. I read his story and we said prayers, and he asked if he could 'read' a book by himself."

Candace's mother, Janet, had taken a seat in her favorite re-cliner. She was still a very slim and attractive woman. If it wasn't for her silver hair, Candace often thought they might look more like sisters than mother and daughter.

As Janet crocheted a baby blanket with fast, efficient motions, she watched *Jeopardy!* and guessed the questions aloud right along with the contestants. She turned down the volume of the large, flat-screen television when Candace entered. "He was so cute at dinner talking about how starting kindergarten will make him a big kid."

Candace chuckled. "He's raring to go, isn't he?"

Her mother nodded. "Yes. He still enjoys preschool, but says he's getting 'too grown-up' for it."

The two women shared a smile. Then Candace's expres-sion sobered. "Oh, Mom, I still can hardly believe that letter." Candace had shared the letter about the hospital closing with her mother when she arrived home. "I hate the thought of looking for another job."

"Could you go back to Princeton?" her mother asked. Before coming to Hope Haven ten years ago, Candace had worked at Perry Memorial in the nearby community.

"If I can't find something here in town, that's really my only other choice," Candace responded. "Tiskilwa and Wyanet don't have hospitals, and Peoria is just too far. We'd have to move, and I really don't want to do that. Brooke loves her school, and the last thing she needs is any more upheaval in her life."

Janet nodded, her expression thoughtful. Brooke had been eight years old when her father had died unexpectedly of a brain aneurysm, and the little girl had taken it very hard. Candace was mindful of the counselor's recommendations that she try to provide as much constancy and stability as possible for Brooke. Surely staying in the same home in the same school district fell into that category.

"I don't want to work in a doctor's office," Candace went on. "But if that's my only option, I'd do it."

"What about an OB practice?" Janet asked. "I know you love working with pregnant mothers and newborns."

Candace smiled. "I really do. I guess I'll get some résumés together when I get a chance." Then her smile faded. "I had some bad news today. One of the ladies in my new prenatal class found a lump in her breast. I went with her for her biopsy, and even though the results aren't back yet, the doctor believes it's malignant." Her mother would have recognized the name instantly, but patient confidentiality laws prevented Candace from offering any information that might identify the patient. She could discuss the case, but revealing any personal information that would identify a patient was strictly out-of-bounds.

"Oh no." Janet's eyes, greener than her daughter's, filled with distress. "That's awful news. What can they do when a woman is pregnant?"

"She still has options," Candace assured her mother. "Surgery, certainly, and I imagine some other treatments as well. I'm not a doctor, so I can't say for certain, but I'm going to stay hopeful. Breast cancer, especially if it's still in stage I, is quite treatable."

"So it was caught early?"

"The doctor thought it was," Candace admitted. "But we don't know yet if it's metastasized." She stopped herself. "And

I'm getting ahead of myself. We don't even know for sure that it's a cancer diagnosis yet."

Janet sucked in a dismayed breath. "I know you can't tell me her name, but I'll pray for her."

"Thanks, Mom. I will too."

"Mommy?"

Candace turned with a start. Brooke stood in the entry from the hallway, dressed in her robe with her long blonde curls anchored atop her head by a large barrette. Her lower lip trembled, and her wide blue eyes, so like her father's, were far too serious for a young girl.

"Hi, honey. That was fast." Candace held out her arms. Her spirits sank as she took in her daughter's distress. "What's the matter?"

"I heard you talking about the lady with cancer. Is she going to die like Daddy did?" Brooke rushed toward Candace, flinging herself into her mother's embrace.

"Oh, honey, I don't think my patient is going to die," Candace said, rubbing the child's back in comforting circles. "You know I work with some terrific doctors at Hope Haven, and they'll take good care of her."

Brooke pulled back, and her eyes were earnest as she said, "But she could die. And who would take care of her baby?"

"She has—" Candace began, but Brooke spoke over her, her little voice soft and determined.

"I'm never going to have a baby. Just in case."

"I really believe she's going to live and be just fine," Candace said firmly, although her heart felt as if an iron fist was squeezing it without mercy. "She and her husband will be taking care of their baby together."

The little girl appeared to think it over for a moment. Finally, she said, "That's good." As if the subject was settled now, she grabbed her mother's hand and tugged. "I'm ready for bed. Let's go read and say prayers."

Then she released Candace's hand and rushed across the room to her grandmother. "'Night, Grammy. See you in the morning."

"See you in the morning, honey." Janet hugged the child and received a good-night kiss before Brooke skipped back down the hallway, her good spirits apparently restored. Candace met her mother's concerned gaze. "I had no idea she was thinking like that."

Candace sighed. "I suppose it shouldn't be a complete shock." She hesitated. "She had a difficult experience Friday when her friend Carla's cat died. That could be what has brought these fears to light. Maybe I should call Tony and set up an appointment to take her to counseling again."

Janet nodded. "Wise idea."

With a heavy heart, Candace turned and followed her daughter upstairs. She had been reading *The Lion, the Witch and the Wardrobe* aloud with Brooke. It had been one of her own favorites as a child, and she was enjoying becoming reacquainted with Peter, Susan, Edmund and Lucy Pevensie and their fantastic adventures. But this evening, she was hard-pressed to keep her mind on the story. After their nightly chapter, she listened to her elder child's prayers, kissed her and turned off the light as she left the room.

Instead of returning to the family room, Candace walked to the end of the hall and entered her own bedroom. Quietly, she closed the door and simply stood at the edge of her bed as the tears began to fall. The bed was a beautiful queen-size, cherry sleigh bed that matched the dresser, end tables, and chest of drawers in the room. She and Dean had picked the entire suite out together. It had been their first purchase of brand-new furniture, and Candace still loved the cherry-wood pieces and the comforting memories they brought back.

Tonight, however, there was little comfort to be had; and she couldn't hold back the flood any longer. Collapsing onto the bed, she picked up the small stuffed bunny Dean had given her for Easter when they were dating and buried her face in a pillow to stifle her sobs.

She tried to never cry in front of her mother or the children. It frightened the children; and although her mother was a tower of strength and dependability, Candace sometimes felt that her mom watched her *too* closely for signs of grief. She supposed she couldn't blame her. Her mother loved and worried about her *and* the children.

It was so hard. Would Brooke ever recover from her father's death? Or would her little girl go through life fearing that she would be left again? What kind of man would Howie grow up to be without ever knowing Dean? Didn't a boy learn how to be a man by emulating his father? Dean had been one of the best men, one of the most principled, kindest men she had ever known. Living the rest of her life without him, trying to raise their children alone, even with her mother's help, felt like the harshest punishment ever devised.

After a few moments, the intensity of her grief began to dissipate. Exhausted, she rolled onto her back and reached for a tissue, mopping her tears and blowing her nose. If she had learned anything in the past three years, she'd learned that crying jags might help to relieve stress temporarily, but they weren't good for much else.

There was an intercom in the hallway, part of a system she'd installed after Dean's death so that if one of the children became upset when she wasn't upstairs with them, she'd be able to hear them from other parts of the house. Walking to the unit on the wall, she pressed the button and said, "Mom? I'm pretty tired. I think I'll just go to bed."

A moment later, her mother's voice responded. "Good night, honey. Everything all right?"

"Yes. Brooke's okay now. Good night."

It wasn't a lie. Brooke had turned off her light and appeared to be sleeping peacefully, and Candace herself was no longer crying. *Sometimes*, she thought sadly, *no longer crying is as okay as I can be.*

The thought of crying reminded her of Robin. Candace realized the younger woman's day had been far more upsetting than her own. On impulse, she took her cell phone from her pocket. She had the numbers of all the expectant mothers in her current childbirth class, and she quickly pulled up Robin's number and hit SEND.

After two rings, a recorded message invited her to leave her name and her reason for calling. Candace hesitated, fearing she might be intrusive. Finally, she cleared her throat. "Hi, Robin and Andrew. This is Candace Crenshaw. I just wanted to tell you that I'll be happy to help you in any way I can while you figure out how you're going to deal with your diagnosis. Also, I will pray for both of you and for your baby."

She ended the call and pocketed the phone. Returning to her room, she kicked off her shoes and picked up her Bible. Reclining on the bed, she began her nightly study and prayer time.

Chapter Four

ANABELLE STEPPED DOWN OFF THE LOW STOOL and stood back to examine her work. "How do these curtains look?" she asked her daughter, as she wiped her hands off on her denim pants. She had spent the last thirty minutes hanging pinch-pleated draw drapes over the double window in the living room of Kirstie's new apartment while Kirstie hooked up her computer, television and DVR.

"They look great, Mother. Thanks," Kirstie said. A pretty girl with long, dark hair and her father's blue eyes, she put her hands on her hips as she studied the drapes. "I can do the rest another day." She picked up the stool and folded it, leaning it against a stack of boxes yet to be unpacked. "You should be getting home. Don't you have to work tomorrow?"

Anabelle nodded. "Yes, but this is no problem. You know I'm happy to help. I'll put up your kitchen curtains too."

"We can talk about that tomorrow." Kirstie began to pick up the packaging from the curtain hooks and tidy up. "Really, Mother, you should go. I'm going to bed soon myself."

"Honey," Anabelle said, "this place is still very rough. Why don't you come home tonight? You should get everything completely shipshape before you start living here."

Kirstie shook her head. "No. I have enough stuff unpacked to get by until tomorrow evening. After school, I have the rest of the day to unpack."

"I can meet you here as soon as I get off work. Maybe Ainslee can come over and the three of us can make a night of it," Anabelle told her, volunteering Kirstie's older sister.

"I'm not sure when I'll get here. You know, grading papers, after-school meetings, that kind of thing. Plus, some of the other teachers offered to come over and help put things away. So I won't need you tomorrow night." Kirstie smiled. "You'll get a night off."

"All right," Anabelle said reluctantly. "Maybe Wednesday evening." She warmed to the idea. "I could get started on the painting. Didn't you say you wanted to do this room?"

"I'm not sure when I'm going to start that." Kirstie yawned widely. "Not that soon."

"You look tired, honey." Anabelle immediately was concerned. "You know you shouldn't let yourself get too exhausted or you're just asking for trouble. Every teacher I know catches all kinds of bugs from the students. And how is your le—?"

"I'm fine!"

Anabelle stopped abruptly, mouth open midword. Since Kirstie had lost her leg more than a decade ago in a bicycle-automobile accident, Anabelle constantly fretted about it, often frustrating her daughter. "You don't have to shout," she said with dignity.

"Sorry." Kirstie made an obvious effort to smile. "I'm just really tired. I'll talk to you in a day or so, all right?"

"All right." Anabelle allowed her daughter to pass her handbag to her. "You can come over for dinner later in the week." She smiled. "At least I can make sure you occasionally eat right."

"I can cook, you know." Kirstie's tone was wry, but good-humored again. "I promise I'll get three squares a day."

Anabelle smiled and reached for the doorknob as she extracted her keys from her handbag. "Good." She reached for Kirstie, feeling all the tension drain away when her daughter's strong, young arms came around her in a tight hug. "I love you, honey."

"I love you too." Kirstie pulled back, and there were tears in her eyes. "It's time for me to be on my own, but I hope you know how much I appreciate everything you and Daddy have done for me."

"We do know." Anabelle sniffed, her own eyes filling. "And remember, if this living situation doesn't work out, your room at home is still waiting for you."

Kirstie burst out laughing. "Okay, Mother. I won't forget."

Candace always packed her children's lunches herself. She took the time to write little notes on their napkins each day, a ritual both children seemed to love. Candace had feared

Brooke might not appreciate it as she got older, but so far, so good.

Already showered and ready for her day, she awakened the children and got them started dressing before walking downstairs to the kitchen. Howie's lunch box and Brooke's backpack both lay on the counter. She opened Howie's lunch box and put yesterday's containers in the sink to be washed. Then she reached for Brooke's backpack to find her lunch sack.

Unzipping the book bag, she withdrew a pink jacket, two textbooks, a school letter about the upcoming book fair, and Brooke's gym sneakers before she came to the lunch sack. When she pulled it out, a small envelope came with it. Curious, Candace turned it over, but it wasn't addressed to her. All right, so it wasn't school correspondence.

Brooke's name was written on the envelope in childish cursive, but the little missive clearly had been opened already. Candace debated for a second before deciding that since it was open, it was fair game for a mother to read.

She flipped up the envelope flap and found a little bifold card that clearly had been made on someone's home computer. It was a birthday invitation. Oh boy. Candace smiled. She hoped it was for a girl. She often had a terrible time helping Brooke buy gifts for boys.

She opened the little card that announced, "It's a Birthday Party!" on the front. Inside was an invitation to Brooke's friend Tiffany's birthday party. But as Candace's eyes skimmed the little card, her brows drew together in a frown. The date was for the previous Saturday. The party was already over!

At that very moment, Brooke walked into the kitchen.

"What," demanded Candace, "is this?" She wagged the invitation beneath her daughter's nose, taking deep breaths to control her exasperation.

Brooke shrugged, appearing supremely unconcerned, although Candace noted that the girl would not look directly into her eyes. "Tiffany's birthday party invitation."

"And when did you intend to tell me about this?"

Brooke shrugged again. "I didn't want to bother you."

"Bother me!" Candace huffed out a breath. "Brooke, you can't just ignore invitations."

"I didn't," Brooke protested. "I told Tiffany I couldn't be there."

"Because?"

"I just didn't really want to go."

"Did you tell her that?"

"No." Brooke was blinking rapidly, as if she was trying not to cry.

"So you lied. Because you certainly didn't have any other plans." Candace crossed her arms, although she made an effort to soften her tone. "Honey, even if you choose not to attend a party, you still should send a gift if you were invited."

"I should?" Her daughter's voice was very, very small.

Candace nodded. "Yes. Remember that little book of etiquette I gave you at Christmas?"

Brooke nodded.

"I bet this situation is covered in there. We still need to give Tiffany a gift." She paused a moment, at a loss to understand her daughter. "Why didn't you want to go? I thought Tiffany was one of your good friends."

"She is." Brooke let one shoulder rise and fall. "I guess we'd better give her a gift."

"Yes, we should." Candace noted that Brooke had detoured around her question, but she let it rest for the moment. "How about tomorrow evening?"

Brooke's head came up. "Why can't we do it right after school one day? I don't want to go in the evening, Mommy."

"All right." Candace didn't really care when they went, as long as the mistake was rectified soon. "Honey, is there something wrong between you and Tiffany?"

"No." Brooke sounded definite. "When can we go shopping for Tiffany?"

"How about today, right after school? I'll bring along a gift bag and a card. Then we can take it straight over to Tiffany's house." Even more puzzled, Candace stared after her daughter as the child walked out of the room. What was going on in that little blonde head?

Perhaps it would be a good idea to request a conference with Brooke's teacher, since Brooke appeared reluctant to explain. Maybe the teacher had noticed something. Brooke had seemed to be dealing with her grief better—until recently. Candace thought of the episode with Brooke's friend's kitty passing away. Brooke's grief had seemed a little outside the bounds of normal for a pet she had met once. And her initial reaction when she'd overheard Candace talking about the pregnant breast-cancer patient had been startling.

Candace sighed. Yes, it might be time for a teacher conference. And it definitely was time for a call to Brooke's counselor.

After she arrived at work, Candace began reviewing paperwork for her shift. She glanced up automatically when the elevator doors opened, and she saw Anabelle Scott and James Bell coming in for their own shifts. "Good morning," she said. "How are you two doing now that you've had the night to reflect on the letter?"

Anabelle snorted. "As you'd expect. I'm anxious, upset, apprehensive. . . ."

Candace nodded. "Same here."

"Hi, gang!" The perky voice belonged to Elena Rodriguez. "I have to talk to you guys," she said. "I had an idea last night that I want to run by you. Can we get together at noon in the courtyard?"

Anabelle glanced at her watch. "That works for me."

"Sounds good," James put in.

Candace nodded. "Count me in."

The four nurses separated, each moving off to his or her unit. As Candace walked briskly into the labor and delivery area, the phone on the counter rang. No one else was close by, so she picked up the receiver. "Birthing Unit, this is Candace."

"Candace? It's Robin Overing. Do you have a moment to talk?" The young woman's voice was hesitant.

"Good morning, Robin. Of course I have time. How are you doing?"

"I've been better," the young woman said honestly. "We got your message. I wanted to thank you for your prayers. That means a lot."

"You're welcome. Have you heard from the oncologist yet?"

"Yes." Robin hesitated. "We have an appointment at one thirty Thursday afternoon. Candace, I know it's an imposition, but would it be possible for you to go with us? I would feel much better with you there to ask any questions I might not think of."

"Of course," Candace said. "That time works fine for me. Where should I meet you?"

"Do you know where Dr. Prelutski's office is? He's going to be my oncologist."

"I do," Candace assured her. "I'll meet you there a little before one thirty on Thursday, all right?"

"Thank you so much." Robin sounded as if she was fighting tears. "We'll see you then."

Candace replaced the receiver slowly. Robin had been a darling little girl, always so sunny and sweet, always eager to please. It was hard to remember that child, full of life and promise, and see what she was going to have to deal with now as an adult. She thought of Brooke, whose childhood security had been shattered when her daddy died. Every child should have the luxury of innocence for that short, magical time during childhood.

Confusion and pain welled up. *Why, God?* If she had a dollar for every time she'd asked that futile question, she'd never have to work again.

Candace was busy all morning, and she got off a few minutes later than normal. When she stepped into the sunny courtyard for the second day in a row, the three other nurses were already there waiting. Elena had soup and a sandwich from the cafeteria, while Anabelle and James both had packed lunches spread out in front of them.

"Candace! Hi!" Elena's voice was enthusiastic. "I was afraid you might not make it."

"I got held up for a few minutes. What did I miss?"

"Nothing yet," Anabelle assured her. "Elena was just about to tell us about an idea she had."

"What sort of idea?" Candace took a seat on the picnic bench and began to unload her lunch items from the insulated bag in which she kept them.

"I was thinking about it last night," Elena said, "and I realized that we—all of us who are employed here—are just sitting around waiting to see what will happen to Hope Haven. But what if we get involved? Maybe we need to pitch in instead of expecting the board of directors to fix it. What would you think of that?"

"Involved how?" Candace couldn't see how the employees could help if the board hadn't been able to come up with the money.

"It's obvious," Elena said. "A fund-raising campaign. Get the community involved. Everyone in Deerford should be concerned about this."

"I agree with you," Anabelle said, "but being concerned and actually getting involved are two entirely different things. And even if we could raise enough money to keep the hospital going for, say, another year, what happens the following year? Remember when the oncology unit was updated a few years ago?"

"They raised millions of dollars," James supplied glumly, "and even then, it wasn't enough to do all that they wanted, so they had to scale back their plans."

Anabelle nodded. "Right. So we raise the money. What happens when it's gone? We'd be right back in the same pickle."

Candace sat up a little straighter. "Not necessarily. My husband Dean was an accountant—"

"Was?" asked Elena.

Candace's throat tightened, as it still did so often, and she couldn't speak for a moment. "He passed away."

"I'm so sorry," Elena said sincerely. "Both for your loss and for my nosiness. I have a bad habit of speaking first and then wishing I'd thought about it before I opened my mouth. This definitely qualifies as one of those times."

Elena's frank words made Candace smile. The lump in her throat eased, and she was able to go on. "I know what my husband would have recommended. A trust or endowment is the way to go, with the principal staying untouched and the interest being used to supplement the hospital budget."

James was nodding vigorously. "If enough is invested, it could become an annual subvention."

"Subvention?" Elena asked.

"Form of assistance or financial support," James clarified. "I wonder how much we would have to raise to have a prayer of saving this hospital." The momentary hope faded from his tone. "It must be astronomical."

"I don't know, but I'll volunteer to find out," Elena said. She grinned, shaking her head with a wry expression as she looked at James. "Subvention. Where on earth did you learn that word?"

James cleared his throat, and the tips of his ears grew red. "Vocabulary is a sort of hobby of mine."

Anabelle, who had sunk onto the end of Candace's bench, rose as she said, "I actually have to get back to work right now. Since James mentioned prayer, I believe I'm going to take a moment to ask for divine intervention. Would any of you like to pray about this with me?"

"I would," Elena said promptly.

Candace extended a hand to Anabelle. "Me too."

James reached out to Candace and Elena, and in a moment the four new friends had formed a circle.

"Dear Lord," Anabelle began, "Hope Haven is a special place. We try to treat our patients with Your spirit as well as with the best that modern medicine can offer. Help us find a way to keep our hospital open."

Each of them added something to the prayer, and finally, Elena closed by saying, "We pray for the future of this hospital, Father. Help us come up with ideas to raise the necessary funds.

Give us the enthusiasm and perseverance to see this through. In Your name we pray. Amen."

Together, they repeated, "Amen."

As they released each others' hands, Elena looked up. Her face was glowing. "I feel much more optimistic after that."

"I do too," Anabelle said, "and when I stepped through that door, optimism was definitely not a part of my day." The older woman looked less stressed than she had since she had burst into the courtyard yesterday.

Candace said, "Perhaps we all could get together a day or so each week for a meal and prayer."

"I'm in," James said immediately. "I can be here most days, barring emergencies and work issues that get in the way."

"What a great idea," Elena said. Candace was beginning to see that Elena was quite the cheerleader, and she smiled at her new friend's enthusiastic tone as Elena added, "I'll be here when I can."

"Me too," Anabelle said.

"We should exchange pager and cell phone numbers," James said. "Then we can get in touch with each other and decide where to meet if it's raining."

"Another great idea!" said Elena. All of them pulled their various communication devices out and a flurry of exchanges ensued.

Chapter Five

*L*ATE ON WEDNESDAY MORNING, ANABELLE HAD A temp nurse cover for her while she attended a meeting of the I've Got Bike Smarts! committee. The hospital presented the bicycle safety program to local fourth-grade classes every year just before the summer vacation began. The project was near and dear to Anabelle's heart. She had been involved in the program since its inception a dozen years ago and continued to serve as an adviser and presenter.

When she entered the conference room, located at the end of the administrative-offices hallway on the first floor, the rest of the committee was already there. The committee chair was Winona Stouffer, a licensed practical nurse in Cardiac Care. In addition to the LPN, the other members included the CFO's assistant, Quintessa Smith, and the manager of the Community Health Office, Bobbi Quarles. The four had been on the committee for several years and routinely rotated chairman duties.

"Hi, Anabelle," Winona said. "You're just in time. We haven't started yet."

"We've been talking about the letter," added Bobbi. It was on everyone's mind—yesterday's news had the power to change the lives of every hospital employee.

"What are people saying?" Anabelle asked. "I've been swamped this morning, and I haven't had time to talk about anything but cardiac issues."

Quintessa spoke up. "I can tell you that the community is up in arms from the article in today's paper. This morning I've already fielded a dozen phone calls from irate folks with a list of reasons why the hospital needs to stay open." She grimaced. "I don't know why the switchboard is referring them to our office rather than the CEO's."

Bobbi snorted. "Probably because they know they can count on you to be polite."

Quintessa laughed, her bright smile lighting up her dark face. Quintessa, Anabelle often thought, had just about the prettiest skin of anyone she'd ever met, a warm, coppery brown that practically glowed at times.

Doing her best to be diplomatic, Anabelle said, "Penny can be less than congenial at times." The CEO's executive assistant, Penny Risser, was the dragon who guarded the executive's door. No one liked to get on her bad side, and it was well known that she had little patience.

"'Less than congenial,'" Quintessa repeated. She rolled her large, expressive brown eyes. "She's a . . . challenge," she added with a grin.

"Ladies, I have to get back to work as soon as possible, so why don't we get started?" Anabelle said, turning to Winona.

"All right." Winona assumed a professional tone as she consulted her notes.

The group discussed visitation times, made minor adjustments to the presentation's content and double-checked the class numbers to be sure they had enough helmets in stock. The price of the helmets had gone up, and Bobbi shared some information about other suppliers. A decision on switching vendors was tabled, since they wouldn't be placing a new order for more than six months.

During each point of discussion, Anabelle shared the benefit of her many years working with the program. She was a sort of historian, she decided, pleased at the thought. With her oversight, nothing could stray too much from the committee's original purpose.

Before the meeting broke up, Winona passed around a sheet of paper. "First, let me know if you see any times here that are going to be problematic for you to go to your assigned schools."

Anabelle glanced over the sheet of paper. "I'd like to be scheduled for Rishell," she said.

Winona glanced at her with her eyebrows raised. "Because?"

"My daughter teaches at Rishell." Anabelle tried to ignore the irritation she felt at the chairwoman's exasperated tone.

"Last year, we voted to not choose favorite schools," Winona reminded Anabelle. "You said it might become too complicated trying to accommodate personal requests. It was a unanimous vote." Winona frowned at Anabelle.

"Yes, and normally I agree. But it's just this one time—"

"I don't think we should start making exceptions," Winona insisted in an unyielding tone.

"It's not a big deal," Bobbi said. "I'm at Rishell. I can switch with you."

Anabelle smiled at the health-office manager, careful not to seem victorious. "Thank you, Bobbi. I appreciate that." Kirstie would be delighted to see her at the school. "Kirstie just moved into her first apartment, and I don't see her nearly as much as when she lived with us."

"That's exciting," Quintessa said. "I bet she's thrilled to be in her own place."

Anabelle bristled. "She was perfectly happy at home. I don't know why she feels the need to move out to prove a point. Her father and I are happy to help her with anything she needs."

"I doubt she's moving out to prove a point," Bobbi said gently. "It's just a normal progression in the growing up process, Anabelle."

"But she's *not* normal!" Anabelle blurted.

There was silence in the room. Anabelle wasn't sure who was more shocked, her peers or herself. "I mean, of course she's normal. But she has physical challenges that—"

"That she has to learn to deal with sooner or later," Winona said briskly. "You can't control everything, Anabelle."

The pointed words stung.

Anabelle glanced at the others. As they all busied themselves gathering their things, each of them studiously avoided making eye contact with her.

"I've got to get back to my office," Bobbi said. "Are we done?"

Winona nodded, and before the words "I believe so" were out of her mouth, Bobbi and Quintessa both were out the door with hasty farewells. Winona smiled briefly at Anabelle before she also departed, and Anabelle got the impression it was meant as a peace offering. "See you at the next meeting."

Alone in the conference room, Anabelle went over the meeting in her mind. What had she done? True, the others were thirty or more years younger than she was, but that didn't matter. She felt that she was forward thinking and that she understood young people. Her own children were in the same age range. If these three had had something to say, she wished they would have just spoken up. After all, she was a good listener.

Of course she was.

One of Elena's new patients in the Intensive Care Unit had had a stroke the previous day, and the poor soul was severely affected. The patient, Barbara, was a grandmother; and Elena tried to talk to her as much as possible, hoping to stimulate speech. As she methodically checked her patient's vitals, Elena told Barbara about Isabel's brick project for school.

Barbara's eyes followed Elena's face as she moved around. "As it turned out," Elena went on, "she was talking about paper bricks. Each child got several to color and then the teacher would help the class build the façade of a house with them. Pretty cute idea, don't you think?"

Barbara closed her eyes and with great effort managed to get out a single syllable. "Yes."

"Yes, I thought so too," Elena said, knowing progress was made in encouraging small steps like the utterance of a syllable.

Suddenly her hands froze. She stood still, arrested by a thought. Bricks! Yes, of course! That might be the answer.

"Barbara, I just had an idea!" Elena was so excited she could barely stand still. As the words spilled out, she paced back and forth at the foot of the hospital bed. "What if the hospital conducted a fund-raiser where people bought bricks to raise money for Hope Haven?" She recounted a magazine article she had read in which a school had done it to raise money for a new stadium. As one approached, there was a lovely plaza with all the donated bricks, many engraved in honor or in memory of loved ones.

"But the hospital doesn't need a plaza," she went on. "It has lovely landscaped gardens out in the front with concrete sidewalks and paths, which are practical for wheelchairs. I'm sure you've seen them."

However, she thought with mounting excitement, *the hospital does need a more attractive lunch area for the staff.*

"Have you ever been in the little courtyard behind the chapel?" she asked Barbara.

The woman's eyes blinked, and Elena took it as a positive response. "Well, then you know how ugly it is." She made a grimace of distaste as she recalled the dismal little picnic area in which she gathered with the other nurses. "What if," she said with rising excitement, "what if it was possible to tear up that courtyard and get rid of those shrubs? The size of the eating area could be doubled. It could be bordered by a brick wall—with donated bricks, of course."

If they could get enough bricks to do the whole project, that would be a start on a fund-raising campaign. And maybe they could follow it up with some additional fund-raising activities.

So how much would they charge for the bricks? She didn't know anything about those aspects of such a project. Then again, why set a price? Elena suspected that people would give more generously if there wasn't a price attached. The bricks could be "free" anytime a donation was made to a Save Hope Haven campaign. Even a certain amount of engraving in honor or in memory of someone could be part of the service.

As she made notes on Barbara's chart and said good-bye to her patient, a bubble of enthusiasm swelled within her. Hurrying back to the ICU nursing station to punch out for her lunch break, Elena thought, *This could work. This could really work!* She considered the congenial group with whom she had met at lunch. They were the kind of people she'd like to run this idea by.

And if they agreed that it could work, she had to figure out whom to talk to in order to make the dream a reality.

Candace stepped into the little courtyard where she'd shared a prayer with her three fellow employees the previous day. She had received a text from Anabelle earlier inviting them to join her for lunch, and Candace couldn't help feeling that God had some purpose in mind when He gathered these particular four people together. They were quite different, yet there was something that simply clicked when they were together.

It was another lovely sunny day, with little humidity and the slightest breeze. Even the bare-bones look of the eating area was softened by the warm light that bathed everything. Candace caught a glimpse of the gorgeous cardinal she had spotted before in the paperbark maple.

Anabelle was already there, seated at one of the picnic tables. Her salt-and-pepper hair was parted on the side and brushed back away from her face with a few bangs that feathered across her forehead. The breeze had caught a few strands and teased them out of the smooth style. She had the daily paper spread out on the table before her, and she glanced up over the top of the reading glasses she wore. "Hello, Candace."

"Hi, Anabelle." Candace took a seat across from her. "What are you reading?"

Anabelle smiled with a certain amount of satisfaction. "I finally got my hands on a copy of yesterday's *Dispatch*. I was interviewed on Monday by a reporter who had heard about the hospital closing. She talked with a number of hospital employees and even looked at Nellie's copy of the letter. There appears to be a shock wave rippling through the community already."

"Good." Candace began to pull her lunch items from the bag, prompting Anabelle to set aside the paper and open her own lunch. "The more publicity the closing gets, the more likely it is that something can be done to prevent it. I'd like to read that after I eat."

"Candace?" Anabelle's voice was uncharacteristically diffident. "Do you think I'm pushy and controlling?"

Candace couldn't prevent a surprised ripple of laughter, but she quickly sobered as she saw Anabelle's stricken face. Her friend thought she was laughing at her, Candace realized.

"Of course I don't," she assured Anabelle. "I wasn't laughing at you. I just wasn't expecting a question like that." She regarded her friend closely. "Why do you ask?"

Anabelle sighed. "I was in a meeting this morning with three young women; and by the time it ended, I felt like a relic from the age of dinosaurs who just didn't understand how to deal with young people today."

"I'm sorry."

Anabelle sent her a wry smile. "Me too."

The door swung open again then, and James and Elena stepped into the courtyard.

"*Ah-h-h.* It's beautiful out here again today," Elena said, her dark eyes sparkling. "I love spring."

Candace nodded. "Me too." The breeze blew a strand of her gleaming, copper-brown hair across her face, and she hooked it back behind one ear.

Elena spied the newspaper Anabelle had laid to one side. "I saw your comments, Anabelle. Excellent job."

"Thank you." Anabelle nodded modestly, as James picked up the paper and skimmed the article.

"Who's Frederick Innisk?" he asked.

Anabelle made a face. "He's on the board of directors of the hospital."

James indicated the article. "He's the only negative voice in the whole piece. He's quoted here as saying that the closing probably is unavoidable."

"He's quite an unpleasant man," Anabelle said. "Unfortunately, he usually has a pretty good finger on the pulse of this town. If he thinks Hope Haven is closing, then we really have an uphill battle ahead of us."

Elena took a seat across from Candace, while James finished reading the article. "Way to go, Anabelle," he said, folding the paper. "Succinct and candid."

"Succinct?" Elena repeated, her tone teasing even though Candace was certain the word wasn't totally unfamiliar. "There you go again with the big words."

"It's not that big—only eight letters. It means concise, without wasted words." He grinned as he folded his tall frame onto the bench opposite Anabelle. "So the closing is public information now," he said. "I wonder what will happen next. Do you think people in the community are as concerned about this as we are?"

"I suspect they are," Candace spoke up. "We'll know soon. I heard that tomorrow's paper will carry local residents' reactions to the possible closing."

"Expletives deleted," Anabelle said, chuckling. "This morning I was in a meeting with Quintessa Smith. She's gotten quite a few phone calls already. People are beginning to get more than a little hot under the collar."

"But will that translate into any beneficial action?" James asked before he took a bite of his sandwich.

Candace sighed. "I guess time will tell."

"Speaking of beneficial action," Elena said, "I had an idea."

James lifted his eyes heavenward. "Why do I have a feeling that those words are an oft-used part of your repertoire?"

Elena grinned. "I refuse to respond on the grounds that anything I say might be incriminating."

They all chuckled, and then James said, "All right. Hit us with this idea."

"Okay." The dark-haired nurse put down her sandwich. Her face was animated and her dark eyes snapped with excitement. "Monday night, my granddaughter was working on a school project that involved bricks; and this morning, I got to thinking: What if the hospital creates some kind of memorial at Hope Haven with engraved bricks? Community members could have a brick personally engraved by making a donation to a fund to save the hospital."

"But what kind of memorial could be created with bricks?" Anabelle asked.

"That's the good part," Elena said. "It could be a Wall of Hope. And it could be right here!" She stood and walked to where the privet hedge divided their small space from the parking lot.

James raised one eyebrow as he considered the plan. "I like it."

"I do too, but do you really think it could raise the kind of money we need?" Anabelle asked doubtfully.

"I don't know," Elena responded. "But I think it's worth considering. Perhaps there are things I haven't thought of that would generate more donations."

"Donations," Candace said in a thoughtful tone. She had been considering Elena's idea carefully, trying to imagine the space transformed. "That might be the key." She looked around at the others. "What if there was no set price for the bricks?

If people simply gave according to their hearts, we might actually raise more than if we put price points on the bricks."

"I think that's an excellent idea." James looked at Candace with approval.

"But how do you keep people from going overboard with the engraving?" Anabelle wondered. "That could cut into profits pretty quickly."

"Maybe we set a limit as to how many letters engraved on any one brick," Candace suggested promptly.

"You should take this to Zane McGarry," James told her. "He's the Chief Financial Officer. He's a good man. He would listen to you."

Elena nodded. "Okay. I'll do it and let you know what he says."

There was a lapse in the conversation as they all focused on their meals for a moment.

Breaking the silence, James said, "Your idea is wonderful, Elena. But the more thought I give it, the more I see that I can't go without a job if Hope Haven does close. I have to have an income, so I've decided to start looking now."

Anabelle stared at him in dismay. "But you can't leave Hope Haven. You're a fixture. How long have you been here?"

James thought for a moment. "Twenty years." His face radiated unhappiness. "I don't want to leave, believe me. But I have to support my family."

Candace nodded. "It's a terrible choice to have to make." Her heart ached for him. She knew exactly how he felt; the same concern had been weighing on her mind as well. "We'll try not to make it harder," she promised him.

Anabelle and Elena looked a bit chastened.

"I'm sorry," Anabelle said. "My reaction was thoughtless. I know you would never leave voluntarily."

"And we do understand the need to support a family," Elena added. "We'll pray for you as well."

"Why don't we spend a moment in prayer right now?" Candace suggested. "Every single employee in this hospital needs God's help right now, even if it's just with managing the anxiety this whole situation is producing."

The others concurred, and after everyone clasped hands, Elena led them in a moment of prayer.

Shortly afterward, she packed her things back in her lunch bag and rose. When Candace looked at her with an inquiring expression, Elena said, "I still have a little time left in my break. I'm going to the CFO's office right now to make an appointment to discuss the Wall of Hope idea with him."

"Good luck," said James. "We'll meet tomorrow and you can give us the latest report."

"Go get 'em," Anabelle called as Elena pulled open the door and reentered the hushed bustle of the hospital.

Chapter Six

ELENA WALKED BRISKLY AROUND THE CORNER AND past the seating area near the registration desk. She turned left into the corridor that housed the administrative offices and walked to the first door on the left. A sign on the door proclaimed, ZANE MCGARRY, CHIEF FINANCIAL OFFICER.

Elena knocked on the door, and a well-modulated woman's voice called, "Come in."

Elena walked into the office. It felt very different from the sterile environs of Intensive Care, decorated with a mauve, gray and green color scheme, thick-carpeted floors and several thriving plants.

"Hello, Quintessa," Elena said. The young woman had worked for the CFO for the past three years. She was one of the sharpest women in the executive department, in Elena's opinion.

"Hello, Elena." Quintessa smiled at her, her dark eyes twinkling and warm. "I haven't seen you in a while. Not since the Christmas decorating committee, right?"

Elena nodded. "I think that's right. How have you been?"

"Great!" Then Quintessa's smile faded. "At least, I was until we got the letter." She waved away the problem with one hand. "But you're not here to discuss that, I bet. Did you want to see Mr. McGarry?"

Elena nodded. "I would like to speak with him, although the letter is exactly why I'm here. I have an idea I'd like to run by him."

Curiosity lit Quintessa's face, but all she said was, "He just returned from lunch. Let me see if this is a good time." She rose from behind her desk—a slender young woman in a smart gray pin-striped business suit and classy gray leather pumps—and disappeared into the inner office.

A moment later, she returned, gesturing with a graceful hand to the door. "Mr. McGarry will be happy to speak with you now, Elena."

"Thanks, Quintessa." Elena moved by her and entered the office of the CFO. It was decorated in more gray and green and less pink, but otherwise echoed the same themes as the outer office.

Zane McGarry rose to greet her, extending a hand. He had an open, engaging grin, short sandy blond hair, and sharp brown eyes that she imagined missed very little. "Hello, Ms. Rodriguez. Have a seat."

"Please call me Elena," she said.

"Only if you'll call me Zane."

She nodded, returning his firm handshake and smile. "It's a deal, Zane."

After she sat down in one of the gray leather guest chairs, Zane returned to his seat behind his desk. "Quintessa tells me you have some kind of idea about the hospital closing."

"It's more an idea of how to avoid a closing," Elena clarified. "Some friends and I were discussing how to raise funds. I'm sure you've given all of this a lot of thought already, but I wanted to share our idea."

"We have given it thought," Zane said, "and I have some ideas too. The board of directors is divided on whether to pursue selling to a larger health care organization—"

"Like Prairie Health," Elena said.

He nodded. "That's one group under consideration. The other half of the board would like to pursue fund-raising efforts. I've been charged with coming up with a potential fund-raising plan before the next meeting of the board." He grinned. "So your appearance here is fortuitous. What do you have in mind?"

Fortuitous. Better file that one away to use on James someday. Then she addressed herself to the question. "Have you ever been in the little courtyard in the back? It's rather basic compared to the rest of the hospital."

"It certainly is," Zane agreed. "I wonder why, especially when everything else around here has been done with such attention to comfort and beauty, like the landscaping in the front."

"My point exactly. I think it would be great if that courtyard could be made into a more attractive, inviting area."

Zane's forehead creased as he frowned. "But what does that have to do with fund-raising? It would just be one more expense on what little additional income we might get."

"Not if we used it as a *fund-raiser*." Elena forged ahead. "What if we created a Wall of Hope in the courtyard? It could be made of bricks that members of the community receive when they make a donation to save the hospital. We could have each brick engraved in honor of loved ones."

Zane sat up a little straighter in his chair. After a moment, he said, "That's an excellent idea. I was thinking more along the lines of soliciting bequests and corporate donations, but your idea would involve the community and generate publicity. I think the more people hear about a possible closing, the more likely they are to become concerned and proactive."

"That's what I was thinking as well—a real community effort," Elena said. "I have to get back to work now, but we could discuss it further if you like."

Zane nodded enthusiastically. "I would indeed. Why don't you mention it to Quintessa on your way out and find a time that works for both of us? We might want her to be here too. That woman is scary when it comes to organizing efforts."

Elena laughed. "I know. She and I get along just fine."

The following day was Candace's day off. It was delightful to have a leisurely morning to wake her daughter before school and share a hot breakfast. She made Brooke's lunch and walked the two blocks with her to school, allowing her mother to sleep in.

Although, she thought with a wry smile, *Mom never did much sleeping in*. On Candace's days off, Janet ran errands, did her volunteer work and visited family. It was an arrangement that had worked well for them for the past three years.

On the way home from the school, Candace picked up her pace and continued to walk for forty-five minutes. She rarely had time for other types of exercise, but she enjoyed walking, even in the winter.

Howie woke up soon after she returned. He rarely slept past eight thirty. She made him breakfast, and then let him choose what he would like to do that morning. Her bet was, "go to the park," and she was right.

"See you later, Mom," she called up the stairs as they departed.

"Good-bye, honey," Janet called. "'Bye, Howie. Have fun at the park."

"'Bye, Grammy," Howie shouted. "Don't forget! Meatloaf for dinner."

As she walked out the door with her son, Candace could hear her mother laughing. Howie adored meatloaf, and she made it once at least every two weeks. It had become a family joke. If Mommy was off, chances were they were having meatloaf for dinner.

Howie loved the enormous sandbox in the Deerford Public Park; as often happened, several of his little friends from preschool and Sunday school were there. Candace spent a delightful morning playing with her son and chatting with several other mothers while she watched him dig in the sand.

She allowed Howie to play until almost noon. Most of his little friends had left by then, and she sat alone on a bench watching him push a yellow bulldozer through the sand. From where she sat, the motor noises he made were clearly audible. Funny, how her son seemed to gravitate toward those kinds of noisy play activities. She couldn't recall Brooke ever doing anything like that. No, her ladylike little girl had been far more apt to swaddle and rock a baby doll or don layers of clothing from the dress-up box Candace kept with the toys.

Thinking of Brooke reminded Candace of Tuesday morning's unwelcome discovery of the invitation Brooke had disregarded. They had gone shopping after school that day and afterward, had taken the gift—a new book Brooke knew Tiffany wanted— over to the birthday girl's home. Tiffany had appeared delighted to see them, and her mother had remarked that Brooke had been missed at the party. Candace had made a general response without offering details. But the whole encounter had raised her antennae even higher. There wasn't even a hint of tension between Brooke and Tiffany. So why had Brooke not wanted to attend the party?

"Mommy!" Howie shouted. "Look at my mountain!"

Snapping herself back to the present, Candace made approving noises, then beckoned to her son. "Time to go home for lunch, buddy. I don't know about you, but I'm starving."

When they had finished their midday meal, Candace dropped her son off at preschool, which he attended three days a week. Then she turned her car in the direction of the oncology center on Cahokia Street to meet Robin and Andrew.

Candace took a deep breath and squared her shoulders as she stepped out of the car. *Lord*, she prayed, *give me the wisdom to comfort this family through Robin's illness and the compassion to calm their fears.* Robin had been so distraught the other day that Candace feared more bad news could make her fall apart completely.

The Deerford Oncology Practice was a building of deep brown brick. Its windows and doors were trimmed in creamy white and the caduceus symbol of the medical profession was part of the practice's bold logo that appeared on a sign out front as well as on the double front doors of clear glass.

Candace pulled open one side of a second set of doors and entered the foyer.

"Candace!" Robin and Andrew already were seated in the waiting area. The young woman leaped to her feet and rushed over to give Candace a hug. "Thank you so much for coming. I've been so frightened about this appointment that I'm making myself sick."

Candace felt a wave of protectiveness wash over her. She put a comforting arm around Robin and led her back to her seat, taking the empty chair on her other side. "This appointment is a *good* thing, Robin. Once we know what we're dealing with, we can begin to consider treatment options."

"If treatment is even necessary," Andrew put in.

Candace smiled at him. "Yes." But privately, she was a little dismayed. Had Robin downplayed the results of the earlier testing? Dr. Hashimi had set up this appointment for Robin because her test results indicated a strong likelihood that the mass in her breast was malignant.

She didn't have time to worry about it, in any case, because Robin's name was called. When the office staffer smiled and said, "Please follow me," Candace and Andrew both moved to accompany Robin.

They were shown to a comfortable room that looked like a very small conference room. The oncologist was

Dr. Joseph Prelutski, a tall, thin man with a craggy, forbidding countenance that melted into a much warmer expression as he introduced himself to them.

Robin was so tense, she was practically vibrating.

"Good afternoon, Mr. and Mrs. Overing." Dr. Prelutski's smile was kind. He extended his hand to Candace as Robin introduced her, telling the doctor, "She's an old friend of mine, and she also teaches our childbirth class."

"Ah." The doctor smiled. "You're an OB nurse. I thought you looked familiar."

Candace smiled as she nodded. "I am."

"Please have a seat." The oncologist waved them to butter-soft leather chairs in front of his desk. Rather than seating himself behind the desk, he perched a hip on the front edge.

"Mrs. Overing, Dr. Hashimi told you that the mass in your breast had classic characteristics of breast cancer. Unfortunately, the biopsy confirms that you do have a malignant tumor."

"Oh no." Andrew's face lost all color as the arm he had placed around his wife's shoulders tightened. "Are you sure?"

"Yes," the doctor said with somber eyes.

Robin cleared her throat. "Shouldn't we get a second opinion, doctor?"

Dr. Prelutski met the question head-on. "Second opinions are always a smart idea. I can give you the names of several other oncologists whom I respect, and my office can set up a speedy appointment with one for you. There is no time to waste here, so everything must move quickly."

"As far as you know," Robin said.

Dr. Prelutski pinned a sober gaze on Robin.

"Mrs. Overing, this type of malignancy typically grows quickly. You should make a decision on how to proceed with treatment as soon as possible."

Robin looked so stricken that Candace began to worry. "Breathe," she said to her young friend. "Let's listen to what else Dr. Prelutski recommends."

"There is some good news." The doctor raised one finger. "A recent study from the University of Texas M. D. Anderson Cancer Center shows that pregnant women respond to treatment in the same way nonpregnant women do, meaning there is no difference in mortality rates."

Andrew Overing looked at the doctor blankly. "Is that good news?"

"Most certainly. For many years, it was believed that higher hormone levels in pregnant women were responsible for an increase in mortality. But in reality, the complicating factor isn't hormones at all. Plus, we're at an advantage because you caught yours quite early."

Robin said, "My obstetrician said it was a good thing I noticed it when I did."

Dr. Prelutski nodded. "It was a very good thing. At present, this is a stage I cancer, which means we have a good chance of nipping this in the bud quickly."

"How?" Andrew sat forward.

The doctor smiled at the young husband, and then returned his gaze to Robin's face. "I would recommend that you have a lumpectomy as soon as possible." He went on to explain the surgery and to talk about following it up with radiation, chemotherapy or a combination of both after she delivered, if necessary.

Suddenly, Robin interrupted him. "But I don't want anesthesia while I'm pregnant. A friend of mine had anesthesia for a root canal when she was pregnant, and her baby didn't make it." Her eyes welled with tears.

There was a brief silence in the room.

Dr. Prelutski cleared his throat. "Are you sure the anesthesia was the reason? It would be unlikely—"

"She didn't say so, but I know that's what it was." Robin clutched at Andrew. "I can't have surgery until after the baby comes. I just can't."

"Honey, you can't afford to wait," the young man said in a worried tone. "The doctor says this cancer is very treatable now, so you need to treat it. Waiting a dozen or more weeks could change everything."

The oncologist nodded. "We won't know exactly what we're dealing with until the surgery is done, but waiting that long would be very unwise. An extremely treatable condition gives you very good odds. Those odds go down dramatically with advanced stages of cancer."

Candace sat in stunned silence as the doctor and Robin's husband attempted to talk the expectant mother into surgery. Didn't Robin want to seize any chance she might have to be there to see her child grow up? Didn't she understand how safe modern medicine made such procedures?

Apparently she didn't. Robin was having nothing to do with it. "I'll think about it," she said, although it was obvious her mind was made up. "But I'm not scheduling any surgery today."

Andrew looked at the doctor, fear plain in his eyes. "How long can she wait to make the decision, Dr. Prelutski?"

The physician shook his head. "Every day of delay changes the possible outcome. I can't tell you what to do, but if you were a member of my family, I wouldn't want you to delay much past two weeks. Four at the very most."

"Because the cancer might spread?" Andrew asked.

The doctor nodded. "Not might. *Will.*"

The appointment concluded on a decidedly unsatisfactory note. As they left the building, Andrew said, "Candace, I'd like to talk with you a little bit. Would you walk over to the Diner on the Corner with us and get some ice cream or something?"

"Sure." Candace had time before she needed to pick up the children from school. She altered her direction, and they crossed Whittington Street, then continued down the block to where the little eatery perched at an intersection right across from the hospital. The staff often came here for a bite to eat, and it was affectionately known as "the Corner" around the hospital.

Andrew held the single glass door open, and Candace and Robin preceded him into the little diner. Robin led them to a booth along the front wall beneath the window, where she and Andrew slid onto one of the dark green vinyl benches. Candace took a seat across from them.

The yellow café curtains all along the plateglass windows gave the room a cheerful look. A long counter stretched the length of the diner, with a small area at one end where there were several tables. Metal stools with green vinyl padded seats stood in a rigid line, while the sizzle of meat on the griddle, the clatter of flatware and the constant hum of animated conversation filled the air.

Candace saw several familiar faces from the hospital but no one she knew well.

A young waitress rushed up with glasses of water. "Hi, folks. My name is Lindy—oh hi, Candace! Didn't recognize you out of your scrubs," she joked.

Candace smiled back. "Hi, Lindy."

"What can I get you folks? Our specials are up on the board." She gestured at a chalkboard near the center of the counter.

"I would like a hot fudge sundae," Candace told her.

"Aha. Going straight for the chocolate fix today," Lindy said.

"I think I'll have one of those too," Robin said.

Andrew opted for apple pie, and as Lindy left to get their food, he said, "So we need to discuss this surgery."

"No, we do not," Robin said. "I will not endanger the life of our baby unnecessarily."

"It's not unnecessary!" Andrew sounded as if his patience was strained to the breaking point. Candace could see the tension in the young husband's face as he went on. "You can't let this tumor grow inside you for three more months. Who knows how big it will get and how much it could spread in that time. You have to have it taken out, Robin."

Robin put a hand over her husband's, which was clenched into a fist. "Honey, I understand how you feel. But it's just too great a risk."

Candace had been quiet as the couple argued. But at Robin's words, she cleared her throat. "That's not exactly true, Robin."

"You, of all people, should understand my position. You've been pregnant. Would you want to risk losing your baby?"

"I think you're being a little pessimistic." When the young woman leaned across the table, eyes flashing, Candace held up a hand and calmly said, "Hear me out. Please."

Robin sat back, altering her taut, aggressive posture. But her shoulders were still set and tense, and her mouth was set in an unyielding line. "Okay. Your turn."

Candace chose her words carefully, not wanting Robin to feel as if Candace and Andrew were ganging up on her. "Dr. Prelutski gave you up-to-date statistics on the risks associated with surgery and anesthesia. I would like you two to go home and read over the information he provided before you make any final decisions."

Andrew's face fell. "But—"

"Those statistics may reassure you," she went on, speaking to Robin. "If you contrast them with the mortality statistics associated with stage III and stage IV breast cancer, which could be the case if you decide to delay treatment for three months, you should be able to see which choice is safer for you."

"It's not *me* I'm worried about," Robin reminded her in a testy tone. "My first priority is the baby."

Lindy returned with their order, and Candace paused before continuing. As the young waitress set down their sweet treats, Candace decided to lighten the intensity of the discussion for a few moments. "Have you decorated your nursery yet?"

Robin's face lit up. Within moments, she was describing their preference to be surprised to find out if the baby was a boy or girl and how they had chosen the gender-neutral Winnie the Pooh theme. That led into the merits of various types of baby accessories.

When a short pause fell, Candace decided to return to the previous topic.

"I understand what you were saying earlier about your baby being your first priority." Candace smiled. "And I don't blame you." She took a breath, deciding that plain speaking was the only choice. And that her own pain came in a poor second behind the need to be sure Robin understood exactly what she might be consigning the rest of her family to. "But do you want your baby to grow up without you?"

Robin froze.

Candace pressed on, though every word was difficult to utter. "Do you want your husband to have to raise your child by himself?"

The questions hung in the air for a long moment. Neither of the couple across the table appeared to even take a breath.

"No," Candace said in a soft tone. "You don't." She paused, then took a deep breath and continued. "You never met my husband, Robin, but he was a wonderful man and an amazing father. He died three years ago when our children were eight and two." As Robin's gaze flashed to her face, she bore down, refusing to cry, though her throat was so tight her words were hard to get out. "I miss him every day. Every time one of them does something funny, or learns a new skill, I want to share it with him. Sometimes I still glance around before remembering he's not there."

"Candace." Robin's voice was a stricken whisper. "I'm so sorry."

Candace made an effort to smile. The knot strangling her vocal cords eased slightly, and she was able to force her lips into a weak smile. "I'm sorry too. I didn't intend to bring my personal life into this."

She couldn't look at either of them, so she dropped her gaze to the scarred top of the white table. "Please weigh the benefits of surgery against the possible negative outcomes. Evaluate your and your baby's chances of surviving with each choice. And trust your medical professionals. Yes, bad things sometimes do happen. In medicine, as in life, there are few guarantees. But most of the time, medicine offers an excellent chance to improve the quality of health and life."

Andrew told her soberly, "You've made this much more real to us. It's very scary to think of being a parent without Robin around to keep herding me in the right direction." He smiled at his wife and put an arm around her.

As Robin cuddled against his side, Candace battled back a pang of envy. *Lord*, she prayed, *fill my heart with joy that these two young people have each other. Fill my mind with the wonderful memories of my years with Dean. And while You're at it, could You please erase this nasty feeling of jealousy? It's hard to see happy couples, and I don't always do such a great job of appreciating the blessing of the years Dean and I had together. And also, if You don't mind, help Robin and Andrew make the right choice to treat her cancer successfully with no lasting side effects.*

Picking up her handbag, she said, "I must be going. But please call me if there are any other questions I can answer for you. I'll see you in class."

"See you in class," both Robin and Andrew echoed. Before Candace could pick up the check Lindy had left on the table,

Andrew slapped a hand over it and grinned. "Nope. Our treat. We really appreciate your taking the time to come with us and to share your point of view."

Robin awkwardly maneuvered her burgeoning belly out of the booth and stood to give Candace a hug. "I don't know what I would be doing right now without you."

Chapter Seven

ON SATURDAY, JAMES ENTERED THE STAFF LOUNGE. IT was nearly deserted, with just one X-ray tech reading a hardback book on one of the couches.

James slowed and glanced at the book as the tech looked up and smiled. It was Dan Brown's latest. "Great story," James said.

He moved on and seated himself at one of the computers kept available for staff use. Pulling a small flash drive from his scrub top pocket, he inserted it into the computer and opened the document he'd been working on. As he began to review and revise his work, the door opened and Anabelle entered the lounge.

Her eyes lit up when she saw him, and she crossed the room to his side. "Hello, James."

"Hi, Anabelle. How are you doing?" As he looked at her more closely, he realized that she seemed disturbed and upset. "Are you all right?"

Anabelle sighed. She dragged a chair over from one of the tables and sank down. "I'm okay. Just a little down. Remember

I told you Kirstie moved into her own place?" He nodded, and Anabelle sent him a wry smile. "I'm not doing a very good job of not worrying about her."

James and Anabelle had gone to the same church for many years. He remembered how long Kirstie was on the prayer list after the terrible bicycle accident in which the young woman had lost a leg. Calculating time in his head, he realized it had to have been more than a decade ago. "What are you concerned about?"

"Her health," Anabelle said promptly. "I'm afraid she'll overdo it, not take proper care of herself. She's completely recovered, of course, but she's always going to have a little bit more to think about than most people."

"Sounds like you're the one who's not recovered," James said, giving her a sympathetic smile.

Anabelle tried to laugh, but it was obvious there was a grain of truth in the comment.

James absently watched the technician close his book and leave the lounge. "I imagine it's hard to let go after so many years of watching over her."

"It is." She twisted her fingers together in an uncharacteristic sign of nerves. Then she inhaled and exhaled deeply. "But I have to." She cocked her head. "What are you doing?"

"I'm working on my résumé," James told her.

"Oh, James, I wish you'd reconsider."

He shrugged. "I wish I could. But I have a family to support; and I'm afraid if I wait, there will be a million other people who all have the same idea."

Ruefully, Anabelle nodded in acknowledgment. "I suppose you're right. So what kind of jobs are you looking at?"

"I don't know. Anything here in town, for starters. And, of course, I have to have a day job so I can help with the boys in the evening, so maybe a doctor's office or clinic would be best." He looked down.

"But you like the hospital setting best," she said.

"I do." James raked a hand through his hair, balancing the chair on its back legs. "I love working in a hospital. *This* hospital. If I didn't have a family, I probably would take my chances. But I do have a family." He smiled. "Thank heavens."

Anabelle smiled too. "Thank heavens for family is right."

"I could go farther away, to another hospital, but I would hate being so far away from Fern. It really bothers her that she can't contribute more. If it came to a choice between being close to home or working in a hospital, I'd choose to stay close."

"Unless the money was amazing," Anabelle said.

"Well, yes," he admitted. "That would change things a little. I've been thinking of remodeling the house to put a master bedroom with a full bath on the main floor. The way our house is set up now, Fern has to go up and down the stairs at least once a day. She has days where her spasticity makes it very difficult, and I don't want to wait until we're desperate, just to end up making hasty decisions."

Anabelle nodded. "I don't blame you."

"What are your plans?" James asked her. "If the hospital closes, I mean."

Anabelle shrugged as she ran her fingers over a scratch on the tabletop. "I'll probably retire. I'm getting a little long in the tooth, you know." Her eyes twinkled, inviting James to laugh with her.

"Right," he said. "I'd like to see the day you grow old. You've got more stamina than most people I know—and that includes my two teenage sons."

"Cam has called me a workhorse on more than one occasion. And I don't think it was a compliment." They shared a chuckle.

"Will you really be content to retire?" James couldn't quite envision Anabelle in that role.

"Maybe not completely," she said. "I probably would take on some private-duty work to keep from growing old and moldy." Her eyes grew wistful. "It might not be so bad. I hope to be a grandmother one of these days, although my children certainly seem in no hurry to oblige me!"

James laughed. "All in good time, I'm sure."

Anabelle's pager vibrated. Checking it, she said, "I'd better get back downstairs. I just need a hit of coffee."

"I'll see you later," James said as she turned and bustled over to the counter where the coffee machine stood.

"All right." She smiled at him as she took a sip and hurried toward the door. "Good luck with your project," she said as another staffer entered the room.

James smiled and waved. He appreciated her circumspection. Even though it probably was a given that many of the hospital employees were quietly evaluating their options if the hospital closed, he preferred not to advertise the fact that he was considering leaving.

On the following Monday, the foursome met for lunch again. Unfortunately, rain precluded having their meal in the courtyard, so they gathered at a square table in the small cafeteria.

Candace arrived at the same time James and Anabelle did, but their fourth companion was running a little late. By the time Elena arrived, Candace and the others had already begun to eat.

"Hi," she said breathlessly as she rushed through the door. "Sorry I'm late. One of my critical patients has not had a good morning, and I waited to talk with the attending physician about his pain management."

"No problem," James said. He was blowing on a large bowl of steaming cream soup.

"Yum," Elena said. "What's that?"

"Cheddar-broccoli," he told her. "When I got Anabelle's message about meeting here, I decided to leave my lunch upstairs in the fridge for tomorrow. This cafeteria has yet to serve a soup I don't like."

"I was in the mood for soup too," Candace said, indicating the cup of soup and tuna sandwich on her tray.

Elena eyed the Hershey bar beside Candace's plate as she opened her lunch bag and began to set out her own food. "That's not all you were in the mood for," she teased.

Candace laid a protective hand over her chocolate. "I need a pick-me-up. It was one of those mornings."

"A bad one?" Anabelle asked. She was idly picking at a mammoth plate of french fries liberally drenched with ketchup.

Candace nodded, her lighthearted moment fading. "We had a mom come in for a scheduled C-section. We already knew the baby had Down syndrome and a heart murmur; but as it turned out, there was a much larger hole than anyone had anticipated. He had to be life-flighted to St. Francis." OSF St. Francis Medical Center was the area's only level I trauma center and the fourth largest hospital in the state of Illinois. "Thankfully, the obstetrician was cautious, and we were prepared for that possibility. They whisked him away like *that*." She snapped her fingers with a crisp, staccato sound.

"I'll keep him and his family in my prayers," Elena said.

Anabelle nodded. "We all will. Those surgeries have a great success rate, you know."

"I know." Candace's eyes filled with tears, and she reached for a napkin. "But when you're facing two absolutely devastated, frantic parents who just watched a helicopter fly away with their newborn, and you can't offer an ironclad guarantee that their baby is going to be all right . . ."

"It's difficult," Anabelle finished. She put a hand over Candace's. "I'm sure you were a comfort to them."

Candace smiled, blotting away the tears. "I tried." There was an awkward pause. Then she said, "Okay. Time for a subject change. Let's talk about something cheerful."

James looked troubled. "With this hospital closing hanging over our heads, I'm having a little trouble finding my 'cheer.'"

"Oh, I know!" Elena raised a hand as if she were a school student, then hastily lowered it when Anabelle grinned. "Let's talk about the hospital *not* closing."

"I can get behind that," James said. "What's up?"

"I have a meeting scheduled with Zane McGarry soon," Elena said. "Last night, it occurred to me that the more information I can present, the more likely he is to look seriously at my proposal."

"What kind of information do you have in mind?" Anabelle asked.

"Cost projections, for one thing," Elena said. "Maybe recommendations for materials and a rough design, but the biggest thing I think we need to know is exactly how much it will cost us for each brick and then for the construction. That probably will be the biggest factor in deciding whether this is worth pursuing." Her brow wrinkled. "I'd like to have that information in my arsenal; but I have to confess, I'm a little lost. Where do I start? I don't even know who engraves bricks."

"A monument company," Candace told her. "Gravestones, statues, that sort of thing."

Elena swallowed. It was obvious that she realized why Candace had the answer at her fingertips. "Thank you."

"You could check with different builders to get bulk prices on bricks," James suggested. "They might also have recommendations on what type of bricks would work best for this project."

"There are different kinds of bricks?" Elena rolled her eyes. "Oh boy. I am in trouble!"

"I have an idea," Anabelle said. "My husband, Cam, owned Scott Landscaping Company until he retired. Now our son Evan has it. I bet Cam would be happy to work with you, Elena." She rose and pulled her phone out of a pocket. "Excuse me for a moment," she said, walking out into the corridor and heading for the front door.

Cell phones were banned in the hospital because they could disrupt the myriad patient monitoring equipment in use. It was not uncommon to see employees standing in the parking lot with mobile phones pressed to their ears.

Anabelle returned within minutes. Her beaming smile told the story. "Cam says he'd love to help," she reported. "He suggested I invite everyone over for dinner tonight so that we can talk about the project."

Candace and James offered their apologies for not being able to make it. Elena looked delighted. "That would be wonderful!"

"Cam!" Anabelle glanced out the window. "Elena and her family are here!"

Cameron Scott's bushy gray eyebrows rose as he glanced over the top of the newspaper he had been reading. "That's good. You did invite them, remember?"

Anabelle frowned. "Put that paper away. And tuck in your shirt."

Cam grinned. "Yes, mother."

Anabelle huffed out a breath. "I just want everything to look nice, that's all."

Cam folded the paper, placed it neatly in the magazine basket and rose. Stepping behind his wife, he placed his hands on her shoulders and gently massaged. "Relax, honey. You're way too worked up about a simple dinner."

Anabelle turned and opened her mouth. Then she halted, took a breath and said, "You're right. I'm sorry."

Cam put his arms around her and hugged her, then moved with her toward the door.

"Hello, hello," Elena called gaily as soon as he opened it. "You must be Cam."

"Guilty." He was smiling as he shook her hand.

"I'm Elena. This is my husband Cesar and my granddaughter Isabel." Elena handed Anabelle a cookie tin. "These are mint brownies."

"Thank you!" Anabelle said, lifting a corner of the lid and taking a deep breath. "They smell delicious. I know what I'm having for dessert."

Elena grinned. "Thank you so much for including Izzy in the invitation. I had completely forgotten it's Monday, and I normally babysit tonight."

"No problem." Anabelle knelt in front of the beautiful little girl with long dark curls streaming over her shoulders. The child carried a slightly scruffy stuffed pig under one arm, and over her shoulders rested the straps of a little pink backpack with Disney princesses cavorting all over it. Kirstie had had long dark curls like that when she'd been small. "Hello, Isabel."

"This is Miss Anabelle, Izzy," Elena said. "The one I told you had a special name like yours, remember?"

Isabel nodded. "We're both bells," she informed Anabelle.

Anabelle chuckled. "You're right."

"She's the lady who's making us dinner," Elena told her granddaughter.

Isabel looked at Anabelle, her striking gray eyes inquisitive. "Did you make something I like?"

"*Isabel Anastasia Rodriguez!*" Elena was aghast. "That is *not* using your good manners."

Anabelle couldn't help chuckling. "It's okay," she said to Elena. "When you're four, that's a perfectly legitimate concern." To Isabel, she said, "I made chicken and mashed potatoes, and I have some green beans and sliced strawberries. And, oh, I almost forgot, some tasty buttermilk biscuits. Do you like any of that?"

"Yes!" Isabel grinned at Anabelle, then looked up at her grandmother. "I like all of that."

"Good." Anabelle rose and pointed toward the living room. "There are some dolls in there you might like to see." To Elena, she said, "I went up to the attic and got some of my girls' old American Girl dolls. I didn't know what she might like to play with."

"American Girl dolls. Anabelle, those are quite expensive." Elena looked worried as she followed her friend and granddaughter.

Anabelle laughed. "They're sturdy and already well loved. My girls got many years of pleasure from those dolls." Her smile faded a bit as she and Elena took seats in the living room to watch Isabel examine the toys, and she gestured at Isabel. "I'd give a lot to have my children be that size again. You're very lucky to have her living with you."

Elena smiled. "I know. Not everyone would see it that way. I have friends who are thrilled when their kids move out. But I really enjoy having Rafael and Izzy living with us."

"I would enjoy that too," Anabelle said. "I wasn't at all ready for Kirstie to move out. This is the third week, and I'm afraid I may not be handling it well." Anabelle sighed.

"I imagine it seems very quiet around here without her. If Rafael and Izzy ever move out, I know our place will seem terribly empty."

Anabelle smiled, watching Isabel work a dress over a red-haired doll's head. "I bet. She's adorable."

"She's a good little egg," Elena said. "Most of the time, she's extremely pleasant and helpful. Although I do occasionally get tired of answering the question, 'Why?'"

Anabelle chuckled. "I remember those days." She looked up as Cam entered the room with Cesar.

"I'd like to show Cesar the garden, if we have time before we eat," he said.

She nodded and rose from her seat. "You do. I'll call you when the meal is ready." To Elena, she said, "I need to take care of a few more things in the kitchen. Isabel is welcome to bring the dolls in there if she likes."

"Could I set the table for you?" Elena walked to the table in the adjacent dining room as soon as Anabelle showed her into the kitchen.

"Sure." Anabelle indicated the counter. "I've got most of the dishes laid out already."

"Oh, Anabelle!" Elena said as she picked up some of the cutlery. "This is lovely." She placed a reverent hand on a table runner in summer prints of lemon, leaf, peach and strawberry that graced the center of the long table. Matching place mats lay in front of each chair.

"Thank you."

"Did you make these?"

Anabelle nodded as she began draining the potatoes. "I'm in a quilting club. Dr. Hamilton's wife Genevieve is also in the group."

Elena was still looking at the place mats as she set the table with a summery set of clear glass plates, bowls, and glasses with a small flower design stretching along one side. "Someday when I have time—and I'm done making costumes and a little girl's clothing—I'm going to learn to quilt." She finished placing soft linen napkins at each place setting and then turned to look at her friend.

"Buela?" Isabel tugged at Elena's hand. "Will you hold this baby?"

"Of course." Elena knelt and smiled as Isabel very carefully handed her a doll, adjusting Elena's hands so that she was cradling the toy.

"She needs a mommy," Isabel told her. "So does this one." She picked up the second doll and held it against her shoulder. "Everybody needs a mommy."

"Izzy." Elena's face looked stricken as she quietly said, "Maybe we should talk about something else."

"But, Buela, she *does* need a mommy," Isabel insisted.

Anabelle quickly joined them and smiled at the little girl. "Are you going to be her mommy? I bet you'd be a good one."

Isabel nodded. "I am, but sometimes I don't know what mommies do 'cause I don't have a mommy."

Anabelle's heart contracted at the innocent statement. "I know. But you have your *abuela*. What kinds of things does she do for you?"

Isabel twisted her little body back and forth, making her eyelet lace–trimmed dress swirl around her body. "She makes me pretty clothes. Like this dress."

"It's a beautiful dress." Anabelle smoothed a gentle finger along the eyelet lace. "What else does she do for you?"

"She makes me eat my vegetables." Isabel made a face and giggled. "An' . . . an' . . . an' she reads me stories an' she listens to my prayers."

"My goodness!" Anabelle infused her tone with wonder. "It sounds like your *abuela* does all the things I did for my little girls."

Isabel considered that for a moment. "You're a mommy?"

Anabelle nodded, a soft smile curving her mouth as she thought of the enjoyable years when her children had been small. "I am. But my little girls and my boy are all grown up now."

"Like my daddy."

"Exactly like your daddy. But guess what?"

"What?" Isabel patted her doll.

"I still know how to be a mommy. And so does your *abuela*. So you're very lucky. You have someone who loves you who can do mommy things with you."

Anabelle could almost see the gears turning as Isabel tried to find a flaw in her logic. But finally, the child said, "My Buela's not my mommy, but she's *like* my mommy."

"Yes, she is." Anabelle rose, stroking a hand over the little girl's glossy dark curls. "And I'm pretty sure she loves you just as much as a mommy could."

The men came back into the house then, and Isabel ran shouting for her grandfather.

Elena threw Anabelle a grateful look, her expressive face unusually sorrowful. "Thanks for smoothing that over. She's a happy little girl, but she does feel the absence of a mother, no matter how attentive I am."

"I think that's only natural," Anabelle said. "The important thing is the first part of that sentence. She *is* a happy child, Elena. And that's due to you."

Chapter Eight

ANDACE WAS BECOMING CONCERNED.

She was fairly certain Robin had avoided her last Thursday evening in the childbirth class, walking out of the room deeply engrossed in conversation with several other women. Andrew had looked back at Candace helplessly, mouthing, "Sorry."

He had nothing to be sorry for, she thought. She sensed the young father was as concerned as she was about her friend's indecision. How could she fail to understand how critical time could be with a malignancy? But she also knew how fiercely protective mothers were; and when a stance was taken, little could be done to sway them.

She picked up the phone on the desk, looking up Robin's number in her cell phone directory. After she called the number, the phone rang and rang. Three times, four, five . . . didn't the Overings have an answering machine? She was on the verge of hanging up when a breathless male voice said, "Hello?"

"Hello, Andrew, it's Candace Crenshaw from—"

"Our childbirth class," he finished for her. "Hello, Candace."

"Is Robin home?" she asked. "I wanted to see what she's decided regarding a treatment plan."

There was a moment of silence. Then Andrew said, "She hasn't decided or made any kind of plan." There was bitterness in his voice. "I've started calling her an ostrich."

The last thing Candace wanted to do was get into the middle of a marital tiff, even if she did sympathize completely with Andrew. "I had hoped to talk to her Thursday, but she left before I had the chance."

"She didn't want to talk to you," the young man told her sadly. "She knows you believe she should treat her cancer, and she just doesn't want to hear that right now." He sounded completely dispirited. "I don't know what to do."

"Support her," Candace said quietly. "Just try to support her. You can disagree with her, but she needs you, Andrew. And I know time is in short supply here, but I believe she'll work through it. At least, that's what I'm praying."

"I'll do my best," he told her. "Thank you for listening. I appreciate the sounding board."

"It's all part of the extra-special Hope Haven service," Candace said, trying to lighten the tone of the conversation. "Enhanced by a little 'former-babysitter' concern."

"Well, it's pretty doggone amazing." His voice was warm. "Thanks again. I guess I'll see you at class Thursday if not before. I'll tell Robin you called."

"Okay, Chrissy, it's time to push!" Candace encouraged a laboring young woman in the delivery room as the mother-to-be gritted her teeth and bore down. Her husband, Shaun, stood near her head holding her hand; Candace sent him an encouraging smile as the obstetrician gave additional directions in a calm, steady voice.

Minutes later, the obstetrician held the baby. While another nurse attended to the remainder of the birthing process, Candace scored the infant's Apgars. It was a boy, healthy and already squalling. Candace wrapped him in a clean blanket and slipped a tiny blue knit hat on his nearly bald head. "What hair there is, is blond," she reported.

Shaun laughed. "My brother and I were both bald as bad tires when we were born."

Candace carried the wee one to the new mother and showed her how to begin breast-feeding while Shaun looked on.

"Shaun, go tell everyone he's here," Chrissy said warily.

Candace smiled to herself. Shaun was too ecstatic, with dazed delighted eyes, to be torn away from the baby right now. "Oh, look," he said. "He's got a little birthmark just like mine!"

"Would you like me to go out and let them know?" she offered. "Then you can take your time in here."

Chrissy shot her a grateful smile. "That would be great. Thank you."

Candace left the young couple in the birthing suite and walked to the visitors' lounge. She stepped into the room and said, "Is the Carlson family here?"

Immediately, a whole crowd of people leaped up and came rushing toward her. There appeared to be two sets of grandparents and several assorted younger adults. One of them was a man in a set of blue scrubs with curly, golden blond hair who looked to be roughly her age. He wore a Hope Haven Hospital ID around his neck, and he sent Candace a warm smile as she announced the baby news. As other members of the family drifted away, chattering excitedly among themselves, he stepped forward and offered a hand.

"Hello. I'm Heath Carlson from Radiology."

"Candace Crenshaw." She smiled and took his hand briefly. "I guess you already know I work in Labor and Delivery."

"I thought you might." His grin invited her to chuckle along with him. "Shaun, the new dad, is my brother. This is my parents' first grandchild, so everyone's excited."

Candace instantly remembered the day that Brooke had been born. "My daughter was the first grandchild on my husband's side of the family. It was quite an exciting time for all of us."

"And how old is she now?"

"Eleven."

"Just on the edge of adolescence."

"Yes, and I'm already beginning to notice flashes of moodiness." Candace gave a small sigh. "I remember my own teen years. You couldn't pay me enough to be that age again."

"I know a lot of people who say that, although I don't remember it as being a particularly traumatic time." Heath's eyes crinkled, and Candace noticed how vividly blue they were. He was quite attractive.

"Maybe it's easier for boys," she said. "I'll let you know in a decade or so, when my son is a teenager. He's still only five and very excited to be starting kindergarten in the fall." Her eyes met his and she smiled. "Do you have children?"

Heath sent her another gentle smile, and deep dimples creased his cheeks. "No. I'm not married." His gaze slid to her left hand.

Candace felt the warmth of a blush stealing up her neck and into her cheeks. Oh heavens. She gestured toward the doorway. "I have to go and do . . . things. I have things to do." An unexpected bubble of something akin to panic rose in her chest.

Heath's smile widened, and his blue eyes sparkled. "It was nice to meet you, Candace."

"You too." With hurried strides, she fled back down the corridor toward the Birthing Unit. At least, it felt like she was fleeing, although she deliberately slowed her steps to a moderate pace.

She had barely thought about relationships since Dean's death. Between the children and her job, it was easy to avoid facing the fact that she was a single woman now. A widow. How she hated that word. *I'm a widow.* A lump rose in her throat. Glancing around and seeing no one, she ducked into an empty room and pressed herself against the wall. *Oh, Dean, I miss you so.*

Heath Carlson had been gentle and warm, and she'd felt herself responding to his smiling gaze with smiles of her own. The way her breath had caught for just a moment had reminded her of the first time she'd met Dean. They both had been undergraduate students at the University of Illinois' Chicago campus. Dean had studied business; she was a nursing student.

She had dropped a folder as she walked to class one day, and several papers had fallen out. It was windy, but she'd managed to grab them all but one. As she'd chased it across a grassy area, a tall boy with hair so blond it almost looked white reached down and snagged it. He'd been laughing as she had rushed up, and she could still remember the *zing* she'd felt when their eyes had met. Neither of them had dated anyone else from that day forward. They'd loved and laughed, and she'd imagined them growing old together.

Then came the day she'd gotten the frantic call from Dean's friend saying he'd been rushed to the hospital. By the time she'd met the ambulance there, a brain aneurysm had taken away the man she loved.

She squeezed her eyes closed and took deep, calming breaths. She rarely gave in to these bouts of grief anymore. Only at night, in the privacy of her own room, did she mourn.

Help me, Lord, she prayed silently. *Carry me and this burden during those moments when it's too heavy to bear.*

She prayed for several minutes, gradually feeling herself calming. The tension in her throat eased. Finally, with a small smile just to prove to herself that she could, she pulled open the door and stepped into the hallway again.

She was a nurse; people needed her.

Elena climbed out of the passenger side of Cameron Scott's truck after they pulled into a parking spot at the monument company. A variety of headstones with different carving effects were distributed in front of the building. CLUDS' MONUMENTS OF DEE-STINCTION, read the sign that fronted the road.

"Dee-stinction?" Elena said, grinning as she pointed to the misspelled sign.

"It certainly makes it dee-stinct," Cam said with a chuckle.

"I can't thank you enough for volunteering to help me with this," she said to him as they started into the building. She glanced down at the notebook she carried in one arm. "Without you, I never would have known what type of brick would make a good memorial wall, and I certainly wouldn't have known where to go to get the best prices."

Cam grinned. He had gray hair and a mustache of the same color, and the way his blue eyes twinkled reminded Elena of the stereotypical illustration of Santa Claus. "My pleasure. And besides, it's self-serving. If the hospital closes, Anabelle says she's retiring. And if Anabelle retires and hangs around the house all day, my honey-do list is going to grow by a mile!"

Elena laughed aloud. "I can't imagine Anabelle retiring," she said.

Cam's pleasant expression altered in a subtle manner, letting her see the concern in his eyes. "Me neither. She loves nursing and working at Hope Haven. She's going to be devastated if that hospital closes. Private duty won't be fulfilling enough for her."

"The community would be devastated." Elena was equally sober.

"That's why we're here—to do our best to stop that from happening," Cam said, clearly attempting to lift her spirits again as he summoned a smile.

The bell over the door of the little shop jangled merrily for a moment as he pulled open the door. Inside, it was cool. At first, it appeared dim; but as Elena's eyes adjusted, she saw there was plenty of white light pouring down from a few utilitarian fluorescent lights.

A woman came through a door on the back wall. "Hi. I'm Andrea Clud. How can I help you?"

"We need to talk to you about engraving," Elena told her.

"Certainly." Andrea gave her a subdued smile as she picked up a pen and set a clipboard with a form in front of her.

"I would like to get a price on engraving a brick. It's for a fund-raising idea." She went on to explain to the woman what she wanted and how the bricks would be used.

"What a wonderful idea!" the woman enthused. "Of course we can help you with that. We have some lovely color choices available at very reasonable prices, and I might be able to give you a discount if you guarantee a certain number." She tapped a few keys on the keyboard at the computer on the counter, then swiveled the monitor to face Elena and Cam. "Here are a couple of different ways we can approach it. I can give you prices on each, and if you would like to choose a couple, we could even engrave the bricks so you would have a sample."

"That would be fantastic!" Elena was thrilled to be putting her idea into tangible form. "Let's check these out," she said to Cam, leaning closer to the monitor.

While they viewed the possibilities, Andrea disappeared through a door at one side of the office, and Elena caught a glimpse of a large, dusty workroom with several solid tables, large chunks of marble and a few unfamiliar-looking machines.

Elena debated the options with Cam, and they chose three different looks, with varying typefaces, ornamentation and surface treatments. Just as they finished, Andrea came back through the door.

"I have some good news," she said. "My husband and I would like to contribute something to your efforts to keep the hospital open. Therefore, we would like to donate the first five hundred bricks and engraving costs."

"Really?" Elena's voice rose with excitement. "Mrs. Clud, that's a very, very generous offer. Are you sure? I mean, that's a lot of money."

Cam laughed and shook his head. "Elena, never argue when someone wants to give you something."

Both women chuckled. Then Andrea Clud said, "We're sure. My husband's brother had a stroke last year. He survived and recovered completely because this hospital was so close by that they were able to administer the new clot-busting drug treatment very quickly. We feel very strongly that Deerford needs Hope Haven Hospital."

Elena was so ecstatic she had to stop herself from jumping up and down and grabbing Cam and dancing around the room with him. "Thank you so much!" she said, taking Mrs. Clud's hand and pumping it up and down enthusiastically.

She was able to focus long enough to give the woman the information on the three samples of bricks they wanted to have. After a final thank-you and farewell to Mrs. Clud, Elena preceded Cam out of the shop. As they got back into the truck, she clapped her hands together in delight.

"The first five hundred bricks. Can you imagine? Five hundred! All of the income from those will be pure donations with no overhead!"

Chapter Nine

SEVERAL DAYS LATER, THE FOUR FRIENDS MET FOR lunch in the staff lounge, where there were several small tables. They had intended to meet in the courtyard, but midway through the morning it had begun to rain once again, so the plan was hastily changed.

James was already there reading a magazine when Candace and Elena came down together from the second floor. "Hello, ladies."

"What are you reading?" asked Elena.

James held up the magazine he'd been perusing. "An article about an orphanage in Romania." He shook his head. "I think it's hard for us to imagine the substandard conditions those poor children live in."

Candace nodded. "A girl from my church went on a mission trip to work in one of the orphanages for three weeks. It changed the whole course of her life. She changed her college major from Biology to Early Childhood Education. After she graduated, she actually moved to Romania and still works there as a volunteer. Our church gives her annual support so she doesn't have to work elsewhere to make ends meet."

"What an inspiring story," Elena said. "I'd like to read that article when you're done and then show it to Anabelle when she gets here."

All four were working that day, although Anabelle had mentioned that she probably would be late; so Candace, Elena and James began to eat without her.

Candace picked up one of the newly engraved bricks that Elena had set in the middle of the table.

"I just picked these up this morning," Elena told them. "These are the three different samples Cam and I chose. I'd like you to look at all of them and rank them from favorite to least."

"And should we choose a color too?" The bricks were variations of the same color family, a light pinkish-brown shade against which the engraving showed up clearly. Candace ran a finger over the engraving before passing the sample to James.

"No, we'll be using several different shades like these. Cam and I originally had chosen a dark brown color, but the lady at the monument company suggested using a lighter shade so that the writing would show up better."

"Looks like she was right," James said. "This is really nice."

"Have you shown these to Zane McGarry yet?" Candace asked.

Elena shook her head. "We have a meeting scheduled for tomorrow."

"Oh, I hope this idea flies." Candace could see a lovely little courtyard in her mind's eye. It would be wonderful if the plan really did stimulate enough income to keep the hospital open. Then she remembered something else. "I had another idea for you," she said to Elena. "If you're interested. If not, that's okay—"

"Of course we're interested," Elena said. "Since I've made this connection with Zane and we're discussing fund-raising, I'd be happy to give him any additional ideas. What did you have in mind?"

"All the departments of this hospital are important as well as helpful to the community," Candace said. "But I think that when a baby is born here, it gives a family an even closer tie to Hope Haven."

Elena and James both were nodding in encouragement, so she took a breath and went on.

"Perhaps the hospital could send out a letter to every person in the community who was born here, or their parents, in the case of children. It would be a good way to let people know what is happening or to reinforce the concern if they're already aware."

"That's a terrific idea," Elena exclaimed. "I wonder how many hundreds of people that would reach."

"Hundreds? More like thousands," James said. He nodded approvingly at Candace. "I think it's an idea *par excellence*."

"Thank you." She cocked her head. "*Par excellence?*"

He grinned. "It's French. Literally, it means 'by excellence.' Outstanding, supreme, preeminent."

Elena and Candace chuckled. Just then Anabelle entered the lounge and came to the table. She set down a wrapped ham sandwich and a cup of soup from the cafeteria and then went to the coffee machine on the counter and poured herself a cup, dropping a quarter into the can beside it.

Anabelle was smiling by the time James had recounted his vocabulary lesson. Candace was glad to see her friend smile. Anabelle had looked tense when she came in. Still slightly concerned, Candace reached over and lightly squeezed Anabelle's hand. "Everything okay? You looked as if you might have had a trying morning."

Anabelle's eyes were warm when she turned to Candace. "The morning was fine. But I had a Bike Smarts meeting right before lunch. It's a great program, but sometimes the meetings get a little contentious." She sighed. "I believe all the other committee members regard me as the controlling type."

"Imagine that," James said in a dry tone.

Anabelle hit him playfully in the shoulder with a balled fist. "All right, so maybe I am. But I'm personally invested in this program. It's been my baby since the very beginning."

"I think it's a terrific program. Brooke got a bike helmet last year after her class completed the program." Candace sat up straighter. "I didn't realize it was your idea."

Anabelle nodded, and her large brown eyes darkened. "Kirstie was hit by a car when she was ten. One leg had to be amputated, and she had head trauma. She probably would have died if she hadn't been wearing a bike helmet. So I feel pretty strongly about them."

"Oh, Anabelle," Candace said. "I'm so sorry. I had no idea." The mere thought of a child almost the same age as Brooke being struck by a car gave her goose bumps and tightened her throat in sympathy. "Your response to the accident is so positive," she added sincerely. "I imagine there have been a number of children who have escaped serious injury thanks to you."

Anabelle blushed. "Thanks to the entire community, who supports it financially when we have our fund-raisers." She looked at the bricks in the middle of the table. "So catch me up. What's going on with our Wall of Hope?"

Elena went straight to the conference room on the first floor after work on Wednesday. She walked in just as Zane McGarry, the Chief Financial Officer of the hospital, entered. Right behind him was Quintessa Smith with a laptop computer.

The CFO's assistant flashed her bright smile at Elena. "Hey, girlfriend. How are you?"

"I'm great!" Elena never failed to be uplifted and energized by Quintessa's ebullient spirits. "How about you?"

"Also great. And I *love* this Wall of Hope idea." Quintessa set down her laptop and powered it up. "Zane gave me a brief summary of what you want to do."

"And you have more information for us today, right?" Zane took a seat at the end of the table, motioning for Elena to sit across from Quintessa.

"I do." Elena set down her file folder and plopped the brick in the middle of the table. "Here is a sample of what one of the bricks might look like." She went on to explain the thinking regarding the light color and the costs for two or for three lines of text. Then she carefully laid out a large sheet of paper that she had rolled up like a poster. "This is one design possibility for the courtyard," she told them. "Anabelle Scott's husband Cameron drew this up for us. He also has indicated that he would be willing to take on the project as a volunteer."

That got Zane's attention. "As in we wouldn't have to pay him? He'd actually build it?"

Elena laughed. "Exactly. He's retired, so he has the time. He used to own a landscaping company, so he has the skill to do masonry work. And he feels strongly about keeping Hope Haven open, so he has the motivation."

Quintessa picked up the brick and ran her fingers lightly across the engraving. "This is really classy, Elena. How much would we charge people for them?"

Elena hesitated. "I'm not sure. There are two schools of thought. The first is to set a price for an engraved brick. The second is not to charge any fee, except for additional engraving, and let people make donations. I believe I prefer this option. I think people would give with their hearts open, considering the need we have."

Quintessa's dark eyebrows shot up. "But what if they don't? What if the donations don't cover the cost of labor, much less any real donation to fund saving the hospital?"

Elena smiled. "It's a question of faith, isn't it?" She pulled out a stack of papers, handing a sheet to each of the others. "Here are several calculations for possible income from this project, just to give you an idea of what we might expect."

Zane glanced quickly down at the page. "I think asking for a donation is a great idea. We probably would make more money that way."

Quintessa shook her head. "In my opinion, that's too risky. The project could end up costing us money, even with Mr. Scott's volunteer offer."

Zane pondered this and then said, "People who make donations for these bricks will know their money is going to help
keep our hospital open. They'll be generous."

Quintessa snorted. "I think you're seeing our fellow citizens
through rose-colored glasses. If we don't set a minimum donation, we won't make the money this place needs."

Elena cleared her throat and held up a hand before Quintessa
could fire another round. She decided she was glad she didn't
work in an office with the two of them. "This committee won't
be making any decisions." She glanced at Zane. "Despite our
personal opinions, our job is to put together recommendations
for the board of directors. They'll be the ones to decide how best
to handle it."

Zane nodded. "I guess we might as well write up both possible
donation ideas to present to the board." It was clear he wasn't
thrilled about it, but Elena knew Zane was highly regarded as
an ethical administrator. Despite his personal views, when he
took it before the board, his presentation would be scrupulously
balanced.

"All right." Quintessa began typing madly on her keyboard,
as professional as Zane was, even though they disagreed. "I'll put
together a packet with an overview of Elena's Wall of Hope idea,
a copy of Mr. Scott's design, the brick pricing, the Clud Monuments people's generous offer, and these donation options for you
to take to the board meeting." She directed the last at the CFO.

"When will the next one be?" Elena asked him.

"We just had a meeting last week," Zane told her. "So there
isn't another regularly scheduled one until next month. I think

I'll call Mr. Telford, the president of the board, and see if we can't call a special meeting to present this. I don't think we can afford to wait long."

The serious note in his voice alarmed Elena as much as the letter they had received. If the chief financial officer was that worried about funds, then it was even more imperative that they raise money.

"Hey, Dad, you fouled me." Nelson Bell stopped playing basketball and glared at his father. "I quit."

James sighed. Nelson didn't enjoy team sports nearly as much as his older brother, and he could only be counted on for about ten minutes of play before he wanted out. Instead, he excelled on his swim team.

"Five more minutes," he said. "Just you and Gid. I'll watch."

Nelson sighed, but he allowed himself to be persuaded to come back onto the "court," which was really just the driveway outside their two-story brick home. James considered himself the victor. He used any opportunity he found to encourage Nelson to participate.

When the game was concluded, Gideon went upstairs to his room to finish some homework while Nelson headed for the shower.

James pulled a load of laundry from the dryer and tossed it into a basket, which he carried into the living room where Fern sat chewing on the tip of a pencil as she worked a crossword puzzle.

"What's a six-letter word that means to absorb or drink in?" she asked without looking up.

"What's it start with?" he asked as he set down the laundry basket.

"Don't know," she said. "But it's blank-blank-*b-i-b*-blank."

James shook out a pair of Nelson's jeans as he mulled over the letters in his head. "Imbibe."

"*I-m-b-i-b* . . . *E! Yes!* Wow, thanks. I can't believe you got that." She looked up at him, smiling. "One more reason I'd better keep you around." Laying the puzzle aside, she scooted forward in her chair and reached for a T-shirt to fold.

As the two of them worked together to get the basket of clothing folded, James decided it was time to mention the possibility he'd been kicking around for some time. "What would you think," he asked slowly, "of renovating the office and making it a master bedroom?"

Fern's hand stilled on the socks she had just matched. "A bedroom down here?"

"Yes." In reality, he didn't think they had much of a choice unless they wanted to move. Although she still got around fairly well, Fern had days when her balance was off enough that she scooted up and down the stairs on her bottom rather than walking, a precaution he'd insisted on after she'd fallen down the stairs and bruised her shoulder badly a few months earlier. "The office could be moved upstairs in our bedroom. We could turn the half bath down here into a full bath with an extra-large shower stall."

"You're thinking of a shower big enough to accommodate a wheelchair."

He nodded. "I thought it would make your life a lot simpler. If our bedroom was down here, you could nap in bed rather than lying on the couch to avoid going up and down stairs."

"And you'd worry less."

"I might."

"It's a good idea," she admitted. "But can we afford it? You're not just talking about swapping some furniture around. A remodel would involve new walls, plumbing and electricity . . . all that gets costly."

James sighed. "We could take out a loan. Though we should probably wait until this job situation is resolved one way or another before taking on additional debt."

Fern nodded. "I agree. But it's a very thoughtful idea." Her smile faded as she added, "One of these days, I may not be able to do stairs at all."

"We'll figure that out if we need to." James patted her hand before he picked up a pair of Gideon's jeans. "I picked up some good paper and envelopes today for my cover letters and résumés."

"Oh, good," Fern said as Sapphire, her cat, leaped into her lap. "*Oof.* You're heavy," she told the enormous feline. Then she looked back at James. "I could print them out for you tomorrow and get them addressed and ready to go. That way, all you'll have to do is sign them tomorrow evening, and we'll pop them in the mail."

"That would be great. If you could update the résumés, I can do the cover letters at work." No way could he let Fern see the addresses of the places he intended to apply. Several were in or around Deerford, but two were in Peoria, well over an hour away. And if he took a job in Peoria, the family would have to move . . . and the remodeling he'd mentioned would be unnecessary altogether.

"All right. How many do you need?" She stroked the cat, which immediately began to purr loudly.

"Six. I've identified six places I'm definitely going to apply." He suppressed a sigh. Fern was distressed enough about her condition. If she realized he was applying to places so far away that they would have to move, it would only upset her more. And she was quite astute, he reminded himself. He'd have to be careful or she'd sense his unhappiness. "Hey," he said. "Remember I told you about the other three nurses I've had lunch with?"

Fern nodded. "Anabelle Scott and two others." She knew the whole Scott family because they also attended the Church of the Good Shepherd. She thought for a moment. "Wait. Don't tell me their names. One is Candace Crenshaw and the other . . . Ellen?"

"Elena. Elena Rodriguez. She's a real firecracker. Lots of energy. And let me tell you about the idea she had."

"Idea for what?"

"She would like to see the hospital do some fund-raising to try to stay afloat."

"Well, me too, but that's not up to us."

"Elena doesn't know the meaning of the word *no*." James shook his head, laughing as he thought about his friend's dogged determination. "She came up with this great idea for a Wall of Hope. You know that rather basic courtyard near the ER outside the chapel?"

Fern nodded.

"Elena thinks we could create engraved bricks—you know, for memorial or honorary purposes—and redo that courtyard with them. Anabelle's husband designed a great wall and walkway for the project."

Fern asked additional questions as James explained Elena's idea. Finally she said, "I think it's a great idea. Anything that would keep Hope Haven from closing is fine with me."

James grinned at his wife, trying not to dwell on the cover letters and résumés he intended to send out. "That's exactly what I said."

Chapter Ten

CANDACE LOOKED OUT AT THE ROOM FULL OF extremely pregnant ladies and their labor coaches. Most of the women had their husbands or partners with them, but a few had a sister, mother, or other friend accompanying them.

Robin Overing sat in the very back row with Andrew at her side. The couple was holding hands. Andrew smiled at her, but Candace noticed Robin avoided her gaze again. If only she could think of some way to get the young woman to listen to reason. She'd been praying about it quite a bit; but if God was sending her any ideas, she was missing the memos.

Turning to the lecture outline before her, Candace put aside her worry and began to speak. Today's class would begin with a lecture on what could happen when a birth did not go as planned, and included a DVD of a cesarean section. During the movie, Candace stood at one side of the room, her gaze constantly monitoring the faces of the viewers. It was not uncommon for a class member to pass out while watching the surgery and blood in the process, even though she warned everyone beforehand and coached them on what to do if they began to feel faint. This class, however, seemed to be fine.

Near the end, she drifted toward the back of the group. Pausing near the Overings, she sent Robin a warm smile. In an undertone, she said, "Can you stick around after class? I'd like to speak with you."

Robin nodded, and Andrew whispered, "Sure." He flashed her a look of gratitude.

Pleased with herself for being proactive, Candace concluded the movie and went on to the next section of the class. It included information on the postpartum process, newborn bonding and breast-feeding. There was another class offered on breast-feeding, so she presented only a general overview.

Finally, they reviewed the breathing and relaxation techniques they had been learning. Each woman lay down on a mat on the floor with her labor coach at her side, and they worked through a series of breathing patterns.

To conclude the class, Candace thanked them all for attending and handed out packets to each mother, which included free samples of infant care products, coupons and rebates and a certificate of completion for the class. She held Robin's until last.

When the last of the mothers had departed, Candace approached Robin and Andrew, who had moved to seats at the front of the room. Pulling a nearby chair around to face them, she said, "Thanks for staying. How are you feeling, Robin?"

The young woman shrugged. "Fine. Except for worrying, of course."

Candace nodded in sympathy. "I'm sure you've been concerned. Have you given any more thought to how you want to handle your breast cancer?" She used the term deliberately—aware that people often danced around terms and wanting to be sure Robin was confronting her illness.

"I'd rather not handle it at all," Robin said, her expression wry. "I know I can't just ignore it, but I still don't know what to do."

"What do your parents say?"

A flood of red color rose up Robin's neck, and her entire face flamed. "I haven't told them," she said, looking down.

Candace was horrified. "But—but Robin, you need support. You need your family around you." Robin was an only child; Candace was fairly certain the Kings still lived in her old neighborhood, although she hadn't seen them more than once or twice in years.

"I know." The girl sighed. "But I have Andrew, and until we've decided how to proceed, I'd rather not upset them."

Candace compressed her lips, trying to stem the concern she felt. "What's holding you back from making a decision about what to do? Do you have any additional questions that the doctor or I can answer?"

Robin shook her head. "I understand what you were saying the last time we talked," Robin said to Candace. "I do." She nodded her head, her eyes wide and sincere. "We read through the information the doctor gave us. Clearly, surgery is my best option." She fell silent.

"But?" Candace prompted.

"But even a small percentage of a chance that the baby might not survive the surgery isn't acceptable to me." She stopped and took a deep breath. "Candace . . . I lost a full-term baby three years ago." Tears filled her eyes.

A chill shivered down Candace's spine. Going through hours of labor only to deliver an infant that didn't live was the worst thing that could happen to a mother. It also was the worst thing that could happen in a labor and delivery unit. No matter how good a nurse was at managing her emotions for the sake of distraught patients, when a baby was stillborn or died during the birth, it was hard to keep one's composure. "Oh, Robin, I'm so sorry for your loss," she finally said. "I understand why you're determined to keep this baby as healthy as possible."

"I just can't do anything that might jeopardize the baby's life. It took a long time for us to conceive the first time, and it took almost three years this time. If I lose this child, I may not get another chance." Her eyes welled with tears. "Although that may be a moot point, given my diagnosis."

"Your diagnosis is extremely survivable for both you and the baby," Candace said gently. Was there any way to get through to Robin? "Ninety-six percent of the women who are diagnosed early and treat breast cancer promptly are cancer free after five years. As for not getting another chance, you're in your prime years to conceive. Even if it doesn't happen right away, women are having babies much later in life now."

"But if I have radiation or chemotherapy, it could hurt my chances of another pregnancy. Or maybe damage me so that if I ever got pregnant again, another baby would have birth defects."

"Who told you that?"

Robin hesitated. "No one. I just know that kind of thing can be dangerous. I read a woman's blog on the Internet—"

"That could have been fiction for all you know." Candace kept her voice gentle and light, infusing it with a touch of amusement, and Robin smiled reluctantly.

"That's possible."

"Internet research is fine, but depending on who wrote it, the information isn't always accurate. It's vital that you share all these concerns with your doctor," Candace urged. "He can give you specific information about birth defects, the likelihood of future pregnancies and anything else you are worrying about."

"Okay." But Robin didn't sound particularly committed to talking with the doctor in more detail, and Candace feared she hadn't changed the younger woman's mind.

"Having treatment could mean—in all likelihood it *would* mean—that you would be there to care for your baby yourself long-term. Don't you want to see your child grow up?" When Candace glanced at Andrew, the pleading expression in his eyes kept her pressing on.

"God has the power to fix this," Robin said. "I'm going to leave it in His hands."

Candace's mouth opened and then closed again. She couldn't believe what she'd just heard. With unusual asperity, she said, "I think you're exactly right. God *does* have the power to fix this. He created doctors and nurses, who are His hands here on earth." Her voice grew impassioned as she leaned forward, her gaze fixed on the pregnant woman. "I believe God uses doctors and other medical professionals to aid in healing. Ignoring medical advice is *not* what God intends, Robin. He guides the hands performing surgery. I know He is with me when I am trying to alleviate a patient's pain or comfort the family of a terminally ill patient."

Robin looked quite taken aback. Candace knew her speech had been a bit more forceful than her normal quiet manner. Had she offended Robin?

Finally, Robin said, "I never thought of it that way."

"Have you prayed about this?" Candace asked. She was usually very careful not to talk much about her faith to her patients unless it was very clear that they would not mind her offering to pray for them, though she had already spoken of faith to Robin the day they had visited her oncologist and then gone to the Corner.

Andrew shook his head in answer to her question. "We don't go to church."

Candace smiled. "We don't need to go to church to talk with God. He listens to everyone. Perhaps you could pray together and try to discern what God wants."

"If we want surgery to be as successful as possible," Andrew said, "we have to make a decision this week."

Robin kept her gaze lowered. "Why don't we do as Candace suggests before we worry about a timeline."

Her husband tossed his hands up in the air and threw himself back against the chair. He looked like he might explode. Tightly, he said, "In case you hadn't noticed, we *are* on a timeline. This is the second week since your diagnosis. You have to get that tumor out of there!"

"I don't *have* to do anything," Robin said in an equally belligerent tone.

Andrew was shaking with anger. Thrusting one finger beneath his wife's nose, he said, "If anything happens to our baby because you can't face dealing with cancer, I will *never* forgive you."

Robin looked stunned by his words.

Alarmed by the level of tension and discord between the two young people, Candace stepped into the momentary silence. Quickly, she said, "Why don't we try this: go home and talk to each other. Don't yell, don't get defensive. I'll be available all weekend. Just call if you have any more questions or concerns." She looked at Robin. "That gives you more time to consider everything we've discussed." She transferred the eye contact to Andrew. "It also addresses your concern about a timely decision."

Husband and wife both nodded.

"Thank you," Andrew said.

Robin reached out and laid her hand over Candace's. "Yes, thank you. I do appreciate your input, even if it hasn't seemed like it."

Candace turned her hand up and squeezed Robin's fingers in return, then extended her hand to shake Andrew's. "I'll be praying for all three of you," she said.

Robin managed a smile as she laid a hand on her rounded abdomen. "Maybe we will do some praying as well."

Elena had butterflies in her stomach as she walked down the corridor toward the office of the Chief Executive Officer. Albert Varner was the hospital's CEO, and she had a meeting with both him and Zane McGarry, the CFO, in just a few minutes.

She wasn't a nervous person, she reminded herself. It was just that she was going to meet with the Hope Haven CEO! If that wasn't cause for butterflies to be wreaking havoc in her stomach, she didn't know what would be.

She was well prepared, she assured herself. At Zane's request, Elena had brought along her brick to illustrate the idea she would be presenting to Mr. Varner.

"Hi, Elena." Zane was just coming out of his own office as she reached his door. "Are you ready to wow Albert with your idea?"

Elena smiled, although it felt distinctly shaky around the edges. "I hope so."

"Relax." Zane patted her shoulder as he steered her toward the CEO's suite. "You'll be terrific."

Penny Risser, Mr. Varner's executive assistant, looked up when Zane and Elena entered the outer office, although she didn't smile. She had a reputation for zealously guarding her boss as well as relentlessly keeping him on topic and on schedule. "He's waiting for you," she said in such a brusque manner that Elena surreptitiously checked her watch to be sure they weren't late.

Mr. Varner stood when Elena and the CFO entered the inner office. Elena smiled as Zane performed the introductions. "Call me Albert," the CEO insisted.

The room was a spacious corner office with large windows providing plenty of light. Several extremely large potted plants towered in the corner between the windows and other hanging baskets spilled over with spider plants, English ivy and silver-and-purple wandering Jew.

As Mr. Varner came forward to shake Elena's hand, he saw the direction of her gaze and laughed. "I take no credit for the plants. My assistant has a very green thumb. If she looks at it, it will grow."

Elena smiled at Albert Varner as her nerves subsided, appreciating his obvious attempt to put her at ease. *What a nice man he is.* "I enjoy plants, but I'm nowhere near that successful," she admitted.

The CEO chuckled. "Few people are. Penny has a gift."

Elena thought of the severe, unsmiling woman who sat at the desk in the outer office. A green thumb—who would have guessed?

Albert gestured toward the two upholstered guest chairs in front of a gleaming black desk. "Please, have a seat. I'm very interested in this idea of yours, Ms. Rodriguez."

Albert's eye contact and warm manner made Elena realize why he was such a good choice as the public face of the hospital. Feeling far more comfortable in his presence than she had expected to, Elena went over the Wall of Hope idea with him, explaining the papers in the file she handed him and sharing the sample of an engraved brick.

Albert leaned back in his chair, steepling his fingers together and regarding her intently as she spoke. When she had finished, a broad smile crossed his face. "I like it," he said. "I like it a lot. It's something that involves the community, beautifies the hospital, and raises our profile as well as working as a fundraiser. I'd like to present it to the board of directors, if you agree, Ms. Rodriguez."

"Elena," she said automatically, her mind on what he'd just said. "Thank you very much."

Albert looked at Zane McGarry. "You're right. We need to contact the board president and get a special meeting scheduled right away. This idea should be implemented as soon as possible, if the board agrees."

"And you think they will?" Elena asked.

The CEO shrugged. "If I said the sky was blue, the board might choose to call it orange," he said with a laugh. "I can never predict their reactions. However, this idea sounds quite exciting to me, and I'm hoping they'll see it my way."

Elena suspected the CEO could convince people of almost anything if he set his mind to it.

Albert flipped through the file she had given him. "Explain this donation page to me more fully. Is Clud Monuments really prepared to make such a generous donation?"

Elena nodded enthusiastically. "Yes. Isn't that amazing?"

"It's certainly noteworthy. You have two methods listed here for the purchase of bricks. Are you proposing to use both?"

Elena shook her head. "No, I believe it's an either/or choice. Either set specified prices for the bricks and sell them at that price, or simply ask people to make a donation in any amount they like."

"*Hmmm*. And do you have a preference for one of the two methods?"

Elena grinned. "I do, but I'd prefer not to tell you until you've thought about the pros and cons of each."

"Fair enough." Albert Varner crossed one arm over his chest and raised his free hand to stroke his chin as he thought aloud. "Setting the price would ensure that we cover costs and make a profit. But it may limit donations, because people might not think about donating larger sums. On the other hand, leaving the donation up to the person requesting the brick might actually yield larger donations. We do, however, run the risk of getting donations too small to cover our costs, unless we set a minimum donation."

"That pretty well sums it up," Zane McGarry contributed. "Exactly what we've been wrangling over."

Albert dropped his arms and stuck his hands deep into his pants pockets, rocking back on his heels. "I think," he said slowly, "that I prefer the second option—leaving the size of the donation up to the giver."

"Because?" Zane prompted.

"Because I believe in people," he said in an impassioned voice. "I think this community will step up with significant donations and that we would raise a larger amount without setting a price."

"That's what I think too," Elena added.

"And me too," Zane said. "But Quintessa thinks we're crazy and that we'd be taking a huge risk."

Albert nodded. "I can understand her caution. I'm certain some of the board members will feel the same way. However, I'm equally sure some others will think as we do." He took his hands out of his pockets and punched the button on his inter-office speaker system. "Penny, can you get Bernard Telford on the line for me, please? We need to see about convening an unscheduled meeting of the hospital board."

Chapter Eleven

CANDACE SAT AT ONE OF THE COMPUTERS IN THE second floor nurses' station when Anabelle came bustling in. She looked frazzled and harried as she dropped several files on the counter and put her hands up to massage her temples.

James stood in front of the automated medication-dispensing station along one wall. "Hi, Anabelle," he said. "Do you have a headache?"

Anabelle took a deep breath. "Yes. Bad day."

Candace looked up from the data she was entering. "Did one of your patients take a turn for the worse?" she asked.

Anabelle shook her head. "I'm just worried about Kirstie. She hasn't called me since the day before yesterday, and I get a little nervous." She massaged harder. "I want to call her, but I don't want her to feel like I'm hovering. But you'd be proud of me. I've resisted the urge to drop in."

Candace laughed, and James asked, "How's the place?"

"It's a cute little apartment, and she doesn't seem to be having any trouble getting around."

"Why would she?" James asked. "She walks so well no one would ever guess she wore a prosthesis."

"I know," Anabelle admitted. "But I still worry that living alone is going to be too much for her."

Candace rose and went to Anabelle's side, wrapping a supportive arm around her friend's shoulders in a gentle hug. "I think I understand why you're worried. It's hard enough to let them go when everything's fine. When your child has a problem, you just want to fix it for them."

Riley Hohmann, the nurse supervisor of the Birthing Unit, stuck her head into the nurses' station, her vivid blue eyes inquisitive. "You okay, Anabelle?"

Anabelle nodded and smiled. "Yes, thanks. Just having a mother moment."

Riley rolled her eyes. "My sympathies. Kids are wonderful, but they sure do turn our lives upside down, don't they?" Barely pausing for breath, she said, "Hey, Candace. Do you want to take your break now? Things are pretty quiet."

"Sure." Candace gave Anabelle's shoulders a final squeeze. "I'm dying for a cup of coffee." Taking her leave of her friends, she slipped up one flight of stairs to the third floor and entered the staff lounge.

A large, polished aluminum coffeemaker that could make anything from one to more than four dozen cups of coffee stood on a counter at one side of the room, along with a microwave and a toaster oven. Paper towels hung on a roll above a stainless-steel sink. Beside the coffeemaker were Styrofoam cups, sweeteners, creamers and stir sticks, as well as a selection of tea bags for the few employees who preferred to brew a cup in the microwave.

Candace tossed a quarter into the basket beside the pot and got herself a cup of black coffee. Blowing on it to cool it, she sat down on one of the vinyl couches, slipped off her clogs, and propped up her stockinged feet on the blocky metal coffee table in the center of the seating arrangement.

"Hello, Candace."

She had to twist to face the far door on the other side of the lounge. Heath Carlson, the man she had met when his brother's baby was born, had just entered the room.

"Oh, hello."

He smiled at her as he went to the coffeemaker and got himself a cup of the brew. "Mind if I join you?"

She waved a hand in a vague gesture of assent. "Please do." She indicated the coffee table. "Ignore my feet."

Heath laughed. "No problem. It feels good to sit down for a few minutes. We've been busy all morning in Diagnostic Imaging."

"We haven't." She grimaced. "Which probably means that ten minutes before my shift is supposed to end, we'll get half a dozen ladies in labor all at once."

"Murphy's Law," he agreed.

There was a moment of silence as they each sipped at their coffee.

"How's your nephew doing?" she asked.

Heath smiled, blue eyes softening in a very appealing way. "Terrific. I think he's starting to recognize me. I go over there almost every day after work to give my sister-in-law a little break."

"That's thoughtful of you." Impressed, Candace gave him her full attention.

Heath shrugged. "No, just self-serving," he said with a chuckle. "I don't get many opportunities to be around little ones, and I don't want to miss out on a minute."

"Every day is an adventure with children around," she said. "What did your brother and sister-in-law decide on for a name?"

"Michael."

"Mike for short?"

Heath shrugged. "So far he's Michael, but we'll see." He looked over at her with a grin that made his dimples flash. "Did anyone ever call you Candy?"

She shuddered. "No. Thank heavens. And my sister Susan has never been called Susie or Sue. I'm not sure why." Then she laughed. "But we're grateful."

Heath chuckled. Speaking of Heath's new nephew made her think back to the years when her own two had been babies. Oh, how she wished she could go back to those days, back to a time when Dean was living and they had two beautiful children and life had been so happy and normal.

"You look sad," Heath said gently. "Is something making you unhappy?"

Startled by his perception, Candace shrugged. "I was just thinking about when my children were babies. I wish they were tiny again. I loved having little ones." Which was true enough, although it wasn't the reason she'd been feeling blue. She forced herself to chuckle. "Not that Howie's anywhere near grown up. But it's really beginning to hit me that when he starts school this fall, my life will change again."

She removed her feet from the table and stood as she glanced at the time and saw her break was nearly over. "I've got to get back to work."

"You have to get ready for that rush of laboring moms," he said.

She shook a finger at him. "Bite your tongue!"

They shared a laugh.

"It was nice to see you again, Heath."

"It was nice to see you too."

James pulled his minivan to a halt in his in-laws' driveway. Switching off the ignition, he pulled the key out and let his head flop against the headrest for a moment.

Lord, help me, he prayed silently. *Fill me with enthusiasm and confidence, and don't let Fern see how worried and upset I really am.*

He lifted the mail that he had picked up when he stopped by the house after work to get out some chicken to thaw for dinner. Flipping up the flap of one envelope, he slid the single sheet of paper out and reread it. Sadly, nothing had changed.

It was the fourth response he'd gotten to the queries and résumés he'd sent out, and it was as negative as the rest. *We regret to inform you that we have no employment opportunities for you at the present time. . . .* The only two positions on which he still awaited answers were the ones farther afield. What was he going to do if he couldn't find work within a reasonable distance of Deerford? Grimly, he decided he'd better take a second look at all the job possibilities around Deerford. Even if they were ones he'd passed over on his first round of letters, he probably should send more résumés out.

"Hey, Dad!" His younger son, Nelson, had come out onto the porch of his grandparents' home, waving madly as he slung an arm around one of the porch posts and leaned far out to one side.

"Hey, Nelson," James replied as he opened the door of the van. Here was a reason to be enthusiastic. Hiding away his concerns, he smiled as he came up the walk from the driveway and approached his son. "How was school?"

Nelson screwed up his face in an expression of utter loathing. "Rotten. It rained all morning and we couldn't go out for gym class and then we had to play dodgeball instead. *Dodgeball*, Dad." He shook his head in disgust.

James passed a hand over his face to disguise his laughter. "Sounds awful."

"It was," Nelson reiterated. "We had to play with the *girls*." He would be finishing seventh grade in a couple of days, and at the ripe old age of thirteen, he still thought girls were an alien life-form. Preferably one he could send far, far away.

"Oh no, not with the girls!" James said, shaking his head. "Sorry, kiddo. Sounds like the worst thing in the whole wide world." *But it won't for much longer*, he thought with amusement. At fourteen, Gideon had already discovered that girls weren't so terrible. His amusement faded. James and Fern had discussed it on more than one occasion. Gideon was bigger than most boys his age, and he looked older as well. It was a worry. He wished he could turn back the clock and have them playing Legos again.

A rush of affection for his sons filled him. Stepping onto the porch, he caught Nelson in a headlock and rubbed the top of his head vigorously.

"Hey!" Nelson's voice was muffled in his dad's shirt. "No fair. I wasn't ready."

James sent his son a superior look as he released the boy and headed for the door. "Excuses, excuses," he said, grinning.

Nelson grinned back as he followed his father into the house. "Aw, Dad."

"Aw, Nelson," James mimicked. "How much homework do you have?"

Nelson shrugged. "English and science. We got some time at the end of class today, and I have most of it done. You can check it," he offered.

"I'll look over it at home," James told him. "Where are Mom and Grandma?"

"Sitting on the back porch," Nelson reported. "They're snapping peas."

"Thanks. Get your things together. We'll be heading home soon."

James made his way through his in-laws' home to the back door. As Nelson had indicated, his wife and his mother-in-law were seated in lawn chairs with a large bowl of snapped peas between them. Each of them had a smaller bowl in her lap, and a trash bag for the snapped-off ends of the peas stood between them. "Hello," he said, opening the door. "So we're snapping peas today, are we?"

"Hello there." Fern twisted in her seat, raising her face for his kiss. "How are you?"

"Fatigued." James leaned back against the doorjamb. "But getting my second wind. It always takes me a little while to make the transition from work to home."

His mother-in-law smiled warmly at him. "We've had a lovely day. Got a lot of peas done." She gestured at a nearby seat. "Why don't you sit for a spell?"

"Thanks. I think I will." James sprawled in the lawn chair.

"I told Mother about your thoughts on remodeling the house," Fern said. "She thought it was a great idea."

James tensed. He was sorry he'd mentioned remodeling at all. What if they had to move away? The depressing thoughts whirled in his head, as they did nearly all the time now.

If they moved, they'd be uprooting the boys from their schools, taking Fern away from her close supportive family, starting over in a whole new community.

"Honey?" Fern was looking at him strangely. "Are you feeling all right?"

With an effort, James forced himself to relax and smile. "Yes, just a little tired, like I said."

"Did something upsetting happen at work today?"

"No." He could answer that honestly. "It was a good day. My prostate cancer patient went home today, and a lady with pneumonia is doing much, much better than we had feared she might." He smiled. "Although Anabelle is worried about her daughter moving into her first apartment."

"Oh, Kirstie. She's a lovely girl," Fern said. "Remember when she taught Nelson's Sunday school class?"

James nodded. "I bet she's a great third-grade teacher."

"Would you like a glass of lemonade or tea?" Fern's mother asked.

"Iced tea would be great." James took a deep breath and slowly released it. He would think about the job situation later.

Candace walked into Rishell Elementary School at three thirty on Friday afternoon. School ended at two forty-five, and Janet had already picked up Brooke. Candace was meeting Brooke's teacher, and she would decide later whether or not to tell her daughter about it. Perhaps Brooke did not need to know. The child would have spent the entire day—no, probably the entire *week*—worrying about what her mother and her teacher were going to discuss.

The doors to the school were locked, so she rang the bell and announced herself on the intercom. When the door unlocked with a little *snick*, she tugged open the door and walked into the school. After signing in at the office and receiving a visitor's pass, she walked to the fifth-grade wing.

Although the fifth graders changed classes for a few subjects, they still received much of their daily instruction from one educator. Mrs. Parker, Brooke's homeroom teacher, was in the second room on the right. She was exceptionally tall and thin. Her dark hair had one dramatic streak of silver right in the front, and her eyes had deep purple shadows beneath them. She was one of the best teachers Brooke had ever had.

"Mrs. Crenshaw," she said, rising from her desk with a smile. "Thanks for coming in. How can I help you today?"

Candace sank down into a student desk, and the teacher pulled another one around to face her. "Thank you for seeing me," Candace said. "I'm concerned about how Brooke is doing socially with her peers." She explained the odd behavior with the birthday party invitation, going on to say that Brooke and Tiffany did not appear to have any animosity or ill will between them. She spread her hands. "As far as I can tell, Brooke just didn't feel like going to the party."

"Maybe that's all there was to it," the teacher suggested. "Although you wouldn't be here if you believed that."

Candace gave a rueful smile. "Right." She shifted in the seat and prepared herself for her next sentence. "You know Brooke's father passed away when she was in second grade."

The teacher nodded.

"She had a number of issues related to that, and we went to counseling for a while. By the end of fourth grade, she was only going once a month. The counselor suggested we take the spring semester off and see how things went." She hesitated. "Everything has been fine, except that I just have this funny feeling that something isn't right."

Mrs. Parker tilted her head. "I almost always find that my intuition is right on the money. When I'm smart enough to listen to it, that is." She chuckled and then took a deep breath. "I'm glad you called, Mrs. Crenshaw. Brooke's grades are fine. She appears to be well liked by her classmates, and I have not seen any behaviors that might indicate otherwise. Nevertheless, I intended to contact you because I also have a feeling something isn't quite right."

"What's Brooke doing?" Candace knew her alarm showed.

"Nothing," the teacher reassured her. "At least, nothing obvious. I'm just a little troubled. I have noticed that Brooke behaves oddly whenever another student's father comes to the classroom. One day, Susie Kelly's father came to help with an art project, and shortly after he arrived, Brooke said she felt sick. I didn't think anything of it, and I sent her to the office. An hour later, she returned, and she seemed fine for the rest of the day."

Candace sat frozen as the teacher went on. "Another time, Jamie Kinnear's father, who lives far away, came in to observe, and Brooke volunteered to take the attendance sheet to the office. Once there, she didn't come back for almost an hour, and when I called up to see where she was, the secretary told me she was lying down in the nurse's office. She returned to class after recess—after Mr. Kinnear was gone."

Oh, Brooke. "Do you think she's ill?" Candace suspected she knew where this was going, but she wanted to be sure she wasn't overreacting.

Mrs. Parker shook her head. "No. I don't think she's ill. When Annie Penn's father helped with the Halloween party, Brooke skipped the group game that he was overseeing. When Josh Trainor's dad showed them how to conduct an experiment to go along with their science unit, Brooke asked to use the restroom and again didn't come back for a long time. I began to connect the dots and realized there appeared to be a pattern, a common denominator, if you will, to Brooke's disappearing acts. She appears to be avoiding her classmates' fathers. There may have been other, earlier ones that I didn't notice." She shook her head. "I hate to even mention it to you, but I think there may be some cause for concern."

Candace crossed her arms and sighed, bowing her head. "I think you're right, Mrs. Parker. Thank you for your diligence. A lot of teachers might never have noticed a pattern."

"Given your family's loss, I thought it might be important to mention it to you," Mrs. Parker said, giving voice to the issue they both recognized.

"I think so too," Candace confirmed in a shaky voice. She drew in a deep, careful breath and then released it, forcing herself to think only of her surroundings, the white streak in the teacher's hair, the slightly sticky surface of the desk in which she sat. "It sounds as if Brooke needs to continue with her therapy."

As quickly as she could, she concluded the conference, thanking the teacher one final time. Then she walked back out to the parking lot and climbed into her Honda CR-V.

Sitting in her small SUV, she fumbled with her seat belt until the clasp clicked into place. Her eyes were swimming with tears that made it impossible for her to put the key in the ignition, much less drive.

Dean, where are you? She couldn't do this alone, she thought as she dug in her handbag for a tissue. She never went anywhere without tissues anymore.

Poor Brooke. Poor precious little girl. Candace laid her head forward against the steering wheel and let the tears flow. Brooke had been devastated, completely unable to function, when her father passed away. And now she couldn't even be around other children's fathers. Had this always been a problem? Neither she nor Janet had noticed it, but Candace wondered, mopping at tears, if they had been so relieved that the most frightening symptom of Brooke's trauma—namely, not speaking—had disappeared that they had fooled themselves into thinking she was fine.

No, not fine, she corrected, recalling the incidents with Carla's cat and Tiffany's birthday. But improving.

A wisp of memory floated into her head, and she saw Dean's face, laughing. The image was so clear that Candace strained to recall more, wanting to prolong the moment. It had been at a parent-teacher conference too, she recalled. She and Dean had gone in for their very first conference when Brooke had been in kindergarten for about two months.

The conference had gone well. The teacher was delighted that Brooke recognized her name and her letters, that she was beginning to write her name, and that she could count to one hundred. There was only one teeny issue she wanted to mention. Brooke normally was the most docile of students, willing to play with anyone, kind to the others with whom she interacted.

But one day on the playground, a classmate had found a large earthworm. He had picked it up and terrorized half the class, but Brooke hadn't been afraid. Instead, she had asked him how he'd like it if he were an earthworm. Then someone picked the worm up and slung him around in the air. She had urged the little boy to put the worm back in the loose soil of the landscaping at the corner of the playground.

Instead, he had thrown the worm on the ground and stomped on it.

And that was when Brooke hit him.

As Dean and Candace had left the building and the door closed behind them, Dean had a mirth meltdown, laughing until the tears ran. Brooke was a gentle, quiet little girl; but she had a strong empathy for others, including animals of all sorts, and seeing someone kill a worm would not have gone over well. As it obviously hadn't. A bubble of laughter worked its way up between the sobs she was trying to get under control.

A tap-tap-tap on her window startled her so badly she nearly screamed as she jolted upright. Turning, she blinked her blurry eyes until the large, dark shape blocking the late day sun coalesced into the face of James Bell.

"You okay?" he asked through the glass.

Too unnerved to start the car and lower the automatic window, she unfastened her seat belt, opened her door and swung her legs out, doing her best to stifle the sobs that still wanted to escape.

"James, what are you doing here?"

James squatted in the open door. "Just waiting a few more minutes until Nelson is finished with Chess Club. You okay?" he repeated gently.

Candace shook her head. "Not really." Her voice quavered, and she pressed her lips together before she attempted to speak again. "I had a conference with Brooke's teacher. It made me think of a parent-teacher conference we had when Dean was still alive."

James didn't say anything, but his silence was comfortable.

She spoke again. "Most days are good now. Really. It's just that every once in a while, something happens that triggers a memory, and it's so vivid that it seems impossible that he's gone. . . ." Her voice trailed away, and she gulped again.

"I can't imagine how you do it." James's voice was quiet. "Losing your partner in life at any age is terrible. But to lose him so young . . . I cannot imagine how you do it. I think you're probably the strongest woman I have ever met."

"I don't think I could go on if it wasn't for the kids," she confessed. "And even then, there are days when I feel like I'm just going through the motions."

James nodded. "I can see that." He shifted position a little. "Are you able to drive home? Because I'd be happy to give you a lift. I could pick you up in the morning and bring you back here to get your car—"

"Thank you," Candace said, "but I'll be all right, James. Talking to you has helped. I can drive home." She smiled at him. "I don't know why God saw fit to bless me with friends like you, but I thank Him every day."

Chapter Twelve

ON SATURDAY MORNING, ELENA WAS ON CLOUD NINE as she returned to the ICU from her morning break. Albert Varner, the hospital's CEO, had spoken with Bernard Telford, who was the president of the board. Mr. Telford had liked the Wall of Hope idea and had called a special board meeting early in the upcoming week to discuss it. Albert had suggested to the president that Zane and Elena should attend, but Telford vetoed it, saying he would handle the presentation.

Elena wasn't sure whether she was glad or sad that she didn't have to speak in front of a whole room full of hospital board members. Either way, she could hardly wait for lunchtime to arrive so she could share the good news with her friends. The Wall of Hope project was one step closer to becoming reality!

On the way back up to the second floor, she shared the elevator with Hospital Auxiliary volunteer Phyllis Getty. The auxiliary was made up of mostly retired older ladies who volunteered in the hospital and performed other service projects to benefit Hope Haven.

Pert and alert, Phyllis reminded Elena of a high-speed hummingbird in her Kelly green volunteer jacket with numerous pins for outstanding service adorning the chest pocket. Despite being eighty-four years old, Phyllis had more energy than any other three people all put together.

"Good morning, dear," Phyllis said as she held the elevator for Elena. "Isn't it a beautiful day? When I came in, the sky was such a gorgeous deep, rich blue that it didn't look real."

"I noticed it too. It was really lovely. What are you up to this morning?" Elena asked.

Phyllis indicated a stack of magazines she held. "I'm distributing reading materials to patients who are interested," she said. "Sometimes I stick around and read to the folks who can't see to read for themselves."

"That's very thoughtful," Elena said as the elevator doors opened on the second floor.

Walking along beside Phyllis, Elena was almost to the counter at the Intensive Care nurses' station right across the corridor from the main second floor nurses' station when she heard a surprisingly loud voice speaking her name.

". . . Elena Rodriguez, and I want to speak with her. Find her right now." The speaker was a silver-haired man standing rigidly in front of the counter.

"Uh-oh," Phyllis muttered under her breath. "I didn't take my heartburn pill today." And with that cryptic statement, she wheeled around and moved off in the other direction.

Winona Stouffer was at the computer behind the desk. Slowly, she swiveled the office chair around and looked up, eyebrows raised in an expression that should have quelled the rude inquirer.

The man appeared oblivious to her unspoken criticism, however. Again, he demanded, "I need to see Elena Rodriguez."

Winona's gaze slid past the speaker and landed on Elena.

"Ms. Rodriguez is right behind you," she said.

The man spun on his heel. When he spotted her, Elena felt like a rabbit without a hiding place while a hawk circled overhead. "You." He pointed at Elena. "I want to speak with you."

It took a lot to upset Elena's equilibrium. She smiled into his grim face and said pleasantly, "I'm going back on duty in Intensive Care, if you'd like to follow me over to the desk." She extended a hand. "Hello."

The man ignored the gesture. "I'm Frederick Innisk. I sit on the Hope Haven Hospital board of directors."

Could the man *be* any more pompous? "Yes?"

"I just came from a meeting with Bernie Telford, who is the president of this institution's board of directors."

"I've met Mr. Telford," Elena said, continuing to smile, although Mr. Innisk's condescension was arousing indignation within her.

"Telford told me about this ridiculous scheme you've dreamed up. Wall of Hope indeed. What's in it for you, girlie?" he said.

Girlie? Elena was so taken aback by the disparaging term that she didn't even know how to respond. "I beg your pardon?"

"It's a terrible idea," Innisk said in a curt, cutting tone. "What's the catch? What are you getting out of the deal?"

"Mr. Innisk," Elena said, "I am not sure what you are accusing me of, but I assure you I am not getting a single thing out of the Wall of Hope idea—"

"Ha!"

"Except for the satisfaction of raising funds to keep the hospital open, and the opportunity to beautify an area that both staff and visitors use on a regular basis. Hope Haven is a jewel in this community. We're so fortunate to have a stellar medical facility easily available to us. I would hate to see that disappear, as would the entire town."

Innisk dismissed her words with a grunt of skepticism. "I'll figure it out," he said as if she hadn't even spoken, wagging a finger in her face. "And I'll warn you now, missy, that I'm going to oppose this ridiculous notion. I don't even know why we're having a meeting to discuss it. No discussion's necessary. We need to close the doors of this money pit before we drown in debt."

Elena barely resisted the urge to bat that offensive index finger out of her face. "You're entitled to your opinion, as are the other board members. Now if you'll excuse me, I have patients who need my care."

"If you were doing your job right, you wouldn't have time for this nonsense," Innisk said.

Elena's eyes opened wide, and her nostrils flared like a bull sensing danger. She was a patient person, but being accused of . . . whatever it was this odious man was accusing her of was just too much.

"Freddie." Before Elena could retort, a low, sweet voice broke the tension between the two. "Do you have a complaint to register about Ms. Rodriguez's work?" The speaker was Marge Matthews, the nurse supervisor of the ICU on the day shift. She had been seated behind the ICU desk where Innisk apparently had not noticed her, or perhaps he'd simply dismissed her. And had she really just called him Freddie?

Before Innisk could respond, Marge continued speaking in her calm, pleasant voice. Beneath the surface, Elena recognized a hint of steel. Apparently Innisk did too, because he didn't attempt to interrupt her as he had Elena. "If you have specific concerns, I would be happy to speak with you and take your issues to the personnel department. If, however, Ms. Rodriguez were to accuse you of slander or some similar action, I would be remiss if I did not send the witnesses to this *discussion* to Mr. Varner to share their perceptions of your confrontation."

Innisk's face grew so red he looked nearly purple. Elena would not have been surprised if he'd gone into cardiac arrest right then and there. "You dare—" he spluttered. "I'll—I'll—"

Marge rose to her full, majestic height, just inches shy of six feet, and looked down at the angry man, who was significantly shorter than Elena's own moderately tall frame. "Why don't we go down to the CEO's office right now," she suggested, stepping out from behind the desk.

Innisk actually backed up a step. "That's not necessary," he said in a tone so frigid Elena wanted to shiver. He turned his attention back to her then, glowering at her as he said, "I will oppose this frivolous notion with every means at my disposal."

And before Elena could form a response, he turned and stalked away. Unfortunately, his exit was spoiled a bit by the fact that he had to wait almost thirty seconds for the elevator to come to the second floor. In that time, not a single syllable was spoken at the nurses' station behind him.

The moment the elevator doors closed, though, Winona rose from her seat behind the desk and said, "I've heard stories about him, but you know how that goes—stories are usually exaggerated." She shuddered. "In his case, there was no exaggeration. Are you okay?"

Elena nodded as she sagged against the ICU desk across the hall. Her legs actually felt unsteady and her hands were shaking. *Lord, pour Your strength into me.* "I'm not good at confrontation," she said weakly, trying to smile. "Do you think he'll really report me for something?"

Marge shook her head. "Not for a minute. He's been a bully since high school. We were in the same graduating class, and I swear he hasn't changed one iota since then. His family is old money in Deerford. His great-grandfather was the first town mayor, and I swear he thinks that gives him ownership or some such silliness." She patted Elena on the shoulder, but her brown eyes were troubled. "Nobody likes the man, but don't underestimate him. Family money often speaks surprisingly loudly."

Elena tried to smile. "Thanks for the warning."

"Did he really say he wants to see the hospital close, or did I dream that?" Winona asked. "He's on the *board*, for pity's sake. How can he want to close it?"

"Apparently, he believes it is too deeply in debt to be saved," Elena said. And the words were a blow to her normally optimistic outlook.

"Huh." Marge gave her opinion of that in one inelegant syllable. "Freddie Innisk," she said, "has never done anything in his life that didn't benefit him. First, last, and always, that man looks after his own interests. If he wants to close the hospital, it's a sure bet that he stands to gain something from it. I suspect it's financial reward."

Just then, one of the Hope Haven Hounds volunteers came by the desk. Charles Washington was African American, a dignified, slightly stooped older gentleman who had never been seen without a bow tie. Some people said he'd been born wearing it. Charles's dark hair was dusted with a frosting of white. At his side walked his beloved beagle, Dixie. She was a popular dog among the patients, because she was small enough to hop up on a bed and lie down with a patient who expressed interest in a visit from a Hound volunteer.

As they passed, Charles inclined his head. "Good morning, ladies."

"Good morning, Charles," everyone chorused.

He smiled and moved on past, but a moment later he stopped when he realized Dixie wasn't walking along with him. The little dog had stopped at Elena's side and was standing on her two hind legs with her front paws against Elena's knee.

"Dixie!" Charles looked mortified. "I'm so sorry," he exclaimed. "She never jumps on people."

"It's all right." Elena chuckled as she knelt. She almost lost her balance as Dixie leapt right into her lap and cuddled up with her head beneath Elena's chin.

"Well, look at that," Marge said, leaning over the counter. "That little dog knew Elena needed a good hug."

Elena blinked back tears as she stroked the warm little body. "They say having a companion animal near you lowers blood pressure and calms folks in distress."

Winona snorted. "No wonder Miss Dixie stopped to visit. Your blood pressure was probably off the chart!"

"I wonder why that is," Marge mused, clearly still thinking about Elena's words regarding pets.

Elena took another minute with the diminutive canine. "I don't care why it works," she said, feeling the tension receding and her customary sunny outlook return, "but I sure feel much better. Thank you," she said to Charles as she gave Dixie one final scratch behind her ear.

Still, she wondered why Frederick Innisk was so determined to thwart her plan to raise funds to keep the hospital open. He'd asked what was in it for her; conversely, she wondered what was motivating him. Was it simply a power play, or was there something more at work?

Candace opened the door to the courtyard and looked for the cardinal that called the paperbark maple tree home. She smiled when she spotted it, then joined her three close friends in the courtyard for a late lunch on Saturday. When she arrived, Elena was recounting an encounter she'd had with one of the

Hope Haven board members. Although Elena made light of the incident, Candace's concern seemed to match James's. Anabelle, who apparently had a passing acquaintance with the man, appeared aghast.

"He couldn't possibly make trouble for you with Human Resources," James said to Elena in a reassuring tone.

"I can't believe it." Candace shook her head and repeated herself. "I can't believe he actually spoke to you like that."

"I can," Anabelle said. "Cam dealt with him all the time when Innisk threw parties and wanted big potted greens and fancy flowering shrubs. He always had to have things that were out of season or quite hard to come by, and he always wanted them cheap. Now Evan has to handle him and his demands. It's a headache for him," she said, referring to her son who had taken over the landscaping business when her husband retired.

"I wonder why he's so unhappy," Elena said. "Something must have gone very wrong in his life to make him turn out this way. I'm going to add him to my prayer list."

Silence.

All three of them stared at Elena until she lifted her head from her lunch. Clearly nonplussed, she said, "What? Do I have food on my face?"

James chuckled and Anabelle smiled.

Candace said, "Elena, I am in awe of your faith. That man was horrible to you, yet you show concern for him. That truly is walking the walk."

Elena beamed. "Thank you. But seriously, can you imagine being him? How very sad."

James nodded. "And you're absolutely right. We should all be praying for the man."

Just then, someone else opened the door and came into the courtyard. Candace was surprised to see Zane McGarry.

"Hello, Zane," Elena said. "Please join us."

Zane smiled warmly as he perched on the end of the bench. "It's nice to see you all. I see names on tax forms and payroll things all the time, but I don't often have a chance to meet the employees who go with those names."

There was a ripple of laughter. Then Zane said, "Elena, the board of directors had a special luncheon meeting over the noon hour to discuss the Wall of Hope. Bernard Telford had all the information you and I compiled, but I'm not sure how comprehensive a job he did sharing it."

Elena grimaced. "I'm certain the vote was *not* unanimously in favor."

"Unfortunately," Zane said in a glum tone, "there was no vote at all. The board felt they didn't have enough information about the project to make a decision one way or the other. They decided to table it until their next monthly meeting."

"What?" Candace exclaimed.

"We can't wait an entire month!" Elena protested.

"Oh boy," Anabelle said. "I bet Innisk will really be on the warpath now."

"His was the loudest protest," Zane told her.

"He was beyond rude to Elena earlier today," Candace said with more heat than she normally expressed.

Zane nodded. "No surprise." He shrugged as if dismissing Frederick Innisk from the conversation.

"What do we do now?" Elena asked. "People have already started asking questions as they hear about the possibility of the project. Waiting a whole month will derail our momentum. Plus we have the added advantage of the recent news coverage of the potential for closing to build on."

"I know," Zane said in a disgusted tone.

"So." Elena looked at Zane, then at the rest of them. "I need to do something. What can I do to get this project moving forward again?"

Zane hesitated. "Well, I suppose we could go ahead and plan the campaign details, with the expectation that the board will eventually vote yes. After all, Mr. Varner and Mr. Telford both liked the idea."

Elena glanced at her watch as she leaped to her feet. "I've got time now!"

Zane looked a bit startled, but he grinned as she whipped her luncheon remains back into the bag and headed for the door. "It was nice meeting you," he said to the others.

As the pair headed indoors, Candace began to laugh. "Mr. Innisk doesn't stand a chance, does he?"

"What should we do first to organize this campaign?" Elena asked as they walked toward Zane's office.

"I don't know where to start," Zane said.

"Okay," Elena said. She began to tick off items on her fingers. "We need a form for ordering the bricks. We need to set up a database so that we can keep track of the orders and contributors. And we need to create a thank-you letter people can use for taxes."

They had reached Zane's office. He held the door for Elena. As they entered, Zane beckoned to Quintessa as he strode by her desk. "Come on in here. We need your input."

Quintessa grabbed her laptop and followed Elena to the inner office. As they took their seats, Zane filled her in on the board's actions and what Elena had just said.

"We'll need a Web site too," Quintessa said. "The guy who does the hospital site offered to do it as a volunteer project whenever we're ready."

"How nice," Elena said with a grin.

"I thought we might be able to use the Hospital Auxiliary to promote it," Zane said.

"Good idea," Quintessa said.

Elena contorted her face as she tried to recall something else that was teasing her memory. "Oh," she said. "You mentioned advertising. Once we're ready to go live with this, we need to get some ongoing newspaper coverage. Could someone approach one of the local reporters?"

"I elect you," Quintessa said.

"All right. When we get approval for this"—she refused to say *if*—"I'll call Valera Kincaid at the *Dispatch* about doing a series of human interest stories. My friend Anabelle volunteered to compile a list of former patients who might be willing to be interviewed."

"We have to be careful about that," Zane cautioned.

"I know. HIPPA privacy and all that. I'll ask Anabelle if she has any ideas about how we can do this." Elena made herself a note on the corner of the luncheon napkin she'd carried into the room.

Seeing what she was doing, Zane began to laugh as he handed her a notepad. "Here you go. It's on me."

Chapter Thirteen

WHEN CANDACE GOT HOME FROM WORK ON SATURDAY afternoon, no one was home. She was almost ashamed of how relieved she was not to have to make conversation and plaster a happy expression on her face.

On the kitchen counter lay a note from Janet. She had taken Brooke and Howie to see the newest animated movie, and they didn't expect to be home much before six. Candace shouldn't worry about dinner because Janet had prepared taco fixings, and everything could be reheated quickly once they returned.

Bless you, Mom. Candace went to her room and changed into casual clothes. She lay down across her bed to take a short nap, promising herself that she would get up in thirty minutes. She'd been wanting to go through the toys in Howie's room and give away or pack up things that were too young for him or that he never used. . . .

"Mommy, Mommy!" The sound of small feet pounding up the stairs dragged her from a deep, dreamless slumber. "We saw the mammoth movie!"

Candace shook her head, propping herself up on her elbows to check the bedside clock just as Howie burst into the room. "You did?" She infused her tone with wonder and enthusiasm.

"Yeah, an' it was cool!"

She laughed, dragging her son onto the bed and hugging him tight. He wriggled to be free, and she began peppering him with big, smacking kisses.

"Lemme go!" he yelled, giggling.

"Never," she said. "I'm the kiss monster."

Howie yelled, "Brooke! Save me!"

A moment later, Candace heard her daughter enter the bedroom. "What will you give me if I save you?" she said to her little brother.

Startled and highly amused, Candace began to chuckle. She released Howie and flopped onto her back, grinning at her daughter. "That's blackmail, Miss Crenshaw."

Brooke grinned back as Howie scrambled out of the room. "I know. And it would have worked if you hadn't let him get away!"

"Oops, sorry." Candace sat up and swung her legs off the mattress as she patted the edge of the bed beside her. "How was the movie?"

"Great. And guess what?" Brooke asked as she seated herself beside Candace.

"What?"

"Tiffany and Jenna were there with Tiff's mom, and they invited us to sit with them."

"Oh, that was nice. So you got to hang with your friends *and* see a movie. Sounds like a good day."

Brooke nodded, smiling. "It was."

"Honey, we need to talk for a few minutes." Candace got up and closed the bedroom door. "I went to your school to talk to Mrs. Parker yesterday."

"You did?" Brooke's face registered confusion, as Candace seated herself beside her daughter again. "Am I in trouble for something?" Her voice rose with anxiety.

"You're not in trouble." Candace put an arm around Brooke and gave her shoulders a squeeze. "Actually, I requested the conference. But as it turned out, Mrs. Parker was going to call me anyway."

Brooke was beginning to look upset. "What did I do?"

"Remember how you didn't tell me about Tiffany's party?" When Brooke nodded, Candace went on. "I wasn't mad, honest. But it did concern me, so I asked Mrs. Parker if you were having problems with any of your friends at school."

"*M-o-o-o-m*." Brooke looked annoyed as well as apprehensive. "I told you there was nothing wrong."

"I know. But it concerned me. Mrs. Parker told me some things that also concern me, honey."

"Like what?" Now her tone was wary.

"Mrs. Parker thinks you are avoiding being in class when other students' fathers come in. She told me about your going to the nurse, or to the bathroom, and not coming back for a good deal of time." Candace hesitated. "Is that true?"

Brooke's shoulders hunched beneath Candace's embracing arm. She didn't respond.

"Brooke?"

"I don't know," her daughter said in a flat voice.

"Did you tell Mrs. Parker you felt sick when Mr. Kelly came in?"

"I don't remember."

Candace went on, asking her daughter about each of the incidents the teacher had mentioned. And each time, Brooke gave her the same response: "I don't remember."

Finally, at a loss for any way to get to the bottom of her concerns, Candace said, "Honey, I'm going to call Mr. Evans. I think it would be a good idea if you went back to talk to him occasionally again."

"What? Mom, no. I *don't* need a counselor."

"Well, then he should be able to determine that in a snap," Candace said. "You need to go at least once."

"I won't go back," Brooke said, shoving herself off the bed. "You can't make me talk." Her fists were clenched, and her eyes shone with tears.

"No," Candace agreed. She knew Brooke only meant that Candace couldn't physically force her to speak to a counselor, but it brought back painful memories of the weeks after the funeral when Brooke had been mute. "I can't make you talk. But I do want you to go, and if you won't talk to him, he'll probably want to see you a whole lot."

"You don't talk to a counselor." Brooke changed tactics, hurling the words at her. "How come you make me go when you won't go?"

Good question. "I'm not the one avoiding my friends' fathers," Candace pointed out. "We're talking about you right now."

"You cry a lot. You think I don't know, but I can hear you at night when you think I'm asleep. I think you need counseling too!" And with that parting shot, Brooke turned and rushed out of the room.

Candace sat on the side of the bed, her daughter's final words ringing in her ears. Aloud, she said, "That went well." Then she blew out a breath of frustration. Regardless of what Brooke said, Candace intended to call Tony Evans on Monday. But Brooke was wrong about her, she assured herself. She really didn't need counseling.

She had worked through the stages of grief already. Yes, she was still sad. Yes, she still missed Dean terribly. But she was functioning just fine.

Of course she was.

Sunday mornings were always a relief for Candace. By the end of the week, she nearly always felt hollowed out and emotionally exhausted from the daily effort of dealing with patients, children, finances, and all the other things that demanded her attention.

The Crenshaws attended Riverview Chapel, a small church at the far southern edge of town, within sight, as its name implied, of a moving body of water, though Candace wouldn't consider it a river. It was a creek at best. But Creekview just didn't have the right ring for a house of God, she supposed.

Between Sunday school and the church service, the congregation held a short social period. Candace was waiting in the social room for church to begin. She nursed a cup of coffee as she watched Howie and another little boy playing Rock Paper

Scissors for no apparent reason other than to see who would come out on top each time.

"Good morning, Mrs. Crenshaw." The speaker was a silver-haired woman wearing a summer skirt-suit in a soft shade of green, with gleaming pearl-and-diamond earrings and a matching necklace. She wore sensible yet stylish low heels that matched her camel-colored leather handbag. Looking more closely, Candace noted the distinctive Prada logo on the handbag. Candace had seen her at church before, although she couldn't dredge up the lady's name from her memory banks.

Embarrassed by her lack of memory, she extended a hand and offered the woman a warm smile. "Good morning. How are you?"

"I'm fine, thank you. I wanted to ask you about the Wall of Hope. I thought since you work at the hospital, you might have the inside scoop." Her blue eyes twinkled.

"I don't really know very much about it," Candace said. She was surprised that word of the Wall of Hope was so widespread already. "It's still very much in the planning stages. The hospital board hasn't approved anything yet."

"So I hear. But I'm sure they will." The lady sounded surprisingly confident. "Will you let me know when the bricks will be available? I'm very interested in donating several, and I really like the notion that this will help keep the hospital open."

"I like it too," Candace told her. "I plan to donate one." She swallowed and focused on her companion, not allowing herself to think of anything else.

"I need three. One brick will be for my parents, and another in memory of my husband. I'd also like to donate one in memory of my horse Gidget," the woman said. "She was with me for thirty-five years, and it would be lovely to have a place where I can see her name on a memorial stone along with the rest of my family."

"I don't have details about the bricks yet but I'll let you know as soon as I do," Candace told her, her interest piqued by the unexpected statements. It had never occurred to her how many people who mourned—whether they had lost a friend, a family member or a favored pet—might like to be able to come and see their loved one's name in an attractive public area. Elena *had* to get the board's approval for that project. Aloud she said, "And I'm sure there will be information about it in the paper." She smiled at the lady. "So tell me more about your Gidget. She must have been a very special horse."

"She was," the lady said. "We competed in dressage together for many years. She was a gorgeous bay Trakehner imported from Germany."

"I don't know much about horses," she confessed, "although I do know what dressage is, mostly from seeing it during the Olympics."

"It's a beautiful sport. Trakehners are known for their athleticism, friendliness and intelligence. Gidget was seventeen hands high, which is quite tall, but it's the breed standard."

As the woman spoke, Candace found herself deeply interested in the woman's ability to discuss the beloved animal, as well as make mention of her husband and parents. Gidget may have been a horse rather than a person, but the relationship had lasted *thirty-five years*. "May I ask you a question?" she said.

"Certainly, dear."

Candace hesitated. "It's about grief, not about horses."

The woman smiled, and her eyes softened. "I know a good deal about both."

"How do you do it?" she asked. "You talk about her—and your family—so calmly, so happily, with a smile on your face. I would love to be as strong as you when I talk about my husband." Immediately, she felt the familiar constriction tugging at her throat. "Three years ago. And I still can't . . . I just can't. . . ."

"It's hard," said her new friend. "Especially at first. I don't think there is a timetable for grief. But I do think it's important to be aware of our reactions over time. Are we moving forward? Do we feel as if our emotions are more stable now than they were, say, a year ago? I think that's the key. And if the answer is no to either of those, then I would recommend you consider getting some grief counseling."

"My children have been in counseling." And the word reminded Candace that she needed to call Brooke's therapist the following day.

"But we're talking about *you*, aren't we?" The lady's silver hair gleamed as she leaned forward and tapped a gentle finger over Candace's heart. "We're talking about *your* heart."

Candace nodded. "Yes." But she didn't need counseling. She was dealing with life just fine, most of the time.

Janet was standing nearby, waiting for Candace when she finished her conversation. As the woman walked on, Candace said, "Mom? Who was that lady? She knew my name, and she looked familiar, but for the life of me, I couldn't come up with her name."

"That's Eulalie Jeffries Hunt," Janet said. "She's the grand-daughter of Winthrop Jeffries."

"The man who founded Hope Haven?" Candace was absolutely dumbfounded.

Janet nodded. "She used to sit on the hospital board, but after her husband died, she began traveling more extensively, so she no longer sits on the board. I imagine that she still keeps close tabs on what goes on there. I'm sure she's not thrilled with all this talk of closing."

Her mother's words gave Candace an idea. Mrs. Hunt might have some influence with the hospital board. It certainly was worth asking. This afternoon, she had a phone call to make.

As always, Elena had found her church service exhilarating and exciting. She attended Holy Trinity Church in Deerford. Holy Trinity was the church whose chimes rang out twice a day except on Sundays, their low, sweet tones floating over the community.

As the congregation spilled out of the historic Gothic-style building, Elena kept a tight grip on Isabel's hand. "Ready for some lunch?" Cesar and Rafael usually went to church twice a year, on Christmas Eve and Easter Sunday, but Izzy looked forward to Sunday school every week and Elena was thrilled to see her granddaughter so enthusiastic.

Ahead of them, a tall, dark-haired man stood, clearly waiting for his wife to finish chatting with a friend. He looked very familiar . . . and suddenly, Elena knew where she'd seen him before. He'd been in a photo in the paper recently. He was on Hope Haven's board of directors.

"Izzy," she said, "I need to speak to that man." They surged forward before he wandered from their view.

"Excuse me," she said as she approached. She extended a hand. "I'm Elena Rodriguez, a nurse at Hope Haven."

The man turned, a pleasant smile on his face as recognition dawned. "Elena Rodriguez—the brains behind the Wall of Hope! I'm Will West."

"Yes, that's me," she confirmed. "I was wondering if you could spare a few minutes to talk."

"I'd love to." Will touched his wife's arm and murmured something to her. Then he drew Elena and Izzy aside. "I think you have a terrific idea," he told her. "I was very disappointed to see it tabled. I think we need to leap into fund-raising mode while there's all this interest in the community."

"Wonderful," Elena said. "Maybe you can help."

Candace had just dropped a letter in the mail during her morning break. As she headed for the stairs, she heard a woman's voice call, "Candace?"

Turning her head, she saw Robin Overing moving toward her. The girl wasn't exactly waddling, but she was getting closer to it. At thirty weeks, she only had ten to go. From now on, Candace knew, the baby would be growing significantly in size with each week that passed.

"Hello, Robin," Candace exclaimed. She had wanted to get in touch with the young mother-to-be after their last discussion, but she was afraid if she pushed too hard, Robin might simply dig in her heels and tune her out completely.

"Do you have a few minutes to talk?" Robin asked as she neared.

"Of course." Candace thought for a second. "If there's no one in the chapel, we could talk there. Otherwise, we'll go to the courtyard."

Robin followed as Candace led the way to the other side of the hospital. As she had hoped, there was no one in the chapel. Pastor Tom, the hospital's chaplain, poked his head out of his small office at the sound of voices; but when Candace gently shook her head, he smiled and withdrew.

"Let's sit here for a bit." Candace took a seat in one of the few pews, and Robin joined her. For a few minutes, Candace simply sat and let the quiet atmosphere soothe her. The chapel had been her lifeline since Dean's death. How many times had she come here and shed tears? God had responded to some pretty tough, angry questions in this room. He also had carried her until she felt she could walk on her own again. She hoped Robin might experience some of the same communion here that she had, the same that she continued to enjoy.

The afternoon sun streamed through the abstract design of the stained glass window above the altar, creating rich hues of color that slid across the interior space. The Hospital Auxiliary had raised money to add the window a few years ago, and it added a lovely dimension to the space.

At the front of the small room stood a simple altar of lightest oak. In the left front corner was a slightly raised platform. A large, dark cross of gleaming cherry stood solidly in its center. At the base, a gentle stream of water recirculated over rocks in a little channel surrounding the cross, creating a delightful, subdued burble. A variety of green plants crowded around the cross and the water's edge. It was, in Candace's opinion, an extraordinary place of peace.

Robin finally stirred, turning toward Candace. "I've never been in here before. It's lovely," she said in a hushed tone.

"It is," Candace affirmed. She took a deep breath. "I've spent a lot of time in here. Since my husband passed away, you can imagine how my faith has been tested."

"And yet you still believe," Robin said.

"And yet I still believe." Candace let the simple statement stand.

After another moment, Robin said, "I'm going to have the surgery."

Relief washed over Candace, though she acknowledged what Robin had said with an encouraging nod. She had been trained in a variety of simple counseling techniques designed to help patients work through the mental challenges illness often presented, so she simply reflected Robin's statement and listened.

Robin sounded more positive now. "But not just a lumpectomy. If I'm going to do this, I'm going to have a mastectomy. That way, I have a much greater chance of survival."

A wave of shock rippled through Candace. She had to force herself not to blurt out her first reaction, which was simply *No!* Nurses were expected to be extremely circumspect about offering medical opinions or diagnoses. They were trained to assist and offer care, not act as doctors. "Did your doctor talk to you about the difference in the two surgeries?" she asked.

Robin nodded her head. "Yes, but he left the choice up to me. If I have to be cut open, I figure I may as well take a more aggressive approach."

Choosing her words carefully, Candace said, "Are you planning to breast-feed?" Circumspect she might be, but there were ways to lead Robin to think about all the varied issues affecting her decision.

Robin hesitated. "Yes. I want to, but not if I still have cancer. I'm afraid of passing something to the baby."

Candace wanted to scream. If she were the patient, she would be talking to doctors and researching everything she could find on the diagnosis. Robin, in contrast, latched onto an idea and clung to it tightly until she was forced to reconsider.

Shifting on the bench, she looked into Robin's eyes. "You cannot pass cancer to your baby through breast milk. But if you're planning to breast-feed, a lumpectomy may be a better route for you to go."

"Why? Wouldn't it be better to be absolutely certain they get it all out?"

Candace wished Robin would talk—and really listen—to her doctor, but for whatever reason, the young woman appeared to be more comfortable talking to her. "What did your doctor recommend?"

"He said he would prefer to do a lumpectomy," Robin admitted, "but that either procedure could be done and the final decision is mine."

Candace reached out and lay a hand over Robin's. She gave it a brief squeeze, then casually added, "If I were you, I might consider the lumpectomy a little more closely. Not only will you retain the ability to breast-feed any other children you and Andrew might have, it's a much less invasive surgery and your recovery time is faster."

"The doctor says neither one will be outpatient surgery because of the baby." The pregnant woman looked anxious. "He wants me to stay at least one night."

"Given your pregnancy, I think that's a very wise precaution," Candace approved.

"He wants me to follow it up with chemotherapy." Robin looked troubled. "But he said that could wait until after I deliver, so it wouldn't affect the baby."

Silence fell between them, broken only by the soothing sounds of trickling water. Finally, Robin looked over and gave her a crooked smile. "Candace, thank you so much. I don't know what I would do without you."

Candace cast her a wry look. "Listen to your doctors?"

Robin giggled. "Maybe. You just seem to have a gift for calming me down and reducing everything to its simplest form."

"Would you like to pray with me?" Candace asked. Since she already had shared her faith with Robin, she felt no constraint in doing so again.

Robin smiled at her. "I would like that. You do the honors."

Candace smiled as she took Robin's hand. She prayed for wisdom, for Robin's return to health, and for the health of her unborn child. She asked blessings on the Overings and guidance in the couple's decision-making process.

When Candace finished her prayer, Robin said, "That was lovely. Thank you." She slid her weight to the edge of the pew and used the one in front for support as she rose to her feet. "I'll talk to Andrew about all this, and we'll go talk to the doctor again."

"Keep me posted," Candace requested.

"Don't worry." Robin chuckled. "I'll probably be back again begging you to explain more of this stuff to me." Her amusement faded. "Sometimes I still can't believe I'm living this, you know? What a nightmare."

"I do know."

Robin immediately looked remorseful. "I'm sure you do. And I feel stupid whining about my problems to you, when there's a very good chance I'll recover and be my old self in a few months."

As opposed to me, Candace thought, understanding the words Robin hadn't uttered. Her life had been irrevocably altered when Dean died—but she refused to dwell on the negative. Life was a wonderful gift, and there was much to savor.

She encircled Robin's shoulder and gave her a little hug as they began to walk toward the exit door. "Worrying about your health is never stupid. I'm glad you feel you can talk to me."

Chapter Fourteen

THE FOLLOWING DAY, CANDACE CAME OUT OF ONE of the birthing suites and walked to the nurses' station to pick up some meds. It was nearly lunchtime, and as soon as she delivered the requested medications, she was going to get her lunch and meet her friends in the courtyard.

As she walked toward the desk, she noticed Elena standing with a youngish-looking woman with some of the brightest red hair Candace had ever seen.

". . . would like to feature an article about the campaign on the front page," the redhead was saying.

The words caught Candace's attention. "Elena," she said, "you didn't tell me you'd gotten the board to approve the Wall of Hope. That's wonderful!"

Elena winked at her. "I didn't. Yet. Valera's doing an interview now so that as soon as we get permission, she'll be able to run it immediately."

Candace skirted around them and entered the nurses' station, wondering exactly what her friend was up to. But her friend was still speaking. "This is Valera Kincaid."

Candace looked at the woman and smiled as Elena continued. "She's a reporter with the *Deerford Dispatch*, and she wants to do a story about the campaign."

"That's wonderful." Candace was sincere. "Elena has worked hard to make her wonderful idea a reality."

"Oh, good sound bite. Can I quote you?" asked the reporter.

Candace nodded, a little taken aback by the young woman's perky enthusiasm. "Of course." At Valera's request, she provided her name and her affiliation with the hospital. Then she went about her work as the two continued to speak. A moment later, she saw them shake hands, and then Elena smiled at Candace. "I'll tell you more at lunch, I promise." And she walked back into the ICU while the reporter headed for the elevator.

"I can't wait to hear this. See you at lunch."

Thirty minutes later, Candace emerged onto the little terrace that Elena hoped to transform with her fund-raising project. Her three friends were already seated, and Anabelle slid over a bit so that Candace could join them at the table. As she did so, the others welcomed her.

"Hello," she said in response. "How are you all today?"

"James was telling us about his son's swim meet yesterday," Anabelle informed her. "Nelson broke a team record in the butterfly!"

"That's exciting. Tell him your friends said congratulations," Candace said, smiling warmly at James. It would be a very long time before she forgot how kind he had been during her post-conference meltdown on Friday.

James's blue eyes twinkled as he looked across the table at her. "Thanks. I'll pass it on."

"Anything exciting going on in your life?" Anabelle asked, directing the question at Candace.

For some ridiculous reason, the image of Heath Carlson flashed through Candace's mind. Instantly setting it aside, she said mildly, "Nothing very exciting, I'm afraid, unless you count Brooke and Howie pleading with me to let them get a kitten. One of Brooke's friends' families let their cat have a litter. There are five little bundles of fluffy joy that need homes, if anyone's interested," she said, eyeing her friends purposefully.

James laughed. "Don't look at me. I've already got one cat. The fact that she thinks she's a dog is beside the point."

Everyone chuckled. James had told them before about Sapphire's retrieving talent.

"No kittens for us," Anabelle said. "We have barn cats. I get them spayed or neutered, but every year there's another new one or two that I have to catch and take to the vet for shots and snipping."

Elena grinned when James winced noticeably. Then she shook her head. "Sorry," she said. "Cesar is allergic to cat dander."

Candace looked at her friend. "All right," she told Elena. "Spill. What, exactly, is going on with the Wall of Hope? I thought it was tabled by the board."

"It was," Elena said. "But let me start from the beginning. On Sunday morning, as I left church, I ran into one of the board members who attends my church. Anybody know Will West?"

"Oh, I do," James said. "Nice guy."

"Very nice," Elena said. "He's very supportive of the idea. He suggested I speak personally with every board member and answer their questions and concerns. So I spent the rest of the day contacting the board members and either speaking on the phone or visiting them."

"Even Frederick Innisk?" Anabelle asked.

Elena grinned. "Yep. At least, I tried. He wouldn't give me the time of day. Anyway, the upshot of all this is that Bernard Telford got a majority of the board to agree to another meeting *this Wednesday* to hopefully approve the project."

"Holy cow." Candace blinked. "I need whatever kind of vitamins you take."

Everyone laughed, and James said, "Terrific job, Elena."

Just as Candace glanced at her watch, the door from the hospital opened and Valera Kincaid stepped through into the tiny courtyard.

"Picture time!" she announced.

"Oh, I forgot," Elena said. "Valera's going to take a picture of the four of us holding bricks. It will accompany her article on the Wall of Hope."

"It'll be in the paper as soon as Elena gets board approval," Valera added. "Can you all step over here?" She indicated the ratty, overgrown privet hedge that divided the area from the parking lot.

"But that's not a very attractive background," Anabelle protested.

"That's the point!" Elena said, gently herding Anabelle into position. "We want folks to see the current setting and be able to contrast it with what we hope to do." She leaned down and grabbed a canvas bag that had been propped against the leg of one picnic table. "Ugh. That's heavy."

Candace realized the bag held several bricks. "No wonder," she said, laughing.

Elena pulled the bricks out one by one, handing one to each of her friends. In just a few moments, Valera had teased them into beaming smiles, as she then showed them on her digital camera.

"I never like pictures of myself," Anabelle announced. "But that one's really good!"

Valera perched on the edge of one of the picnic tables, pulling a notebook from her pocket. "Now. I assume each of you will be contributing a brick to the Wall of Hope?"

Candace nodded. Together, James and Anabelle said, "I will."

"Who will your bricks commemorate?" the reporter asked.

Elena immediately said, "Mine will be in memory of my parents."

"Mine is in honor of my wife, Fern," James said, going on to explain that she suffered from MS.

"My brick," Anabelle told Valera, "will honor Dr. Drew Hamilton, who is on the staff here at Hope Haven."

"Any special reason?" Valera asked, her pencil poised expectantly over her pad.

"Oh yes." Anabelle nodded. "He saved my daughter's life after she was badly injured in an accident ten years ago."

"My goodness," Valera said. She lifted her head and looked at Candace. "How about you?"

Candace took a deep breath. "My family will donate a brick in memory of my husband, Dean Crenshaw. He passed away unexpectedly three years ago." It was startling to hear Dean's name spoken aloud. She rarely had cause to use it now, and she bit her lip as her voice faltered.

Elena put an arm around her.

Valera let the silence hang for a moment. Then, in a quiet voice, she said, "Thank you all for sharing your stories with me. They will give the Wall of Hope a very personal face. I hope I can convey that to our readers."

Anabelle was late. *Doesn't it just figure*, she thought as she rushed into the cafeteria the next afternoon. She had invited Marge Matthews and Phyllis Getty to have coffee with her, and she wasn't even on time to greet them.

"Hi, Anabelle." Marge waved one beefy arm aloft, and Anabelle immediately turned toward the booth where the two women sat. They were a study in contrast, with Marge planted as solidly as a mountain while Phyllis resembled a tiny humming-bird as she dashed over to get a napkin from the dispenser on the counter.

"Hello," Phyllis said as she returned. "Rough day?"

Anabelle blew out a breath and sank onto the red vinyl seat beside her. "When it rains, it pours," she said. "We've had three cardiac admissions this morning."

"We've been busy in the ICU too. I wonder if there's a full moon or something." They all laughed as she referred to an old wives' tale that said more people got sick or did crazy things on the night of each full moon, but Marge looked sympathetic as she pushed a steaming Styrofoam cup of coffee toward Anabelle. "Here. I got you a drink. No sweetener or creamer, though."

"Thank you." Anabelle plucked one of the small blue packets of artificial sweetener out of the little metal dispenser and tore it open. Adding a tiny amount to her drink, she stirred it vigorously for a moment.

"So what's up?" Phyllis asked. "Marge and I were trying to guess what you wanted while we waited. I told her you might want us to pool our funds and buy lottery tickets together," she went on with a gleam of humor in her eye, "but she was sure you were going to invite us to join you on a white-water rafting trip."

Anabelle choked on the sip of coffee she had just taken as she began to laugh. "I have an extremely detailed mental image of two sixtysomethings and an eighty-four-year-old in bright orange life vests and fluorescent helmets paddling like mad as our raft gets tossed toes-over-nose into a Class V rapid."

Phyllis began to laugh, her deep, hoarse tones sounding as if they couldn't possibly come from such a tiny little person.

Marge grinned too. "You'd have to knock me out to get me to go white-water rafting. Terrifies me even to watch it on TV."

"I agree." Anabelle took another sip of her drink. "No, as much as it pains me, I have to confess. I need your help with a hospital-related matter."

"A hospital-related matter?" Phyllis repeated. "Not nearly as exciting as we were guessing."

Anabelle leaned forward. "Have you two heard about the Wall of Hope?"

"Of course," Phyllis said promptly. "You can't walk through this hospital without hearing about it."

Marge nodded. "Elena told me about it. That woman's got some serious ideas for saving this hospital, doesn't she?"

Anabelle nodded. "She's a marvel."

"So," Phyllis prompted. "The Wall of Hope."

"Right. Elena has some publicity lined up with the *Dispatch* if she ever gets the board to approve the project. Valera Kincaid wants to do several human-interest stories in conjunction with the launch of the fund-raising campaign to save the hospital. And I need your help."

"Doing what? We're not very interesting." Marge blew on her coffee.

"Speak for yourself," said Phyllis. "I find myself extremely interesting."

Anabelle hid a grin. She suspected Phyllis was only half kidding. "Valera needs a list of people to contact to interview," she told the others. "I would like you to help me come up with a list of maybe a dozen or so of the most interesting and compelling cases that have come through the hospital."

"Within what time frame?" Phyllis wanted to know.

Anabelle shrugged. "I don't know that there is one, although I would think the patient should still be living. These are success stories that showcase the reasons the community needs us."

Marge's broad brow wrinkled; she looked troubled. "We can't turn over the names of former patients to a reporter," she said. "That goes against every privacy law ever created."

"We won't be giving these names out at all," Anabelle explained. "I'm going to run our list by Dr. Hamilton and ask him to rank them in order of interest. Then Albert Varner, the CEO, will send out letters asking these people to *volunteer* to be interviewed. Once we get a list of volunteers, Valera can take it from there."

Marge was nodding. "That works for me," she said.

"I've already drafted a letter," Anabelle said. "I'd like you to read over it to see if you think it sounds appropriate. Now, put on your thinking caps. Let's make a list."

"How about the fellow who was struck by lightning last year?" Marge asked. "I still can't believe he didn't suffer brain damage. His heart stopped three times."

"What was his name?" Anabelle snapped her fingers impatiently as she thought, but the name remained firmly lodged in her memory just out of reach.

Phyllis, of course, knew the name immediately.

Anabelle pulled a small notepad and pen from her pocket and began to write. "Good one. Who else?"

"The boy who fell out of the tree house," Phyllis said.

"That family with two sets of triplets."

"Oh, I know a good one. How about that pregnant woman who was in the car accident a couple years ago? Her baby was delivered by C-section in the ambulance. . . ."

Chapter Fifteen

ELENA HAD JUST SETTLED A NEW PATIENT IN A BED when she saw Zane McGarry standing at the nurses' station as she came down the hall.

"Hello." She greeted him with a warm smile. "What are you doing up here?"

Zane looked at her soberly. "I just thought you ought to know Freddie Innisk is gunning for you. He is hopping mad that you managed to get that board meeting rescheduled."

"Oh no." Elena's heart sank as she recalled the unpleasant scene she'd already had with the board member.

"I'm sorry, Elena," Zane said. "His wealth makes him a powerful man in this community."

"Can he stop the project altogether?" she asked in a stricken voice.

Zane shrugged. "I think he's trying. And I think he's probably got a fifty-fifty chance of success. Although from what I hear, you were extremely persuasive with your home visits and phone calls on Sunday." He looked away from her. "The board is having another meeting tomorrow."

Elena took a deep breath and straightened her shoulders. "I'm going to 'let go and let God,' as they say. I've done everything I can. I don't want to become a pest."

Zane searched her face as a slow smile began to chase away his grim expression. "'Let go and let God.' Can't say I've ever really tried it, but I may go home and say a few prayers."

"All right." She held up her hand in a high five, and with a laugh, Zane slapped his palm against hers.

Candace left the hospital after her shift ended on Tuesday. Spring had yielded to summer, and the days were often muggy and hot now. She opened her car door, ducked in, and turned on the engine, then pushed the automatic buttons to roll down all the windows to let out some of the accumulated heat, while she waited for the air-conditioning in the vehicle to start churning out cold air.

"Candace?" She turned at the sound of her name.

"Mrs. Hunt, hello." She remembered that the woman's grandfather had founded the hospital. It shouldn't be surprising to see her here.

"I was visiting a friend," Mrs. Hunt said. Her silver hair gleamed in the bright sunlight, and she was as impeccably attired as she had been at church, in a skirt ensemble of pink and lavender. "May we speak for a moment?"

"Of course. Would you like to go inside and get something to drink?"

Mrs. Hunt smiled at her. "That's all right, dear. This will only take a moment."

Candace returned the smile. She could only hope to be as vibrant as Mrs. Hunt in a couple more decades.

"I did a little bit of sleuthing after our telephone conversation," the older woman began. "And I got some very interesting information. After that, I visited Fred Innisk." She smiled. "I think it's safe to say he won't be bad-mouthing any more attempts to save the hospital."

Candace was both surprised and curious. "Just like that, he's going to stop? Why?"

"Apparently, dear old Freddie has invested heavily in the medical center that is projected to open in town in two years."

"I didn't know he was involved in that. There will be several new specialists taking office space there. If the hospital stays open, that is." Her smile dimmed. "I'm afraid that if it doesn't, we won't be able to keep *any* of our doctors in town."

Mrs. Hunt nodded. "It's a legitimate concern."

"But why is it significant that Mr. Innisk is involved in that project?"

"Because, dear . . ." Mrs. Hunt allowed the suspense to build for another moment. "One of the things he's pushing for is an emergency clinic in the medical center. The only way that would be feasible is if Hope Haven Hospital could no longer handle emergencies."

Candace's mouth fell open. "What a sneaky little man!"

"Exactly." Mrs. Hunt made a face as if she had smelled something very rank. "Fred's investment will be worth a great deal more if this emergency clinic becomes reality. So although I don't believe he's actively sabotaging the hospital, he certainly is doing his best to sabotage any efforts at fund-raising to keep it open."

Candace was dismayed. "So what can we do?"

Mrs. Hunt's smile reminded Candace of the Cheshire cat in Brooke's illustrated version of *Alice in Wonderland*. "Oh, you don't have to do anything. I took the opportunity to point out to Freddie that his credibility in this town will suffer significantly if anyone finds out what he's been up to. Image is very, very important to him. He might not be happy about it, but he won't be making any more trouble for your fund-raising team."

Candace could hardly believe it. "Thank you, Mrs. Hunt. Thank you. My friend Elena, who came up with the Wall of Hope, will be so relieved."

"As will we all, if we can keep our little jewel of a hospital open," Mrs. Hunt reminded her.

James didn't meet his friends for lunch on Wednesday. Instead, he took the latest lunch on his shift, and he used the computer and printer in the staff lounge to prepare several more résumés and cover letters, which he signed, addressed and stamped. He couldn't let Fern see these. They were mostly in Peoria, although two were clear over in a suburb of Chicago.

He was becoming increasingly convinced that the hospital couldn't stay open. Elena had a wonderful idea with her Wall of Hope, but he couldn't imagine how that could possibly raise enough money to keep the hospital afloat.

Placing the stamp on the final envelope, James sealed it, then took the elevator down to the first floor. On one side of the registration desk was a special bin for staff members' outgoing mail, and he tossed the new batch of job inquiries in there. Then, still brooding about the idea of changing jobs, he returned to the second floor.

Candace was alone in the nurses' station when he approached. As he clocked back in, she said, "Hi. We missed you at lunch."

He knew there was no accusation in her tone. Candace was the last person on earth who would fuss at him. Still, he felt defensive as he said, "I had some things to take care of," without looking in her direction.

"You missed the big announcement."

He looked over at her. "What big announcement?"

She was grinning a very wide, excited un-Candace-like grin. "Elena's project was approved by the board today!"

He was stunned. Yes, stunned. Despite all his encouraging words, he hadn't really expected Elena to come out on top in a battle with an influential Deerford heavyweight. "That's terrific!" And now he felt *really* badly for missing lunch. "I'm sorry I missed it," he said sincerely.

"Me too. Life does tend to get in the way of fun, doesn't it?" Her voice was light and warm, and suddenly he felt regret for not letting the others know he wouldn't be at lunch. At the very least, he could have notified one of them. For Pete's sake, they all worked on the same floor of the same building.

And then he realized he also felt the need to share his worries with her.

"I'm sending résumés out of the area," he said baldly.

Her fingers stopped flying over the keyboard, and there was a moment of silence in the little area. "Have you tried finding other work in Deerford?" she asked.

He nodded. "No luck. I really don't want to have to move my family, but I have to have a job."

She nodded as she swiveled her chair around to face him. "I know."

Then it struck him. She really did know. Unlike Anabelle and Elena, Candace was the only provider in her family, which also included three other people. "Aren't you worried?" he asked, searching her eyes as he turned to face her.

"I'm concerned," she said carefully. "But I have faith in this little community. I believe enough people care about Hope Haven to help keep the hospital open."

"Maybe that's my problem," James mused. "Not enough faith."

"I understand your feelings, though. It's not prudent to ignore reality."

"Is that what you're doing?"

"I don't think so," she said. "I'm just not ready to look for another position yet. I'm going to do my best to support and encourage the Wall of Hope and see what happens."

"I wish I had your optimism," he said.

A startled laugh escaped Candace, and he looked up. She was often the most serious one of their little group, and he rarely had heard her laugh aloud. "I don't consider myself particularly optimistic," she said. "But I've been praying about this, and I believe God will answer our prayers. We may not always like the answers; but with His help, we can live with whatever comes along."

James was acutely aware of the way in which his friend had come by her apparent serenity. Despite the gravity of Fern's illness, he suddenly felt self-absorbed and not very trusting compared to her.

As if she read his mind, Candace said, "We all have different challenges to surmount, and we all deal with them in different ways. You'll meet and surpass this challenge, James."

He only wished he could be as certain.

That evening, Candace and her mother were working together on dinner. Janet was getting an eggplant Parmesan dish out of the oven while Candace set the table.

"Mom?" Candace waited until her mother had set the piping hot casserole dish atop the stove before she spoke.

Janet turned with a smile on her face. "Yes?"

"Do you think I should be job hunting?"

Janet's smile faded, and two vertical lines appeared between her eyebrows. "I don't know. I don't know enough about what's going on at the hospital to answer that. But the fact that you're mentioning it tells me it's a concern. Why do you ask?"

Candace shrugged. "I honestly hadn't thought much about looking for a new job. I thought the Wall of Hope would solve the insolvency problems and all the hospital's money woes. But I guess I'm naive. One of my friends has been actively looking for a new job. He hasn't found anything local, so he's begun sending résumés out to other areas—so far away that if he's successful, his family would have to move."

Janet grimaced in dismay. "Move? Having to adjust to a new school might be very difficult for Brooke."

Candace nodded. "That's exactly what I thought. It's bad enough that she's still having grief issues, but she's also on the verge of adolescence."

"Do you feel as if you should be job hunting?" her mother asked.

Candace shrugged. "I didn't until today, when James and I discussed it. But just like him, I'm the primary supporter for our family; and I shouldn't be waiting until the last minute to think about it."

"I'm going to put my trust in the Lord," Janet said. "Listen to Him, honey. In your heart, you'll hear what you need to do. And if that means moving to Peoria or who-knows-where, we'll all find a way to make it work. Even Brooke."

Candace tried to chuckle, although it was a poor effort. "As if living through adolescence isn't hideous enough without other complications."

Janet did laugh then. "Yes, I don't know many people who would willingly relive it. Especially the middle-school years."

"Grammy? Why are you talking about school?"

Candace whirled around. One of these days, Brooke was going to give her a heart attack with the way she silently drifted into a room. Had she heard any of the discussion about moving? Given the problems Brooke was having right now, that would be extremely upsetting for the child. "Grammy and I were just thinking about you being in sixth grade next fall." She tugged on a lock of her daughter's hair as Brooke moved to her side. "How did you grow up so fast?"

"I don't want to go to sixth grade." There was a hint of fear in Brooke's voice, but Candace relaxed as she realized Brooke had only come in on the very tail end of their chat.

"Sixth doesn't sound like fun?" Candace filled water glasses, using a plastic one for Howie rather than the glass the others were using.

"No," Brooke said definitively. "Some of my friends are excited, but I'm not."

"I suppose you could stay in fifth at Rishell," Candace said. "But it might be weird with your friends all in sixth."

"Mommy." Brooke gave her a look that Candace suspected she would be seeing all too often over the next few years. "You know I'm going. But I'm not looking forward to it." Her tone was both dignified and melancholy.

Brooke was such a little adult sometimes that it broke Candace's heart. If her life hadn't been rocked by the loss of her daddy, might she have been different?

"I know you're not." Candace gave her daughter a hug before handing her napkins and nudging her toward the table to put one by each place. "But at least keep an open mind. You may like it better than you expect."

"I'm not so sure. We'll be changing rooms for every single class. Changing for every subject doesn't sound very efficient to me."

Candace stared at her daughter. "I suppose it's not. Although I don't know that I ever thought about it quite that way."

"So why do they do it?"

"Because by the time you get to middle school, your subjects get more and more complicated and teachers have to specialize." That sounded like a good rationale, and she warmed to her theme. "An algebra teacher isn't going to be as good as a teacher who focuses purely on English. And an English teacher would have a hard time knowing as much as someone who only teaches science."

Brooke's eyebrows rose. "Oh." Setting down the last napkin, she wandered out of the room.

"Go find your brother and wash your hands," Janet called. "It's time to eat."

Candace stared after her daughter. "My explanation satisfied her?" she asked incredulously. "What's the date? I'm going to write this down."

On Thursday morning, Elena arrived at the hospital early. She closed and locked the door of her Jeep Liberty, and then she started toward the building, deep in thought.

She needed to write thank-you notes to Quintessa, Zane, Albert Varner and the board of directors. Well, all the directors except for Mr. Innisk. And her three closest friends here at Hope Haven too. They deserved thanks for being such terrific supporters.

"Elena?" A pleasant masculine voice made her look to her left.

Dr. David Weller was coming toward her. One of the ER physicians, Dr. Weller was barely a year out of medical school, driven and enthusiastic. Elena didn't know him well, and she hadn't realized he knew her name.

Dr. Weller extended a hand and introduced himself, as if she didn't know who he was. His handshake was so vigorous she decided it was a good thing she didn't need her fingers for anything important like surgery. "I heard about the Wall of Hope. It's a terrific idea," he told her. "I'd like to help in any way I can."

"Thank you." She matched his bright smile with one of her own. "I could give you some brochures to share with patients you see in the ER, if you think that would be all right."

"I'm sure that will be fine," he said confidently. "If you think of anything else, don't hesitate to call me."

"Thank you." There were not many people who Elena felt matched her energy level, but Dr. Weller certainly was right up there with her, she realized as she watched him stride toward the building. She supposed, she thought with a small grin, that some people might characterize her as overzealous.

"Good morning, Ms. Rodriguez." The stiff female voice belonged to the equally stiff Leila Hargrave, the nursing administrator. Mrs. Hargrave oversaw the entire nursing program. A short, plump woman, she always wore her gray hair in a tight bun at the back of her head.

"Good morning, Mrs. Hargrave." Elena would no sooner have called the woman Leila than she would leap off the Willis Tower. There were not very many people who intimidated Elena, but Mrs. Hargrave was near the top of her short list. Possibly right ahead of Albert Varner's scary executive assistant with the green thumb.

"I wanted to speak with you," Leila said, her gray eyes looking Elena up and down.

Checking to be sure her uniform was properly put together, Elena suspected. She braced herself.

"Yes, ma'am?"

"Your Wall of Hope project is an excellent idea."

Elena blinked. *Really?* "Thank you."

"I would like to offer my services in any manner befitting my position," the nursing administrator went on.

"That would be terrific," Elena said sincerely. "Organization is something we may need, and I suspect you would excel at that."

Leila nearly smiled; Elena could see her lips quiver. "I suspect I would be. Contact me when you know what you need." Inclining her head as regally as a queen, Leila walked on.

Elena stood where she was for a moment, until someone came along behind her and bumped her shoulder companionably. "The middle of the parking lot probably isn't the best place for daydreaming," Candace said. "Good morning."

Elena laughed as she fell into step beside her friend. "Good morning."

Candace was wearing pink scrubs today. The color emphasized the soft bloom of color along her cheeks. Candace, thought Elena, was a lovely woman when she smiled. All too often, she had her head down in serious contemplation of who-knew-what.

"You seem happy," she said. "I thought maybe Mrs. Hargrave would leave you needing to be cheered up."

"Nope. The exact opposite. Would you believe she offered to help with the Wall of Hope?"

Candace looked appropriately stunned. "Amazing."

"I know!"

As the two women continued into the hospital and headed for the elevators, several people stopped them. Elena received several more offers of help, a number of people informing her they were keeping the project in prayer, and more encouragement than she had ever anticipated. By the time she and Candace had stashed their lunches and purses in their lockers in the staff lounge, she needed a paper and pen to write down all the new volunteers.

As she swiftly divided them into prayer partners, flyer distribution and other tasks, Candace looked over her shoulder. "I couldn't organize anything that quickly if my life depended on it."

"Yes, you could. You're very organized."

"I'm a good faker."

The two women chuckled together as they headed to the second floor to begin their respective days. And Elena's heart felt light. Surely with all these good people ready to support the project, the townsfolk would step up financially.

Wouldn't they?

Chapter Sixteen

"DR. HAMILTON?" ANABELLE STUCK HER HEAD INTO the office of the man who had saved Kirstie's life. He had been practicing medicine at Hope Haven Hospital for nearly forty years, and there were few people in Deerford who didn't recognize his name. Anabelle had worked with him for quite a bit of that time. Long enough, she thought fondly, that she could remember him with dark brown hair. Still, the silver was striking; it made him look even more distinguished.

"Hi, Anabelle," the physician said, swiveling his chair away from his computer monitor and leaning back. He wore a lab coat unbuttoned over a white shirt and a deep red tie.

"How do you know I want anything?" she asked. "Maybe I'm just visiting you out of the goodness of my heart."

"Are you?"

She laughed and shook her head. "No, you win. I need your assistance with something."

Dr. Hamilton was grinning too. "Gotcha!"

She came all the way into the room and took a seat in front of his desk. "Have you heard about Elena Rodriguez's idea for a fund-raiser called the Wall of Hope?"

"Maybe a better question would be to ask who hasn't?" he said, smiling. "Oh yes. I've heard about it. And heard about it, and heard about it."

"That's great! We're preparing to publicize it within the community—"

"I know," he said, grimacing. "I got a phone call this morning from Frederick Innisk. Have you ever met him?"

"Not personally," Anabelle said. "Which I believe is a good thing for me." That man hadn't succeeded torpedoing Elena's wonderful idea, she thought with satisfaction. "And if a fraction of the things I've heard about his temperament are true, I probably don't want to. He's bad-mouthing the Wall of Hope, isn't he?"

The physician nodded. "Yes. He tried to tell me the hospital will be leaving itself open to lawsuits if we use patients for publicity purposes. I don't know where he got a ridiculous idea like that, and I told him I couldn't imagine any health professional would do something like that."

Anabelle crossed her arms. "I know where he got the idea. Well, maybe I don't know exactly how he heard it, but clearly someone has been talking 'out of school.'"

"What do you mean?"

"Mr. Innisk must have heard something about the plans for publicity and misunderstood. He already blocked the newspaper from running an article, but now that the board approved the project over his objections, he won't be able to stop it."

Dr. Hamilton pursed his lips. "Freddie Innisk wields a lot of clout in this town. It's about time someone reminded him we live in a democracy."

Anabelle laughed. "Let me tell you what the Wall of Hope plans really include."

Dr. Hamilton listened with interest as she explained Valera's initial news article's focus. Then she went on to tell him about the reporter's interest in doing a series of stories with former patients who were successfully cared for at Hope Haven. "And that's where you come in," she added. "Although if we can't even get the first article published, I'm not sure what good the rest of these interviews will do."

"Tell Elena not to give up," the doctor advised. "I think of Freddie as a tsunami—he rushes in and overwhelms; but as his influence recedes, people come to their senses and begin to fix the damage he's done."

Anabelle snorted. "I hope that's true."

"So how can I help?"

"Other than counteracting the Innisk Effect?" she asked.

He laughed aloud. "Oh, the fellows I play golf with are going to enjoy that." Then he sobered. "I'll do what I can outside the hospital to set things right. What else?"

His words gave her hope. Dr. Hamilton was well known and widely respected in the community. His words carried a lot of weight. "I have a list here," she said, waving a sheet of paper at him. "It contains the names—or cases, in places where we couldn't remember names—of fifteen people who are former patients. Marge Matthews and Phyllis Getty helped me come up with the list. I'd like you to look over this list with me and see how many of these would be good possibilities for the interview series." She went on to explain the letter she hoped to send out inviting them to volunteer.

"I'll be glad to look at it." He held out a hand for the list. "Once we have the list finalized, I'd be happy to send the letters out personally. The people who are interested could contact my office, and I could have a list compiled for the reporter."

Anabelle's eyes widened as she handed over the sheet of paper. "Thanks. That's a generous offer."

"It's the least I can do. After all, my job is on the line here too."

His words were serious, but Anabelle realized it wouldn't be exactly the same for him. If the hospital closed, he still could have a private practice, as could most of the other physicians. It was all the other hospital staff who would be most affected by a closing. They stood to lose their jobs and their livelihoods.

When Dr. Hamilton had finished with the list, he laid it on his desk. "All right. Do you trust me to take care of this?"

Anabelle nodded. "Of course. Zane McGarry's office has the sample letter, if you'd like to use it."

He nodded. "No sense reinventing the wheel. I'll call down there right now and ask them to e-mail it to me."

"Thank you," she said. "You're a peach."

"I know." He grinned modestly. Leaning back in his chair again, he said, "So how's my best girl doing these days? She hasn't been in to see me in a long time."

He was referring to Kirstie, with whom he had developed a special relationship after his heroic efforts to save her life when she'd been hit by that car. Kirstie still had a stuffed animal he'd brought her while she was in the hospital, a little white plush kitty with the softest fur imaginable. It had occupied a place of honor on her bed for many years; and while Anabelle doubted it still lived on Kirstie's bed, she knew for a fact that her daughter had packed it and taken it along when she moved.

"All grown up." To her horror, Anabelle felt her chest tightening. She would *not* cry, she told herself fiercely. Releasing a deep breath, she said, "She got a teaching job."

He nodded. "I heard. What grade?"

"Third. She loves it." She managed a smile. "She moved into her own apartment last month."

"Wow. I bet you've got empty-nest-itis in a big way."

Anabelle chuckled, and it sounded shaky even to her. "You could say that."

"It's natural," he said gently. "Especially after everything your family has gone through with her. Instead of stepping back gradually as she grew and matured, you needed to be front and center again through a lot of her adolescence."

"Once she got comfortable with her prosthesis, she became Little Miss Independence again, though, and we didn't have so much to do for her. Cam still drove her to school in any kind of bad weather so she didn't have to try to walk to and from the bus stop. And I checked her stump every night for any kind of skin lesion," Anabelle admitted. "Even a tiny scratch can become a big problem if it isn't treated immediately."

"You're good parents," he told her. "You encouraged excellent habits and routines, so she's adept at caring for herself." He smiled. "Genna had a tough time when the last one of ours went off to school. Anytime a child moves away from home, it leaves a hole."

Anabelle nodded. "I avoided it earlier because she lived at home while she was in college. So it's time. I'm just having a little trouble adjusting." She sent Dr. Hamilton a wry smile. "Unlike Kirstie. She seems to be having absolutely no trouble spreading her wings and flying on with her life."

He grinned at her expression. "That's the way you want it," he assured her.

"I know," she admitted, "but I don't have to like it!"

Candace was helping Brooke with a project on seahorses to be displayed in the summer science exhibition at the local Children's Museum. Scanning the sheet of instructions, Candace said, "Okay. You know what they look like and how many kinds there are. Now you need to research what they eat and where they can be found. And it says you should include any other unique or interesting facts about your animal." She set down the paper. "How did you decide on seahorses?"

Brooke shrugged. "I saw a show about them on the Discovery Channel last week, and I thought they were interesting. Mommy, did you know the fathers are the ones that have the babies?"

Now *that* wasn't a sentence she'd expected to hear from an eleven-year-old. "Are you sure?" she asked. "Females almost always are the ones—"

"No, it's the fathers," Brooke insisted.

Her words reminded Candace that Brooke had a counseling appointment set up for next week. Tony Evans had squeezed her into his schedule right after Candace called.

"They said it on TV." Brooke arched her eyebrows as if the TV's authority ended the discussion.

Candace resisted the urge to tell Brooke not to believe everything she saw on television. It was such a clichéd motherly statement. Instead, she said, "All right. Get on the Internet and find me three separate references that say that. And they have to be knowledgeable sources, like zoos or national aquariums."

Brooke heaved a sigh. "All right," she muttered. "Boy, are you going to look dumb when I find them."

"Brooke!" Candace decided she and her mother had jinxed themselves when they talked about adolescence the other day. But her daughter had already trudged out of the room.

The telephone rang then, and she rose to answer it. "Hello?"

"Candace?"

"This is Candace."

"Hi, it's Robin Overing." The young woman sounded chipper and relaxed.

"Hi, Robin. How are you feeling?"

"Fat," the woman said with a laugh. "But I wanted to tell you that this morning Andrew and I had a joint meeting with my oncologist, the surgeon, the anesthesiologist, my obstetrician and the pediatrician who will be caring for our baby."

"My goodness. That's quite a powwow." Candace was ecstatic. "Did the group of you come to any decisions?"

"Yes. I wanted you to know right away that I listened to you and asked a whole lot of questions about the surgery. I've decided to have the lumpectomy. You were right—it sounds much less complicated and invasive than a mastectomy. And the anesthetist made me feel a lot better about that part of it." But then she stopped, and Candace felt a hesitation in her silence.

"But?" she prompted.

"It's not really an objection," Robin said. "The one thing we didn't resolve is really just a question my oncologist, the pediatrician and I need to discuss a little more. My doctor wants me to have chemotherapy as soon as possible after I give birth."

"All right," Candace said slowly.

"But I had really gotten excited about breast-feeding," Robin said wistfully. "It would be so much better for the baby."

"Better, perhaps, but not critical to good health under most circumstances," Candace offered.

"You think I should start chemo and not breast-feed, don't you?"

"My opinion isn't important, Robin," she said patiently. "You and Andrew have far more information than I do about all the complexities of your case, and you can make your own decisions. But I want to congratulate you on being proactive and talking with all those doctors. I think you're making the best decision possible with the information available to you."

"I hope so," Robin said in a small voice. "I have a few weeks yet to decide about chemo. It can't start in any case until after the baby's born."

Candace chuckled. "Not too long to go, then. Babies have a way of wreaking havoc on any attempts at scheduling," she advised. "You and Andrew had better be ready to make that last decision at any time."

"Oh, I don't think I'll deliver early," Robin said confidently. "My mother was two weeks late with me."

Candace and her friends had agreed to meet for lunch at the Corner the following Monday. James joined Candace first, with Anabelle only moments behind him. The three exchanged family stories while waiting for Elena, who came flying in five minutes later.

"Great news!" she crowed as she slid onto the dark green vinyl seat of the booth beside Anabelle.

Candace smiled at her friend's enthusiasm. "What's that?"

"The paper printed the introductory article about the Wall today. Look!" She passed out copies of the day's *Deerford Dispatch*. "Hot off the presses, with our smiling faces right on the front page."

James smiled. "Honestly, Elena, why don't you show a little more enthusiasm?"

She made a face at him, and they both grinned.

"I'm so glad Frederick Innisk didn't manage to squash this," Anabelle commented. "I still can't understand why he'd object to any attempt to keep the hospital from going under."

"Zane told me that Dr. Hamilton is speaking to people," Elena confided.

Anabelle looked just a teeny bit smug. "I may have mentioned to him that Innisk was causing trouble when we spoke about the letters."

Elena threw her arms around her friend. "You're amazing! Thank you!"

Candace had to laugh. "You're pretty amazing too," she told Elena. "You've taken this project from a mere kernel of an idea to something the whole town can support."

Elena's cheeks bloomed with color. "It wasn't really such a big deal."

"It will be if this hospital stays open." James's tone was serious and dampened everyone's high spirits.

"You're right," said Candace. She thought of the conversation she had had with her mother. "It's almost impossible to fully appreciate what a wonderful thing it will be if the hospital stays open. I'm sure local businesses share our concern."

"The pharmacy's business would decrease without the hospital," James said. "And the town's tax base will be significantly smaller if a lot of hospital employees are without work or are forced to move to new locations."

Candace nodded. "If people move and take their families away from Deerford, it's going to affect how many teachers are needed in the schools. And if there are fewer teachers, that affects the tax base even more."

"Fewer people to spend money locally," Anabelle said. "Which directly affects any retail businesses, from the dry cleaners to the bicycle repair shop."

"It creates a chain reaction," James said.

"Wow," Elena said. "I guess I didn't realize just how significant the economic impact on this town will be if Hope Haven closes."

"And the last thing any of us need is more financial stress," Anabelle said. "So good work, Elena. We're behind you all the way."

Chapter Seventeen

THE PERSONNEL DIRECTOR AT THE CHILDREN'S Hospital of Illinois in Peoria looked across her desk at James. He'd made the ninety-minute drive earlier that morning and had undergone an extensive interview. "And moving your family from Deerford would not be a problem for you, Mr. Bell? What if the Deerford hospital stays open?"

James swallowed. *Lord, don't let me blow this.* "I love my current job. But I support a family of four, and I have to think of them first. The thought of moving doesn't make me jump up and down and cheer, but I can't live on what-ifs."

There was a short silence when he finished speaking. The personnel director tapped away at her keyboard, presumably entering a few notes on their conversation. Or maybe, James thought with a sudden burst of humor, she was checking on her friends' status updates on Facebook.

The woman rose and extended a hand across the polished surface of her desk. "Thank you for speaking with me, Mr. Bell," she said. "Would you have time to take a tour of the hospital?"

James did his best to hide his relief. Would she bother with that if she wasn't seriously considering him? "Certainly," he said. "Children's has a wonderful reputation. I'd love to see it in action."

The personnel director smiled. "And we love showing our facility off, believe me." She beckoned to him to follow, and James realized to his astonishment that she intended to conduct the tour herself. "Children's cares for more pediatric patients than any other hospital in Illinois outside of Chicago. We offer five key areas of service, including neonatal and pediatric ICUs, pediatric surgery, hematology and oncology, and our congenital heart center. . . ."

An hour later, James was invited to lunch with one of the nurses from the heart center. The work sounded fascinating; and he was engrossed in the conversation until he realized that if he didn't leave soon, he'd be late picking the boys up from their summer activities. After thanking the nurse for her time, he made his way back to the parking lot in a daze. That certainly had gone as well as he ever could have dreamed.

His cell phone rang as he slid behind the wheel of his vehicle and he answered it before putting on his seat belt.

"Hi, honey." It was Fern's voice. "I've been dying to hear how your interview went."

"I'm sure you have been. Believe it or not, I've been at the hospital all this time. I had the interview, took a tour and then had lunch with one of the nurses." He went on to give her a brief overview. "I'll tell you more when I get home," he promised.

"But it went well?" she persisted.

"I would have to say I think it went very well," he told her. "But I'm not going to get excited yet. I'm sure they're interviewing lots of qualified candidates."

Fern laughed in a shaky voice. "I'm glad it went well, but it's really beginning to sink in that we could be moving if you get this job."

"I know." He glanced at his watch. "Look at it this way. We wouldn't have to do any remodeling. We could find a house with a master bedroom on the main floor right off the bat."

"There is that," she agreed, although she didn't sound exceptionally enthusiastic.

"I'm going to get on the road now," he told her. "I'll see you after I pick up the boys."

"Drive carefully. I love you."

"I will. Love you too. 'Bye."

As he drove home, his euphoria faded. It was nice to feel that he'd done a good job with the interview. But the bottom line was that he didn't want to move. Peoria was a city of more than a hundred thousand people. The boys might find it very difficult to adjust after growing up in Deerford's small, close-knit community. And he'd be taking Fern far away from her family and all the others who helped and loved her . . . and then there was Hope Haven.

He loved his work. He loved the setting, the people, the special relationships he'd developed with Anabelle, Elena and

Candace. It would be very difficult to tear himself away from them; they had become his own little support network of a sort.

But support network or not, he didn't think he would mention this interview. If he was offered the job—or some other one—there would be time enough to break the news. Still, the whole topic took up a great deal of his mental energy as he worried it back and forth. He couldn't speak frankly to Fern about how sad and upset he felt; it would devastate her. She already hated not being able to work, and he feared she would see it as her fault for not contributing to the family coffers.

On the day of Robin's surgery, Candace stayed with her throughout her pre-op. The surgery was scheduled for eleven. Andrew held Robin's hand until they got to the doors beyond which only staff was allowed; and the couple exchanged a hasty, whispered conversation.

Then Robin held out a hand for her. "Candace, would you pray with us?"

Touched beyond measure, Candace stepped forward and grasped both their free hands as Andrew uttered a brief prayer for Robin's and their baby's safety and a successful surgery. Then she continued to clasp Robin's hand as they went into the OR suite, leaving Andrew standing forlornly in the hallway.

Candace rarely spent much time in the operating room. When there were scheduled cesarean sections, the OR and pediatric nurses were usually involved. Only in emergency sections, which often were completed in the small emergency OR right there in the Birthing Unit, did she attend surgeries. She held Robin's hand at her request until the young woman was anesthetized, then she stepped back out of the way.

"Candace, you want to watch what we're doing here?" the surgeon asked her. "After all, this little lady is your patient too."

Her eyes widened above her surgical mask. "I'd love to," she said.

The doctor's eyes crinkled. "Then elbow your way in here."

The surgery was quick, as surgeries went, and within an hour Robin was in the recovery room. While she still was out, Candace walked over to the surgical waiting room on the third floor.

Andrew, his parents, Robin's parents, and an assortment of other people greeted her eagerly. Andrew had tears in his eyes as she quickly reassured him that the lumpectomy had gone well and no secondary spread appeared to have occurred, although they would be doing lymph node biopsies to be sure.

By the time Robin fought her way out from under the anesthesia, Candace was back at her side. After a few minutes of disorientation, Robin's eyes managed to focus on Candace's face as she leaned over the gurney on which her young friend lay.

Robin reached out and clamped her fingers around Candace's wrist with surprising strength. "My baby?" she whispered.

Candace smiled. "Your baby's fine," she said. "Just fine. And so are you."

"No problems?"

"No." Candace shook her head. "The surgery went very well. The lump was contained and there didn't appear to be any secondary involvement."

"Thank heavens," Robin said before her eyes closed again and her grip on Candace's arm relaxed.

An hour after that, Robin was installed in a room in the Intensive Care Unit. It wasn't usual for women to be admitted for a lumpectomy; the procedure normally was outpatient surgery. But given Robin's advanced pregnancy, it had been deemed wise to keep her under close observation and keep her close to the Birthing Unit, just in case.

When Candace walked into the room later that day, Robin burst into tears.

"You can't cry now," Candace said, going to her side and drawing her in for a hug. "It's over and everything's fine."

"I feel a hundred pounds lighter," Robin said, pulling back and drawing a tissue from a box on the bedside tray table. "I guess I didn't realize the extent to which this whole ordeal was preying on my mind."

"You should feel much better now," Candace confirmed.

"Now I just have to get healed before this baby comes." Robin's smile faded a little. "Did the doctor say anything to you about follow-up treatment?"

Candace shook her head. "Has he been in to speak to you since the surgery?"

Robin nodded. "As soon as the baby is born, he wants me to have radiation treatments and then a short course of chemo."

Candace looked around. "Where's Andrew?"

"He went to get some coffee," Robin said. "I want him to go home tonight though. I'll be fine."

The women chatted for a bit longer. When Andrew returned, Candace rose to take her leave.

"Candace?"

She paused in the doorway and looked back. "Yes?"

"I know you said everything was fine, but . . . you don't think there's any chance this hurt the baby, do you?"

Candace shook her head. "No, I don't. If anything was going to go wrong, it already would have happened. You could have gone into pre-term labor. But you didn't, and your body seems to have handled the anesthesia and the surgery very well. In a few short weeks, you'll be holding him or her in your arms."

"But I won't be able to breast-feed," Robin said sorrowfully.

"True. But the ability and opportunity to breast-feed has nothing to do with your parenting, or with the bond you and your baby share. Many mothers who don't breast-feed have wonderful relationships with their infants."

Robin sighed. "I know. I guess it's just a dream I'll have to let go of."

"Think about all the years you and your child will have together," Candace suggested. "You have given yourself the very best chance to live a long and healthy life."

Anabelle did not work on Saturday. She buzzed around the house all morning, catching up on laundry, vacuuming, cleaning the kitchen and bathrooms, watering her plants and sweeping out the barn.

Shortly before lunchtime, she stopped and changed into clean khaki slacks and a chocolate blouse nearly the same color as her eyes. She took a picnic basket from her pantry and loaded a chicken casserole she'd baked and cooled into it, then stacked a divider atop it before adding a pie made of sour cherries from one of their fruit trees. It was her daughter Kirstie's favorite type of pie.

Humming "Abide with Me" softly to herself, Anabelle climbed into her little Ford and set off for Kirstie's. Her daughter would love the surprise meal.

It was a glorious summer day with temperatures in the upper seventies and a pleasant breeze. The drive from the farm to Kirstie's new apartment took less than ten minutes.

Parking along the quiet street in front of the brick building, Anabelle hefted the heavy basket and walked along the sidewalk, up several steps to Kirstie's apartment door. Knocking firmly, she braced the basket against her hip as she waited.

In moments, she heard her daughter's familiar tread. Although Kirstie walked so well that many people who didn't know about the accident never realized she had an artificial limb, she had a very slight limp and favored her right leg just the tiniest bit. To Anabelle, it was as clear as glass. When she was away from Kirstie for any reason and first saw her again, she always had to stifle an urge to cry over the injustice of the injury sustained by her beautiful child.

When the door opened, Anabelle was wiping away a tear.

"Mother! What are you doing here?" Kirstie looked more surprised than pleased to find her mother on her doorstep, and she didn't immediately invite her in.

"I brought you a meal. And a pie," Anabelle said, smiling warmly. She held out the picnic basket. "What are you up to this fine day?"

"I'm grading summer-school tests," Kirstie said, finally stepping back. "I can only take a short break."

Anabelle laughed, although she was disappointed she wouldn't be able to share lunch with her daughter. "I can take a hint. I won't keep you." When Kirstie didn't protest, Anabelle felt her smile wobble around the edges.

Kirstie led the way into the kitchen, where she had a laptop set up and papers spread out over the surface of the table. Anabelle stopped in consternation as she came into the room. There was a man at the other end of Kirstie's table. A husky, blond young man with vivid blue eyes who also had work spread everywhere and looked quite comfortable.

"Mother," Kirstie said, "this is Mark Holcher. He teaches at the high school."

The man had already risen, and Anabelle noted his neat appearance, with a navy sport shirt that emphasized broad shoulders tucked into his belted chinos. He extended a hand. "Hello, Mrs. Scott," he said. "It's nice to meet you. Kirstie's spoken of you often."

Kirstie had spoken of her? Anabelle barely stopped herself from blurting out, *She hasn't mentioned you at all.* "It's nice to meet you too," she said.

"Let me take that basket for you."

Anabelle let him slide the basket from her arm and carry it to the counter, too surprised to speak further. After he'd deposited the basket, he resumed his seat.

Kirstie had gone to the basket and lifted out the pie. "Oh, thanks, Mother," she said as she stored it and the casserole in the refrigerator. "You know I adore your cherry pie." To Mark, she added, "Wait until you try it. Your taste buds will sit up and beg for more." From that, Anabelle inferred he would be sharing at least one meal with her daughter.

Mark laughed. "Kirstie tells me you're a great cook, Mrs. Scott."

"Call me Anabelle," she said automatically. She summoned a smile. "Are you from the area, Mark?"

The young man shook his head. "No, I grew up in Traverse City." Seeing her blank look, he elaborated. "It's in Northern Lower Michigan—the top part of the mitten that sticks up into Lake Michigan." He held up his right hand and pointed to the tip of his ringfinger. "I got my teaching degree from the University of Illinois, though, and Deerford was the first job offer I got." He smiled across the room at Kirstie. "This is a wonderful little town."

Anabelle watched her daughter smile back at the other teacher. She felt distinctly like a third wheel. The silence that fell was obviously awkward.

"Well," she said briskly. "I'll just be getting along. I have a million things to do at home." She bustled across the kitchen and picked up her empty basket, then wheeled and hurried toward the front door. "It was nice to meet you, Mark," she tossed over her shoulder.

"Thanks for thinking of me, Mother," Kirstie said from behind her. She hastened to Anabelle's side and caught her elbow, slowing her down long enough to kiss her on the cheek.

Anabelle grabbed Kirstie in a tight hug that lasted only a moment. Releasing her daughter, she opened the door and started down the walk. "Good luck with your grading," she said without looking back. "I'll see you at church tomorrow."

"See you at church," Kirstie echoed.

Anabelle jammed her hand into the pocket of her pants, searching for her keys. She wrenched open the driver's door of the car and threw the basket inside as her breath hitched, and she suppressed a sob. The interior of the car already had heated uncomfortably in the summer warmth, and by the time she'd fumbled the proper key into the ignition and rolled down her window, she couldn't pull out of her parking spot because she couldn't see through her tears well enough to drive.

Holding onto the wheel, she leaned her forehead against the hot vinyl as tears rolled down her cheeks. She knew she was being ridiculous. Kirstie was twenty-three years old. An adult in the eyes of the world.

But she was Anabelle's baby girl, and she'd nearly lost her once. Now that Kirstie had moved out and obviously was enjoying her independence, Anabelle felt as if she was losing her child all over again.

Why hadn't her daughter said anything about Mark Holcher? They couldn't have been dating long; she couldn't possibly know him well. Had she even told him about her leg? How long would she have waited to tell her family about him if her mother hadn't stopped by unannounced? Anabelle felt almost betrayed, in a way, even though a part of her recognized that her feelings were less than rational at the moment.

Rummaging through her handbag, she pulled out a tissue and wiped her eyes, then blew her nose and took a deep breath. Turning on the car, she put it in gear and drove out of town again.

Chapter Eighteen

CANDACE WAS ENJOYING A RARE, LOW-KEY MOMENT at the nurses' station with her three friends. It was a gray, rainy day outside; and it appeared that everyone had decided it was a good day to not get ill or have a baby.

"More good news," Elena told the rest of them. "Our network of volunteers has placed brochures for the bricks all over town, and the first of the three interview articles will be in the paper later this week. Would you believe we already are beginning to get our first donations from outside the hospital staff?"

"That's great news." James pumped a fist, and Candace had the whimsical thought that Elena was usually the one doing the cheering.

"Yes, it is," Elena agreed. "And there's more. A bunch of kids from the high school are doing their own fund-raiser to donate a brick in memory of the vice-principal who passed away last year. They already have over two thousand dollars!"

All three of the others made sounds of surprise. "People are really embracing this, aren't they?" Candace said.

"They are." Elena paused and looked around. "If the campaign is successful, it will keep the four of us here together."

Candace looked around dubiously. "Well, not exactly *right* here—"

The others all laughed, and she blushed, unaccustomed to the role of clown.

The elevator at the far end of the central hall dinged, and the doors slid open. Marge Matthews stepped out. She was carrying an envelope which she extended to Elena. "A girl I didn't know in Reception asked me to give you this. She said you'd know what to do with it."

"Another donation. I'm taking it straight to Zane." Elena waved the envelope and then did a little dance right there in the hallway. Dashing toward the elevator, she called over her shoulder, "See you later."

"See you," James said. He too started toward the far end of the hall.

A nurse who had grabbed the ringing receiver said, "Candace, phone. It's a patient in labor."

"Thanks." As Candace went toward the phone, she saw Anabelle pick up the second telephone at the desk. Candace turned away, speaking calmly to the agitated patient. Then, after the woman agreed that it was time to call her doctor and let him know she was in labor, Candace pulled up an intake form and accessed the preregistration file.

Anabelle ended her call and dialed another. She looked upset, but Candace didn't want to intrude. Eavesdropping, however, was another matter. It was practically impossible *not* to in the confined space behind the desk.

"Cam," Anabelle said, "you might as well save that roast for another night. Kirstie can't come for dinner."

While she went on with her conversation, Candace did her best to concentrate on the monitor before her.

Finally, Anabelle hung up the phone. She sighed, drawing Candace's attention again. "I assumed Kirstie was coming over for dinner tonight, but she's going out with a couple of other teachers. And when I suggested to Cam that maybe we could drive over and check on her later tonight, he practically *yelled* at me."

"Are you all right?" Candace felt real concern when she saw the stricken expression on Anabelle's face.

The older woman shook her head and sat down heavily in one of the rolling chairs. "I'm overly protective and interfering," she whispered, resting her elbows on the desk and pressing the heels of her palms against her eyes. "But I just worry so much. . . ."

Candace rose and went to her friend, kneeling beside her and rubbing her back with one hand. "You're her mother," she said softly. "Of course you worry. It's part of the job description."

Anabelle lifted her head.

"And your job description was complicated enormously by her accident," Candace said. "It's perfectly understandable that you don't want to let go."

"Part of me does," Anabelle said. "I'm so very proud of the way she insists on living a normal life. But I wish she would carry a tiny video camera around with her so I could have a live-feed! Then I'd worry less."

Candace laughed. "You should patent that idea," she said. "Mothers the world over would be lining up to buy a system like that."

Both women rose, and Anabelle gestured toward Cardiac Care. "I'd better get back to work." She reached out and clasped Candace's hand, squeezing warmly. "Thank you."

Candace smiled. "No need for that. Just be ready to wipe my tears the day Brooke moves out." She sobered as she tried to imagine it, then fanned her hand beside her eyes to dry incipient tears. "See? I can't even talk about it and it's years away!"

Finally, a small smile lifted the corners of Anabelle's lips. "I'll be there for you," she promised.

Candace and her three friends had concluded one of their lunch get-togethers in the courtyard. Anabelle, James and Elena all went back to work; but Candace had gotten a late start on her lunch break, and she still had ten minutes.

It was an extraordinarily beautiful day again, with temperatures in the low eighties with plenty of sunshine. Candace left the picnic table and walked across the gravel to the lone bench in the little courtyard. She took a seat and leaned back, tilting her face up to the sun. Oh, it felt wonderful.

She thought of Robin and Andrew Overing, and she hoped Robin was able to enjoy her last weeks of anticipation before her baby's birth now that the surgery was over. It must have been terribly difficult to relax knowing she was walking around with a malignant tumor eating away inside her body. But Robin was or soon would be cancer free, and she'd be there to see her baby grow up.

A sound disturbed her lethargy. She opened her eyes and squinted into the bright sunlight as a broad-shouldered figure walked toward her.

"Hello, Candace."

It was Heath Carlson, her friend from radiology whose brother had the new baby. Figuratively speaking. "Hi, Heath. Is this your lunch break?"

He was carrying an apple, a sandwich from the cafeteria and a bottle of water. He grinned. "How'd you guess?"

Candace tapped her temple. "Nothing gets by me."

Heath laughed. Then he looked up. "There's a cardinal."

"He's been there all summer. He's gorgeous."

He pointed to the small maple tree that shaded the picnic tables. "Look up there. He has a mate."

"How do you know that?" What Candace knew about birds would fit on the end of a pencil. She could identify cardinals, robins, crows and blue jays and that was probably about it.

"See the nest?" Heath pointed to the fork of a branch high in the tree. "The female has a lot of brown and gray on her, with just a little red shading. They both have that funny pointed crest and red bills, although her crest isn't nearly as striking as the red on the male."

Candace watched as both adult birds flew off.

"Keep watching." Heath unscrewed the top of his water bottle and opened his sandwich without looking away from the nest. "I bet they're feeding babies."

Moments later, he was proven right as the small red-and-brown bird returned. Candace could see something protruding from its beak; and as she watched, several tiny beaks appeared just above the edge of the nest, making tiny high-pitched peeping sounds with their little mouths gaping as wide as they could. The mother bird leaned down and the thing Candace realized was a worm dropped into one of the babies' mouths. The others protested loudly as this happened, and then they all subsided when the mother flew away again.

"Thank you," Candace said, smiling broadly. "I never would have seen that if you hadn't pointed it out. How do you know so much about birds?"

Heath shrugged. "I've always been a bird-watcher. They fascinate me. I'm a member of the National Audubon Society and the Bureau County Audubon Society." Then he said, "I saw the article about the bricks in the paper. It's a terrific idea, and not just because it'll raise money. This little area could be really beautiful." He cleared his throat. "I hadn't realized you were a widow. I'm sorry for your loss."

"Thank you," Candace said formally.

Heath kept his gaze on the nest. "I was engaged to be married when I was twenty-three. She died when a drunk driver hit her car head-on."

"Oh, Heath," Candace said. "I'm so sorry."

"It was a long time ago." His voice sounded contemplative. "I hate it that I can't remember her face anymore without seeing a picture first."

"I have dozens of photographs of Dean. I realized a few months ago that almost all my memories now are scenes from pictures. I'm starting to forget the sound of his voice, the goofy way he laughed." She chuckled. "The way he sang—really loud and really off-key."

Heath smiled. "It happens. Time does indeed march on. It's like waves against the beach. Very slowly, your memories erode."

They were quiet again. The sun was warm. Candace felt so peaceful. Reluctantly, she said, "My lunch break is almost over. I'd better get back." She turned and started for the door to the interior.

"Candace?"

She turned around. "Yes?"

"I could build you a bird box. One of our projects is putting up bluebird nest boxes. Your children might enjoy watching them."

She nodded, turned and grasped the door handle. "I think they would."

Chapter Nineteen

CANDACE LOOKED UP FROM THE BOOK SHE HAD BEEN reading while Brooke was at her counseling appointment. Brooke came through the door from the back part of the office with Tony Evans right behind her.

"Mrs. Crenshaw?"

Candace rose. "Back in a few," she said to Brooke.

Candace and Tony had established a standing routine throughout his years of working with Brooke. She spoke with him after he had talked with Brooke at each session. They exchanged pleasantries, and she sank into the comfortable chair in front of his desk. Around the other areas of his office, toys, musical instruments and art supplies were scattered and stacked. Tools of his trade, she supposed, as a child therapist.

Tony leaned back in his chair and steepled his fingers. "So," he said. "I think I have a handle on what is going on with Brooke right now."

"I hope so," Candace said. "I've been worrying about it. I just can't come up with any good reason for her to be avoiding her friends' fathers."

"This has nothing to do with manners."

"Well that's a relief," Candace said in a tone that indicated manners were the last thing on her mind. "Then what is going on in that little blond head?"

Tony straightened up. He laid his hands flat on the desk. "Brooke is avoiding these men because she is pretending that her friends don't have fathers either," he said simply.

What? Candace stared at him, while a white-hot streak of grief pierced her heart. "Why would she do that?"

Tony's eyes were sympathetic as he said, "Because she doesn't want to be different. Because she doesn't want to accept that her friends have their fathers while hers is gone. Because she can't bring herself to talk about him to her friends so it's easier just to pretend there are no fathers in her world. It's become a coping mechanism for the pain of her own loss."

"And here I thought she was doing better." Candace felt sick. "Pretending. She's pretending none of her friends have fathers." She knew she sounded like a parrot, but it was a shocking explanation to absorb. But as she thought about it, it answered some of her own questions. "That's why she didn't want to go to that birthday party," she realized. "And the reason she wanted to take Tiffany's gift over early was so she wouldn't have to be there when Tiffany's father was home."

Tony nodded. "Both of those incidents illustrate her avoidance of the fact that fathers exist."

"She hardly ever talks about him," Candace said.

"Which also fits." Tony nodded.

"So what do I do?" How on earth could she make Brooke acknowledge something she wanted to hide from?

"Nothing," Tony said. "At least, nothing overt. I wouldn't try to address it with her and try to get her to talk. The last thing you should do is make a big deal out of it. One thing you *should* do is make certain that she doesn't get any more opportunities to do her vanishing act. Talk with her teachers about it. But be sure they don't bring up the topic with Brooke. At home, watch for instances—like the birthday party—that she might be trying to avoid other fathers. Don't let her take those opportunities. She and I have talked about strategies for dealing with these feelings, and she needs chances to practice using them."

Candace immediately thought of Brooke's desire to deliver Tiffany's gift while the father wasn't home. That would have been quite easy to alter. "All right."

"Another thing you can do," Tony said, "is talk more about your family life with your husband. Share the good memories. Help Brooke patch up her memories of having a father."

Candace stared at him. Did he have any idea what he was asking? How painful that was going to be?

"I want to see her again in two weeks," Tony said. He rose and extended a hand. "Thanks for coming in, Mrs. Crenshaw."

"No, thank *you*," she said, forcing herself to smile. "Hopefully, in two weeks Brooke will have had a few chances to practice your coping strategies."

Kirstie came to her parents' home for dinner on Monday evening. She had not been able to come the night before, as Anabelle had assumed she would. Anabelle hoped in the future they could make Sunday night a family dinner evening now that she no longer lived at home. From now on, she would invite Kirstie early in the week rather than assuming anything, she promised herself.

"Stuffed shells?" Kirstie asked as she sniffed the air when she stepped into the house. "One of my favorites."

"I know." Anabelle hugged her daughter. "Come talk to me while I make salad."

"I'll set the table," Kirstie said.

"Already done. Would you like a drink?"

Kirstie nodded. "I'll get it."

"No, you sit." Anabelle waved her off as she went to the cabinet and took down a glass.

Kirstie settled onto one of the tall stools at the counter.

"Are you comfortable there?" Anabelle asked as she set a glass of ice water in front of her daughter. "If you sit at the table, you won't have to perch up there and put pressure on your leg."

"Mother," said Kirstie, "I am perfectly capable of taking care of myself. I know my limits. Stop."

Anabelle smiled. It was a familiar complaint. "Sorry, honey. So," she said casually, "your friend Mark seemed pleasant. How did you meet?"

"We met at a cast party after the high school's spring musical. Remember I told you I helped with costumes? He was in charge of the stage crew."

"And have you gone on dates other than study get-togethers?"

Kirstie grinned. "Yes. We went to the movies twice. But it's not serious, Mother, so don't get excited. Ainslee is the only daughter you're going to be getting grandchildren from for a while."

"I was just curious." Anabelle thought for a moment. "So you like your apartment?"

"Love it," Kirstie affirmed. "I'm going to paint my bedroom this week."

Mother and daughter chatted casually while Anabelle chopped carrots, cucumbers and tomatoes and added them into a bowl of spinach and lettuce and tossed the mixture. Placing the salad in a pretty glass serving bowl, she added a pair of salad tongs and carried it to the table.

Then she slid a heat-proof mitt onto her right hand and opened the oven door. Pulling out a tray full of slices of buttered Italian bread, she quickly transferred the bread to a linen-lined basket and pushed it across the counter at Kirstie. "Set that on the table for me, please."

Kirstie turned and slipped off the stool, depositing the basket on the already-set table. "I'll call Pop," she said, correctly assuming the meal was ready. While she left the room, Anabelle set the pan of stuffed shells on a large trivet in the middle of the table and got a large serving spoon.

Cam and Kirstie came in together. In one large hand he carried a brightly colored bunch of dahlias, which he stuck into an empty jelly jar and added tap water. Then he went to the sink and washed his hands; he'd been outside weeding their garden.

Anabelle carried the dahlias to the table. "These are so pretty. I really like the mixture you planted this year."

Cam nodded. "It mostly has dinner plates, but there are a few other decorative dahlias too. And it's a great color mix." He put an arm around Kirstie's shoulders and squeezed. "I'll cut you some to take along when you're ready to go."

"Thanks, Pop," she said. "My favorite flowers from my favorite guy."

As she took her seat, Anabelle noticed that her daughter appeared to be limping a bit, and she had to bite her tongue—almost literally—to keep from commenting; but she managed not to say anything. What had Kirstie done to cause the limp?

She was distracted by Kirstie's description of a recent in-service writing workshop she had attended. The method used to encourage children to write sounded interesting, but Anabelle had a concern. "Don't you think that having them spell things the way they sound will be a problem for them as they grow older? Whatever happened to spelling words?"

"We still have weekly spelling tests," Kirstie assured her. "The point of invented spelling, as it's called, is to give children a tool to help them write without getting stuck. For instance, a first-grader who visits a wildlife center might want to write about rabbits, opossums and raccoons. Since none of those words are on a first-grade spelling list, the child isn't going to be able to write her story unless she is able to come up with a good guess for each of those words."

"But how will she ever learn to spell them right if she learns them wrong?" Anabelle asked.

"Inventing a spelling for an unfamiliar word isn't going to keep a child from learning the correct spelling," Kirstie said. "And the wonderful thing is, that child can read the story she wrote, because she understands what she was trying to say. We often forget that the goal of spelling is to aid in writing."

Anabelle pushed her hair back. "I'm glad I'm not the one who has to figure out how to teach all these new-fangled methods."

"And I'm glad I'm not the one who has to learn how to use new health technologies on patients," Kirstie said. "Hey, I almost forgot. Very nice article in the paper about Elena and the Wall of Hope. I hope it generates a lot of donations."

"People seem very interested so far. Whether or not they'll be interested enough to save the hospital is anyone's guess."

They cleared the table after the meal, and Anabelle poured coffee before setting out a plate of brownies.

"Yum." Cam patted his belly beneath the denim overalls he wore. "How many can I have?"

"One," Anabelle said severely.

Cam looked crestfallen. "One?"

"I noticed your belt was getting a little tight, mister." Anabelle relented. "Two, if you take a walk with me after dinner."

He grinned. "Okay. It's a deal."

The thought of walking reminded Anabelle of the way she had observed Kirstie walking earlier. She turned to her daughter, unable to resist voicing her concern. "Your leg seems to be giving you a little trouble," Anabelle said. "Are you overdoing it?"

Kirstie shook her head. "No. It's the end of the day, and I'm just tired. That's all."

"You know," Anabelle said, "I've been meaning to tell you that I'll be happy to pick up your laundry once a week and do it over here. That way, you won't have to walk up and down those steps so many times." The shared laundry room in the building where Kirstie rented was in the basement.

But Kirstie shook her head. "Thanks, Mother, but it's not a problem."

Anabelle knew she should stop now. Kirstie had made it clear she could take care of herself. But what if Kirstie overdid it? Before she could stop herself, the words tumbled out. "Honey, that can't possibly be good for your stump. It's no wonder you're limping—"

Kirstie rose from the table and took her dessert plate into the kitchen, completely ignoring Anabelle. Putting it in the dishwasher, she said, "Thank you for dinner. I have work to do, so I'm heading home now."

"Kirstie!" Anabelle was shocked. She hadn't raised her daughter to be rude. "I was speaking to you."

"No, Mother," Kirstie said. Her tone was very even, although she was actually shaking, and her face was red with anger. "You were lecturing again, trying to browbeat me into doing things your way." She took a deep breath. "I'm an adult. I will take care of myself. I love you, but I don't need to be babied." She let a frozen beat of silence hang in the air. Then she said, "Good night. Thank you for dinner." And she turned and walked toward the front door.

Cam was standing in the doorway to the kitchen. As she brushed by him, Kirstie rose on her tiptoes and brushed a kiss over his cheek. "'Bye, Pop. Love you." And she was gone.

There was an awful silence in her wake.

Anabelle felt tears rising. "Oh, Cam," she said, "I'm so worried about her—"

"Anabelle, just stop."

Stunned by the curt, annoyed tone of her easygoing husband's voice, Anabelle fell silent.

Cam sighed. "She's right. You have to stop trying to baby her," he said in a quieter tone, although the words were uncharacteristically blunt. "She's an adult and can make her own decisions. If she makes a poor one, she'll learn from it. You can't keep doing things for her forever."

"I wasn't—I didn't mean to. . . ." But she had. If she was honest with herself, she had to admit she wanted to wrap her daughter in cotton batting and keep her safe for the rest of her life. She rose from the table and rushed toward the bedroom. "I'm sorry," she said in a choked voice.

"Anabelle . . ." Cam sounded as if he was coming after her.

"Don't," she got out. "You're right. I need to step back. It's just so hard. . . ." She rushed into their room and threw herself on the bed, burying her face in her arms.

"I know, honey." Cam ignored her resistance. Sitting down on the edge of the bed, he rubbed her back. "I'm sorry if I was harsh."

"You were honest," she said in a muffled tone. "I never know what to say to her anymore. She doesn't want to hear my concerns."

"Maybe," Cam suggested, "you should try just being her friend for a while. She seems to be handling herself just fine. If she needs us, I'm sure she'll ask."

Anabelle sighed. They sat in silence for a long time. Cam rubbed her back until finally, she sat up and slid over to perch beside him on the edge of the bed. "Thank you," she said, heaving a sign that caught in the middle. "I owe Kirstie an apology, don't I?"

"And a promise that you'll stop trying to manage her life for her," Cam said, uncompromising despite the love he was offering. He put an arm around her, and she laid her head on his broad shoulder.

"All right."

Cam released her and stood. "I'm going out to cut some flowers for her. I'll drop them off on my way to Bible study breakfast tomorrow." Cam met three of his friends for breakfast and a Bible study at the Parlor, a downtown restaurant, each week.

Oh no. Anabelle realized Kirstie had left in such a huff that she'd forgotten the dahlias her father had promised her. She felt even more awful. No wonder Cam was annoyed with her. How was she going to make herself stop being so frantic and worried?

Exhaling heavily, she dropped her head and clasped her hands in her lap. *Lord, I surrender to You. I need help letting go of Kirstie. I need help trusting that she can take care of herself, and I need help accepting that she'll make mistakes, and I can't always fix them.*

Elena walked into Quintessa Smith's office. She carried a large paper bag which she handed to Quintessa with relief. "These are all brick orders! People have been handing them to me right and left all week."

"We've gotten dozens of brick orders from the community already and a few other outright donations." Quintessa smiled. "I was here until eight o'clock last night trying to get them recorded in the database."

"Oh, Quintessa, thank you." Elena was dismayed. "We need to get more help, don't we?"

Quintessa shrugged. "It's okay. It's not a problem for me to stay late. And I expect this mad rush to settle down soon, don't you?"

"Probably." Elena grinned. "Although it would be nice if we kept getting this many donations continuously. Do you have any idea how much we've brought in?"

Quintessa hit a few keys and looked at her computer screen. "We were close to seventy-seven thousand before today."

"Are you serious?" Elena was elated. "Seventy-seven thousand dollars!"

Quintessa smiled. "I know. It sounds like a lot of money, doesn't it?"

Elena's excitement slowly faded. She knew what her friend was trying to say. "Yes, it does," she admitted. "Until I look at the hospital budget for one year and see that we need millions of dollars."

"Millions is right," Quintessa confirmed.

Elena's face fell. "This fund-raiser isn't going to make one little bit of difference, is it?" She sat down in a chair near Quintessa's desk, her shoulders slumping.

"Hey, now," Quintessa said. "Keep the faith, girl. You're the upbeat, positive force around here. You've made me believe we can do it; you can't stop now."

Elena smiled, but her heart wasn't in it as she rose. "All right. I'll do my best." She glanced at her watch. "I have to meet my friends. I'll come by after work and help you enter these forms and information if you like."

"That would be great. See you then." Quintessa turned back to her keyboard as Elena left the office.

Candace was waiting for her friends in the little hospital cafeteria. It had been raining earlier in the morning; and although it appeared to have stopped, the sky was still overcast, so no one wanted to take a chance on lunching outside.

James came in, and then Anabelle, with Elena right behind her.

"What's the special today?" Anabelle asked.

Candace indicated her tray. "Broccoli-cheese soup and a chicken sandwich. They're both terrific."

One by one, the others ordered and returned with their own trays, and soon the four of them were digging into their meals. Everyone seemed a little preoccupied, Candace thought. The mood was oddly subdued.

"What's the latest on the Wall of Hope?" She directed the question to Elena.

Elena sighed—a heavy sound that matched her somber expression. "The latest," she mused. "Well, Quintessa has been keeping track of the donations coming in. As of this morning, we're at a little over seventy-seven thousand."

Anabelle leaned forward, smiling for the first time since she'd sat down. "I know. Isn't that great?"

Elena shrugged. "It is nice, I know. But do you have any idea how much money is required to keep this place in business for just one year?"

"Millions of dollars," James said. "I can't begin to come up with an accurate guess, though."

"Millions is right," Elena said. "It's hopeless. We don't stand a chance of raising that much."

"Wait a minute," Candace said. "Why do you have to raise that much?"

Elena's eyebrows rose as if she didn't understand the question. "Because that's how much it takes to meet the hospital budget."

"But the hospital brings in money," Candace said. "It hasn't been operating in the red, according to the last budget I saw. The problem is that there's a gap between the annual projected income and the projected expenses, right?"

"Oh, I see what you mean." Elena's eyes suddenly lit with hope and determination. "So we don't really have to raise millions. Well, maybe one million, but that might be doable."

"And not just through the brick campaign," James said. "There may be other ways to raise money that haven't been explored yet. The board must be discussing it."

"I wouldn't count on that," Elena said. "Mr. Innisk is still going to fight every effort, I'm sure."

"Why?" James asked.

Elena shrugged. "Because he's a curmudgeon."

"Good word," James said approvingly.

They all laughed. Then Candace said, "I don't think you have to worry about Mr. Innisk trying to derail your project anymore."

The other three turned and stared at her. "What do you know that we don't?" demanded Elena.

Candace chuckled. Then she shared with them the information she had received from Mrs. Hunt.

"Oh, Candace, thank you! I can't believe you managed to render Mr. Innisk ineffective!" said Elena.

"It wasn't me," Candace demurred. "It was Mrs. Hunt."

"Who never would have known about it if you hadn't spoken up." Anabelle squeezed her hand.

"And thank you for reminding me that I don't have to come up with the entire year's income," Elena added. "I got so wigged-out worrying about all that money that I completely forgot the fate of the entire hospital doesn't rest solely on this little fund-raiser."

"You're welcome," Candace said.

"There's nothing little about the Wall of Hope," Anabelle said in a firm voice. "It's an excellent idea, and I have faith that it will prove to be a good way to help save this place."

Elena beamed. "What would I do without you?" she asked rhetorically, looking around at her friends.

"I don't know about you, but I would be in a poorer place spiritually," Anabelle said, "without this group's support."

"Me too," Candace said. She looked at Anabelle. "You've been quiet today. Is something bothering you that you'd like to share?"

Anabelle was silent for a moment. She set down her soup spoon and picked up her napkin, dabbing at her lips. "I don't want to share it, mostly because it makes me look like a controlling, interfering mother, but I'm going to anyway."

Candace, James and Elena listened as Anabelle confessed her recent attempts to direct Kirstie's life. "It's so hard to stand back and not say anything," she said, lowering her head.

"I'm sure it is." Candace smiled sympathetically. "We're all parents here; we all can imagine how difficult it must be to step back after years of pouring your energy into protecting and helping your child."

Anabelle nodded. "That's exactly it. And the worst part is, I know better. While I'm babbling away, a part of me is looking on, horrified, thinking, *Shut up, shut up!*"

James chuckled. "Sorry," he said. "It's just that I know that feeling. Sometimes when Gideon and I are at odds over something, I can hear my father's voice speaking right out of my mouth. And believe me, channeling my dad is the last thing I ever want to do."

Elena's eyebrows rose. "Bad memories?"

James shrugged. "He was a good man and a hard worker. But he could find more things to criticize than anybody I ever met." He shook his head ruefully. He looked back at Anabelle. "So what are you going to do now?" he asked.

The older woman raised her hands helplessly. "I'm not sure. Apologize, for sure. Any suggestions?"

Silence fell over the little group.

"Prayer," Elena said after a moment. "When Rafael got his girlfriend pregnant, we had some very harsh exchanges of words. If I had been a person of faith back then, I might have handled it very differently. I like to think I would have given it to God."

"That's easy to say, but tough to do," Candace commented.

Elena nodded. "I tried to fix everything when I saw the relationship crumbling. I was constantly after Rafael to get counseling, to get the girl into drug rehab—"

"She was doing drugs while she was pregnant?" Candace asked.

Elena nodded. "It was not a good time," she said in what was clearly a massive understatement. "Looking back, I see I should have stepped back, and let God be with him through his troubles. I should have prayed for them and invited them to pray too."

"That's exactly what I should do," Anabelle said. "As difficult as it is, I have to let God be with Kirstie as she makes her own way as an adult. I need to back off and ask God to guide and protect her." She looked around at her friends. "And I need all of you to pray for me to have the ability to do so."

"We'll be glad to," Candace said.

"While you're at it," James said, "please continue to pray for me." He took a deep breath. "I was offered that job at Children's in Peoria."

Anabelle took a deep, dismayed breath, and Elena looked stricken. Candace rushed to fill the silence. "Congratulations," she said warmly. She felt her smile slip a little, and she firmly pinned it back in place. "When do you start?"

"Well, that's the thing." James rubbed the back of his neck and then caught himself. It was a gesture he only made when he was stressed. "I haven't accepted it yet. They've given me a week to decide."

"What's holding you back?" Elena asked.

"I just found out this morning," James said, "and I haven't even told Fern yet. She's going to be uneasy at the thought of moving away from her family and friends. And honestly, it's a scary idea for me too. She has a strong support network here that gets her through the bad days. If we move and she's alone most of the time, she's going to have trouble getting back and forth to doctors' appointments and therapies; and I'm afraid she might get depressed being by herself so much."

"But surely there are support groups she could join in Peoria," Candace suggested. "I know it wouldn't be like family; but still, it might be a good way to meet some people."

"And when you find a church, you'll make friends there," Anabelle pointed out.

James sighed. "Those are exactly the things I'm going to say. I would appreciate any prayer support you've got around, say, four o'clock today."

"You've got it," Anabelle said.

"Prayer support," Elena said. "I have another idea."

"Uh-oh." James mimed cowering behind his raised hands. "She's got another idea. Everyone take cover."

Elena balled her fist and gently tapped him on the arm. "Very funny." Then she sobered. "I'm going to talk to the chaplain. The four of us have been praying on a regular basis, but what if we had a prayer service to lift up the Wall of Hope and the hospital's budget crisis?"

Anabelle cocked her head thoughtfully as James and Candace nodded. "Excellent idea. The more prayers we can muster, the better."

"I'll talk to Pastor Tom today," Elena said.

Chapter Twenty

*J*AMES PICKED UP HIS SONS FROM SUMMER activities when he got off work.

As the three of them headed home in the mini-van, Gideon said, "I can't wait until I can drive."

James was taken aback. His kids were growing up too fast as it was. "You've got a while to wait," he pointed out to the fourteen-year-old. "And even when you do get a license, we aren't going to have a vehicle for you to drive." Which was true. They had sold Fern's car several years ago when it became apparent she would no longer be able to drive safely.

"I can buy one."

"With what? Your imagination?"

Gideon was sitting in the front passenger seat, and James saw his son's jaw set as he responded. "I want to get a job when I turn fifteen."

Not a chance. But James said nothing aloud.

"Dad? Can I?"

"We can discuss it after your birthday," James told him. "But I'll be honest. I would have a lot of concerns about your working. I'm afraid it would interfere with your schoolwork, Scouting and your other activities." He smiled over at his son. "You have the rest of your life to work."

Gideon scowled. "I'll have the rest of my life to drive too, if I ever get a car."

James sighed. He was not going to get sucked into a fight about this subject, when it was still almost a year and a half away. "We can talk more about it later. In the meantime, why don't you estimate a budget of how much a car might cost, plus your costs for insurance, maintenance, registration and gas?"

"Huh?" Gideon looked shocked. "I have to pay for all that stuff?"

"Someone does," James told him. "Cars aren't free."

Gideon glared at him for a moment and then turned away, slouching in his seat and looking out the window.

From behind them, Nelson said, "Hey, Dad! Wanna play basketball when we get home?"

"I can't tonight, son," James replied. "Your mother and I have to discuss something important."

"Can't you do it later?" Nelson's voice held disappointment.

"Sorry, sport. We can't play ball tonight," James said. He hated to turn Nelson down; it wasn't often that his second son *wanted* to play basketball.

When James and the boys arrived at the house, Gideon and Nelson rushed inside. James followed more slowly.

Fern wasn't in the kitchen this evening, but the room was filled with the delicious smell of the vegetable soup that he'd been simmering in the Crock-Pot throughout the day.

"Hi, honey," he called.

"Hello." Her voice came from the living room.

Moving into the adjoining room, James found Fern seated in her favorite chair. "Hey. How was your day?"

She had been using the computer; but she turned as he came closer, lifting her face for his kiss. "Not bad at all. How about yours?"

James hesitated. "Mine was interesting. I'll tell you about it after I go change." Rising, he crossed to the stairs, ascended to the second floor, and poked his head into his son's room.

Gideon was hammering something out on his keyboard. When James asked him about it, he replied, "Chatting online," without even looking up.

Gideon still was stewing about their car conversation, James realized. Quietly, he backed out of the room.

Across the hall, Nelson was playing a Nintendo game, complete with the sounds of explosions and gunshots. James winced. Despite the example he tried to provide for his sons, pop culture was a powerful influence.

He stuck his head into the room. "Have you practiced your saxophone this week?"

"Only a little." Nelson didn't look away from the screen.

James opened the door wider. "Practice before game time," he said firmly. When Nelson still didn't respond, he said, "Or I take the Nintendo."

"*Aww*, Dad, just one more minute."

"All right." James stood there and counted off the seconds on his watch. At the one minute mark, he said, "Okay. Time's up. Game off."

Nelson sighed, but he turned off the Nintendo, knowing there would indeed be a consequence if he didn't practice his saxophone, which he had begged his parents to buy him.

"The sooner you get started, the sooner you'll be done." James waited until his son unclipped his case and pulled out the shiny instrument.

He paused at the top of the stairs as he heard the first several notes of Nelson's scales. Oh, how he wished it wasn't necessary to have the conversation he was about to initiate.

As he started down the steps, Fern called from the kitchen, "Honey, would you like a glass of lemonade?"

"Sure. I'll get it." He walked hastily toward the kitchen. Fern liked to do things for herself, but he'd noticed the heavy pitcher had been a problem for her lately. His train of thought was interrupted by a loud crash. The sounds of splashing liquid and hard plastic hitting the floor told him what had happened.

James ran the last few steps. "Are you okay?"

Fern was standing near the open refrigerator in a lake of lemonade. She nodded, then put both hands to her face. "I'm sorry."

"You don't need to apologize." James slipped off his shoes. He scooped up the pitcher and tossed it in the sink before grabbing several dish towels to spread over the liquid on the floor. Then he set his hands at Fern's waist and lifted her out of the moisture, setting her on a tall chair at the bar. "Just give me a minute to wipe this up, and then I'll clean off your feet. Mine too," he added, forcing a grin, trying to get her to smile.

"Thank you," she replied in a small, sad voice.

James knew she needed to be reassured, but he also needed to clean up the mess, while he figured out how to tell her about the job offer. He'd thought about it the whole way home, but he still hadn't come up with any brilliant ideas.

Quickly, he sopped up the lemonade, then washed and rinsed the floor so it wouldn't be sticky. Next, he tackled his feet and Fern's, and finally he wiped down the cabinets and the refrigerator where the liquid had spattered as it hit the floor.

When everything had been cleaned, he looked up at Fern. "How does iced tea sound? I'll make some more lemonade tonight." He wanted to tell her not to try to lift something as heavy as a full pitcher anymore; but he knew it would upset her, so he bit his tongue.

Fern sighed. "I'm not thirsty. You go ahead."

James didn't respond, but he poured two glasses of tea anyway, then perched on a bar stool next to her at the counter. He realized she was trying not to cry. "Hey," he said. "This was no big deal. Nothing was damaged, and you weren't hurt. I'll take an accident like that any day."

"You had a long day, you came home and dealt with the boys, and I made more work for you." She sighed. "I'm so sorry."

"I know. Let it go."

"I'm having more muscle spasms than I used to," she said. "I really did have a pretty good day, but mid- to late afternoon seems to be my worst time." James put a hand over hers, and she turned her palm up and laced her fingers through his. "I really thought I could lift that lemonade from the fridge to the counter," she said. "Guess I won't be trying that again."

A small wave of relief rolled through James. He hadn't been looking forward to trying to talk her out of lifting heavy pitchers and containers. "A good idea," he commented. Then he had an idea of his own. "I could put several glasses of water or juice, whatever you like, in the fridge for you in the morning, so you wouldn't have to try to lift anything during the day. I could use those tall Tupperware cups with the lids."

Her eyebrows rose as she considered the idea. "I wonder if I could get the lid off without spilling the drink."

He hadn't thought of that, and his shoulders sagged. "It's worth a try."

She nodded. "It's a good idea, honey. I'll go you one better. What if we got lidded cups that a straw will fit into? Then it would be even easier, and I wouldn't have to try to take off the tops at all."

"Good idea." He knew his response was flat; he was trying to figure how in the world to open the conversation. No point in tiptoeing around it. He might as well just say it.

She reached over to rub his back. "What's wrong? You seem preoccupied. Did something bad happen at work?"

He dropped his head forward and let her continue to massage his neck and his shoulders. "No," he said, "but something did happen that involves work."

Her hand stilled. "Did you hear something from one of your interviews?" she asked.

James nodded, although he didn't lift his head, loath to discontinue the soothing massage.

"Oh, honey, I'm sorry," Fern exclaimed after waiting an expectant moment. "There will be other jobs. I'm sure that—"

"Whoa, whoa." James sat up straight with a resigned smile. "No, it's not bad news. Fern, I got the job."

His wife's pretty brown eyes lit up. "You did? Congratulations, honey!"

James smiled. "Thanks. Although you may not be as delighted when I tell you the whole story."

As Fern's smile faded and a questioning expression took its place, James went on to explain the position and the new location. He couldn't look at her, but played with a spoon lying on the counter while he spoke. She asked a few questions, but for the most part she didn't say much.

When he had finished, there was a large silence. "The benefits and the salary sound excellent," she said quietly.

James nodded. "They really are. But there are also some cons we need to discuss."

"We don't have to make a list, honey. We both know what they are."

"But—"

"If we have to move away from Deerford, I'll manage," Fern said before he could list his concerns. "I know it won't be easy. I do depend on my family, our friends and our church a lot. And I'll be honest. The thought of having to ask a whole group of strangers to step up and help out is daunting. But James, we can't afford for you to be out of work. I know that. So if you want to take this job, I'll make the best of it. The important thing is that we are together enjoying raising our sons."

He smiled at her and wrapped an arm about her shoulders. His heart felt at least twenty pounds lighter. "Every day, I find another reason to be glad you married me, you know that?"

Fern leaned over and lifted her face for a kiss. "I feel the same way. And after twenty years, that's a lot of reasons!"

The little chapel in the hospital was packed two weeks later. Every pew was filled to bursting, people sat in the aisle and others stood around the edges of the little room.

In the front row, Elena whispered to Candace, "Wow! I never expected so many people to show up for this prayer service."

Candace looked around at the crowd. "It's amazing. And what a lovely testament to the power of prayer." Her eye was caught by the sight of a tall blond man near the very back of the chapel. Heath Carlson.

He was watching her, his blue eyes intense. When he realized he had caught her eye, he winked and smiled.

She lifted a hand in a brief wave and smiled. Then she quickly turned around again.

Pastor Tom rose from his seat at one side of the front, wearing his customary navy slacks with a matching navy clerical shirt and a detachable white collar. The Hope Haven Hospital chaplain was a man of deep, quiet faith. Warm and personable, he could be found more frequently at a patient's bedside than in the chapel. His neatly combed brown hair was frosted with silver and his eyes were a striking light blue, nearly the color of a summer sky.

"Good afternoon, friends," he said. "Welcome, and thank you all for joining us. This might be the first time I have ever wished for a larger chapel in this hospital."

Laughter ripples through the room.

"We are gathered here today," he continued, "to lift up the future of this hospital in prayer, to ask God's blessing on our efforts here. We will lift up both the medical miracles that so many of these extraordinary caregivers administer every single day as well as the efforts to raise funds to keep this very special place of healing open for many more years. This is a nondenominational chapel. Our services are available to anyone seeking dialogue with our heavenly Father. Will you please pray with me?"

After the prayer, a young African-American man with a guitar rose from the front pew at the other side of the room and took a seat on the steps. Candace recognized him from the lab. He was Quintessa Smith's twin brother, Dillan, who was one of the lab techs. She hadn't known he played guitar.

He began to play, nimble fingers flying over the strings. In a clear, perfectly pitched tenor, he started to sing "Shine, Jesus, Shine." Candace had heard the popular song on the radio and in her own church many times, and she hummed along under her breath. Then she felt a motion at her side as the first chorus began.

Elena popped up out of her seat and faced the crowd. She began to sing, waving her hands to indicate that everyone should join in. Candace began to sing, and from James's place on the other side of the aisle, she heard a strong baritone. Within moments, the little room was filled with the sound of many voices worshipping together.

When the song concluded, Pastor Tom rose, beaming. "Thank you, Dillan, thank you. What an inspiring way to share our faith." He scanned the congregation. "Now I'd like to introduce to you the woman who has been instrumental in organizing a fund-raiser for your hospital. It includes a Wall of Hope to be constructed in the courtyard. Friends, this is Elena Rodriguez, an LPN in the Intensive Care Unit."

Elena rose, blushing, and thanked the pastor. In short, concise sentences, she shared the idea for the courtyard, the fund-raiser with the bricks and her hopes that it would result in a significant contribution to the financial crisis. She concluded by encouraging everyone present to donate a brick and to share the project with their families, friends and churches.

When she had finished, the pastor rose again and offered the Lord's Prayer. Dillan's guitar provided accompaniment for the doxology, and finally Pastor Tom offered a benediction:

"Throughout the journey of your life, may you reach out to those in need of comfort, share God's blessings with those who need to hear His voice and offer care and comfort to those in need of your healing grace. Let your love touch the least as well as the first. Let God be your teacher, the answer to the questions in your heart, the wisdom in your thoughts and the example you show to all those around you. Do these things, and know eternal life."

Dillan began to play a simple instrumental postlude, and the buzz of conversation filled the air as people began to depart. There was a buoyant energy in the air.

Elena's eyes were shining as she turned to Candace. "Wasn't that terrific?"

Pastor Tom joined them. "It was, indeed," he said, catching Elena's question.

"I was rather surprised by the size of the crowd," Candace said honestly.

"As was I," the pastor concurred. "However, I found it enormously encouraging to think of all the faithful people that make up the staff of this place of healing."

Candace nodded, smiling; but as she opened her mouth to respond, her beeper alerted her to a message. "Excuse me," she said, checking the small device. "Gotta go," she told Elena. "Patient in labor—oh no!"

"What's wrong?" Elena asked with concern.

"It's my patient with breast cancer," Candace said as she turned and began to rush away. "Pray for her," she tossed over her shoulder. "She's only thirty-five weeks along."

Chapter Twenty-One

RILEY HOHMANN, CANDACE'S SUPERVISOR, WAS IN the hallway preparing to go back into one of the two birthing suites. She wore a stylish set of light blue scrubs with clouds and tiny angels scattered over the top. It had been a busy morning and her blond hair, usually so sleekly styled, was falling out of its once-elegant french twist.

"Riley! Where's Robin?" Candace asked.

"She hasn't arrived yet," Riley said. "She called Dr. Carpenter a few minutes ago and said she is having contractions. Dr. Carpenter told her to get in here right away."

"She's still got five weeks to go," Candace said. "She's not due until mid-August. I was really hoping she wouldn't deliver for another few weeks."

"How long has it been since her surgery?" Riley asked.

"Not long enough," said Candace darkly. Then she stopped and thought about it. "Actually, it's been close to a month."

"Oh, good. That shouldn't create any special problems," Riley said, clearly relieved. "We should have a birthing suite opening up in an hour or so. I'll reserve it for her, since she's the next incoming," Riley promised in a soothing tone. "One of our moms just delivered, so we'll get it ready as soon as she's transferred to a room." She rubbed Candace's arm. "Calm down. You're as nervous as if this were *your* labor and delivery."

Candace relaxed and chuckled. "No, not quite *that* nervous, believe me. Sorry," she said sheepishly. "I'm a little personally invested in this case."

Riley grinned as she stepped back. "I have to get in there. This mom is going into transition, and she's liable to get panicky." Riley was referring to the shortest but most intense stage of labor during which a woman's body suffered through a variety of physical changes as it prepared for delivery. Many women needed extra reassurance during this time, others felt like giving up and still others became belligerent and aggressive.

Candace could already hear the woman's voice rising. "Go, go!" she urged.

She turned and walked back to the nurses' station more calmly. There was no one on the computer so she was able to call up Robin's chart and review everything yet again. She'd looked at that chart so many times she probably could have rewritten it in her sleep.

Thirty-five weeks, she thought. A thirty-five-week delivery was considered a preterm baby. There could be untold complications, or it could go as smoothly as a full-term one. Troubled, she leaned back in her chair. It really would be best if Dr. Carpenter was able to postpone the delivery for at least a day, preferably more. Candace hadn't talked with Robin yet, so she didn't know how intense or frequent her contractions might be. Perhaps it wouldn't be difficult to settle her down again.

The elevator dinged, and the doors opened. Anticipating Robin, Candace glanced up; but it was Dr. Carpenter approaching, a white lab coat flapping around her as she trundled down the hall.

Dr. Frances Carpenter was one of three OB/GYNs in the Deerford Mother & Child medical practice and the only woman. She was in high demand because many women preferred female obstetricians.

Short and undeniably stout, Dr. Carpenter had black hair with dense spiral curls, which tended to stick out wildly in all directions, and black eyes set a little too close together. When she drew her thick eyebrows into an annoyed line, she could look quite forbidding; but normally she was exceptionally pleasant and surprisingly soft-spoken.

"I bet I beat her here, didn't I?" she said, laughing. She lived just two blocks from the hospital. It was quite practical, since OB doctors were sometimes woken from a sound sleep and asked to get to the hospital within minutes.

Candace nodded. "If you're talking about Robin Overing, yes."

The obstetrician nodded. "Got her records handy? I want to look over them." She sighed. "How long ago was her surgery?"

Candace reviewed the record with her, giving Dr. Carpenter her own observations.

The physician scanned the record. "*Hmm.* Thirty-five weeks. Let's see what she looks like. If the contractions are mild and she's not far along, I might try a tocolytic to postpone labor for a day or so. If that works, we'll administer corticosteroids to allow the fetal respiratory system to develop more."

Dr. Carpenter was hoping to keep Robin from delivering her baby for at least twenty-four hours so that she could receive shots of a special drug designed to speed up the development of the baby's lungs. It was a tried-and-true approach that had helped preemies for many years.

Candace clasped her hands together beneath the desk and said a brief prayer. Her prayer was aimed at Robin and her infant receiving the best possible care and being as healthy as possible postdelivery.

Candace paced for twenty minutes. Since it was early afternoon, she called her mother because she expected she might be at the hospital for quite a while yet. Her mother was excited when Candace explained that it was her breast-cancer patient.

"I'll pray for a short and swift delivery," she said. That was Janet, ever-practical.

True to her word, Riley got the newborn's family out of the birthing suite and they began their cleanup protocol. Candace smiled wistfully as the beaming new mother came down the hallway in a wheelchair, her husband at her side and their new baby in her arms.

She should be used to the sight, but every single time she saw a new family, she still immediately thought of Dean. He'd been so thrilled when Brooke was born. When they had come out of the delivery room, a nurse had pushed Candace down the hall while Dean carried Brooke. Every time they passed someone— usually a perfect stranger—Dean had announced, "We have a daughter!" The memory still made Candace chuckle even when she couldn't stop the tears.

She took a moment to carefully wipe her eyes with her fingers, blotting incipient tears without smearing the touch of mascara she wore. When she glanced up again, Robin Overing was waddling down the hall with her husband Andrew at her side.

"Hi, Robin," Candace called. "How are you doing? Are your contractions strong?"

Robin smiled, and Candace could see both excitement and apprehension in her expression. "No." She shook her head. "I called as soon as I realized what was happening because I know it's too early."

"It's a little early," Candace admitted. "But we are going to take excellent care of you. Let me get Dr. Carpenter to talk to you right away."

As it turned out, Candace didn't have to get the doctor. Riley had notified her as soon as she saw Candace and her patient coming down the corridor.

Quickly, Candace ushered the pair into an exam room. Dr. Carpenter came in; and after a moment of small talk, she performed a pelvic examination on Robin as Candace watched and Andrew held his wife's hand. Afterward, the physician seated Robin in a rocking chair in the birthing suite and pulled a stool over.

"When did you start having contractions?" she asked.

"About an hour ago," Robin said. "I called you right away." Tears rose in her eyes. "After what happened the last time, I was afraid to stay at home for a single minute."

Candace had gotten some additional information from Robin about her first pregnancy, and the child who hadn't survived. It had been a horribly sad yet simple birth defect in the baby's heart that had not been apparent in utero. Labor, however, had stressed the tiny, damaged heart beyond bearing. Candace understood exactly why Robin was afraid, although exhaustive prenatal testing had revealed no heart troubles with this baby.

The obstetrician made a note on the chart she held. "And how far apart are your contractions now?"

"At first they weren't very regular, but now they're about five minutes apart." She squirmed in the chair. "My back is *killing* me."

Dr. Carpenter smiled. "You're definitely in the early stages of labor," she told her patient. "It's a little earlier than I would have liked, but I don't think we have too much to be concerned about. Here's what I'd like to do, though." She proceeded to explain the procedure involved in slowing Robin's labor and administering drugs to speed the development of the baby's lungs.

Robin looked a little panicked by the idea. "I know it would be good for the baby," she said, "but will you really be able to slow down my labor? And what happens when you're ready to speed it up again?"

Dr. Carpenter talked to the couple at length, reassuring them and explaining exactly what medical procedures would occur and what the desired outcome would be. After a few more minutes, Robin nodded. "Let's get started. The sooner we do, the better the baby's chances are for optimal lung development."

Candace smiled to herself. Robin clearly had been absorbing all the "medical speak" she'd heard.

As Dr. Carpenter left the room, Candace explained to Robin that they were going to admit her to a regular room until it was time. Hopefully, the Overings would be able to get some sleep tonight. If her labor began again tomorrow afternoon, Robin might be a mother before the end of the day.

Candace monitored Robin closely for the next two hours. The young woman's labor did indeed stop; and soon afterward, the medication for the baby's lungs was administered.

"I'm going to go home now," Candace told the young couple before she left the unit. "The evening and night shift nurses are terrific; they'll take good care of you."

"When will you be back?" Robin was trying to look calm, but her eyes were huge and worried.

"I come in at seven in the morning," Candace told her. "But I've left word that if something happens, and you go into labor, they'll call me right away. I don't live far; I can be here pretty fast."

"Have a good evening," Robin said. "I want to see Brooke again, all grown up."

"She'd love that and she'd love to meet your little one," Candace said. "Brooke adores babies." She walked to the bed, bent and hugged Robin, then squeezed Andrew's shoulder. "I'll see you two in the morning. I can't wait to meet the newest member of your family."

The Church of the Good Shepherd was holding a fellowship evening and potluck dinner at the pavilion on the church grounds each week over the course of the summer. So after work that day, James made brownies and a taco salad to contribute to the food offerings, and the family hopped in the minivan for the trip to the church.

Their church was a large brick structure trimmed in gleaming white paint. The congregation was equally large, and there was quite a crowd buzzing around when James parked the family's van in the handicapped spot in the parking lot.

Good Shepherd was fortunate. When the church had been built, there was a sizeable additional parcel of empty acreage next to them. Owned by a church member, it had been deeded to the church after his passing.

Now it contained a large picnic pavilion, two small playgrounds, a softball field, a volleyball court, and a basketball court. There also was a small restroom and storage building with water fountains, although it wasn't heated during the winter. The church youth group often held retreats during which the kids slept and communed in the church's social room and used the outside area for group activities. Other churches in the area even rented the land for their own gatherings.

James glanced over at the pavilion, where picnic tables already had been covered with paper. Anabelle had said she and Cam probably would be here, but he didn't see her.

He brought Fern's walker around to her side of the van and helped her stand. Then, knowing she didn't like when he hovered, he signaled to Gideon to keep an eye on his mother's progress. Although the lawn was quite smooth and newly mown, it was still far more uneven than walking around in the house.

Gideon was becoming a wonderful help in situations like this. Fern would accept his company at her side more easily than she did James's. Fortunately, Gid didn't mind assisting his mother, and his mature attitude impressed James. Scouting had been partially responsible for that, James was sure; but he liked to think that Fern and he also had something to do with the compliments they often received on their well-behaved, friendly sons.

As James retrieved the large picnic basket with the food and joined them, Fern waved him on. "Go ahead and get that over to the food table," she said. "Gideon will keep an eye on me."

Over her head, James winked at Gideon, who flashed him a thumbs-up behind her back. "All right. If you're sure . . ."

"I'm sure."

James still didn't see Anabelle, but he knew a great many others. He was thanked for donating canned foods, recruited for the softball game to take place after the meal, and reminded that he had agreed to substitute teach for the third and fourth grade Sunday school class next month.

Finally, he delivered his dishes to the proper table and turned to find his family's table.

Standing right behind him was Kirstie Scott, Anabelle's daughter about whom he had heard so much recently.

"Hello, Kirstie," James said.

"Mr. Bell!" she said, her blue eyes warm and welcoming as she gave him a spontaneous hug. She looked a lot like Cam, James thought, except her delicate features made her extremely pretty. "Hello. I haven't seen you in ages." She chuckled. "I bet you go to the earlier service at church. I can barely make myself get up in time to get to the ten forty-five service."

James chuckled as he nodded. "We usually do attend the nine fifteen service." He held her at arms' length. "How are you?"

"I'm great. How about you?" She lowered her voice. "Are you worried about the hospital closing?"

"We're all worried," James told her. "But I guess your mom probably has told you about the Wall of Hope. We're trying to stay positive."

Kirstie's eyes dropped, and her smile faded. "I haven't seen much of my mother lately." She sighed. "In fact, I'm a terrible daughter. I've been avoiding her."

"You're not a terrible daughter," James said. "Trust me, I've met some children I wouldn't wish on my worst enemy, and you don't even come close."

Kirstie laughed as she studied his face. "She needs a new project," she told him, "to draw her attention and energy away from me."

James's eyebrows rose as he realized she wanted him to casually pass that thought along without Anabelle knowing where the suggestion came from. "A new project?"

"Maybe something involving children." Kirstie warmed to her theme. "Particularly children with handicaps."

The statement triggered a memory from several weeks earlier. "You know," he said, "I may have just the thing. I'll look into it."

Suddenly, Kirstie dodged to one side. "Uh-oh, there are my parents." She gave him a quick hug. "It was good to see you, Mr. Bell."

"You too, Kirstie." He expected her to head for her parents' car, but instead she turned and walked the other way, putting the crowd between them. Chagrinned, James realized the rift between his friend and her daughter was more than a simple misunderstanding.

Chapter Twenty-Two

*H*EY, MOMMY, LOOK WHAT I MADE AT DAY CAMP!"
Candace was barely through the door before Howie
pounced on her, eager to show her the rhythm
instrument he had made from a potato-chip can and rice kernels,
some paint, and heavily glued construction paper with the help
of his camp leader.

"This is beautiful," Candace told him. "I can see you worked
hard on it."

"Uh-huh, and everybody in my whole group has one."

"And did you all play them at once?" Candace looked over
her son's head and made a "silent-scream" face at her mother
as she envisioned a dozen preschool-aged kids all shaking those
things.

Janet turned away, shoulders shaking as she tried not to laugh.

"Yeah," Howie responded, oblivious to the adults' amusement. "We all shaked 'em while we sang the Days of the Week
song. Wanna hear it?"

"For the hundredth time," murmured her mother.

Candace grinned at her as she clapped and sang along with her son. "Go take a break, Mom. I'll do his bath."

As her mother disappeared into the family room, Candace shepherded Howie toward the stairs.

Brooke came out of her bedroom when she heard her mother. "Mommy!" She rushed to Candace and threw her arms around her. "I didn't think you'd get home before bedtime."

Candace nodded. "The lady who's having a baby is going to sleep all night, so I got to come home." She stroked her daughter's long, silky hair. It was so fair it looked white in many lights, just as Dean's often had. "How was your day, baby?"

Brooke considered it as seriously as she did nearly everything else. "Pretty good," she finally said. "My summer book club order came in. I forgot you let me order *four* books last time!"

"Have you started one?" Her daughter was a voracious reader, and she read well above her grade level. Candace was constantly searching for age-appropriate material that would keep Brooke interested.

The child nodded in response to her question. "I'll let you read them all when I'm done," she offered.

"Thank you. Have you had your shower yet?"

Brooke shook her head. "I was waiting until after Howie got his bath." Because, in the Hierarchy of Chronological Age, an elder sibling absolutely couldn't get ready for bed earlier than a younger one, Candace knew. It was a rule.

"All right," she said, "I'm going to get your brother in the bath right now. As soon as you hear the water stop running, you start your shower, okay?"

Brooke nodded. "Okay. Just as soon as I check my AllyKatzz." She was referring to a social networking site frequented by the girls around her age. It was a safe, parent-approved site, and Candace often sat with her when she was on the computer just to keep abreast of what the kids were talking about.

"All right, but just check. Five minutes."

Brooke nodded. "And then shower. I promise." She started down the hallway, hesitated and turned back. "Is your lady going to have her baby in the morning?"

"I don't know." Candace knelt to hug her daughter fiercely. "But she told me she wants to meet you, so maybe one day after she and her baby are home, we'll go see them."

"Oh, goody!" Brooke twirled in a circle, suddenly more care-free and giddy than she usually was. She loved babies, and Candace knew there would be no forgetting this conversation until Brooke got to see Robin's baby.

It had been a long day. Candace got both children in bed, ate a late bite of supper while she caught up with her mother and then tumbled into her own bed, almost too tired to give proper attention to her Bible study.

Just before she turned out her light, she turned onto her side and smiled at the framed photo of Dean that she kept on her bedside table. It was a close-up, taken one day when they had been vacationing along Lake Michigan. His hair was blown into odd tufts by the breeze, and his blue eyes sparkled with love. She had been the photographer, and he had just told her he loved her. It was a memory she cherished.

"Good night," she murmured as she snapped off the lamp. "I love you too."

Robin did not have her baby the following day, because Dr. Carpenter decided to try to hold off her labor for at least another twenty-four hours.

Andrew went to work after speaking with the doctor during rounds, although he made Candace promise to call immediately if anything changed. He was looking the worse for wear after getting very little sleep in the reclining lounge chair in Robin's room.

"I hope you don't work with machinery," Candace teased him before he left. "I'd be afraid you might cut off a finger."

"Nothing more dangerous than a pencil," he said. "I'm a loan officer at a bank."

The day was a busy one. Candace noted that Robin had plenty of company from family and friends, so she didn't worry about checking on the young woman too frequently.

She went in to say good-bye again before she left, and Andrew already had returned after cutting his workday short.

"You can't stay away, can you?" she asked, chuckling.

"I might," he said. "Tonight I'm going home to sleep in my own bed."

"Which you desperately need." Robin was out of bed, standing in front of her window looking out. "You're going home, too, aren't you?" she asked Candace. "I wish I were!"

"I'm sure you do. Try to relax, though. Remember that the longer the baby stays in the womb, the better. It may not be wildly wonderful for you, but every hour is helpful at this stage."

Robin nodded. "I know. Dr. Carpenter told me to stay off my feet. I'm just anxious."

Andrew looked solemn. "We'll be anxious until our baby is born living, breathing, kicking and healthy," he said. "It's worse this time, in a way, because now we know what can go wrong."

"Your baby is healthy," Candace reassured them. "This labor is going to be fine." She stopped, deliberately rolling her eyes in an exaggerated manner. "If labor can ever be called 'fine.'"

Robin and Andrew both laughed, and then he took her hand. "Come sit down, honey. I'll let you trounce me at backgammon again."

"Let me? You wish," she retorted as he tried to tug her toward a seat.

It was nice to see their banter.

That was something she missed so much. She and Dean had teased each other with gentle humor.

"Hey, honey? You've got something on your lip." Dean's blue eyes looked so earnest and innocent.

"Where?"

"Right here." And before she knew it, Dean had flicked her face with a jam-smeared finger, and then she really did have something on her lip.

Now his eyes were laughing as they gazed into hers. "Guess I'll just have to get it off."

"Ahhh! I fall for that every time!" But she was giggling, as he leaned forward and gently laid his lips against hers.

The memory was all the sweeter, because she had forgotten how Dean had teased her. She was so gullible, and he'd always been tricking her into kissing him in one way or another.

It had been nice being part of a couple. Now that she no longer was, she was acutely aware of all the little things she once had taken for granted.

Candace left the couple as they were laughing, Robin playfully slugging Andrew on the shoulder, to tend to her other patients.

Several hours later, Candace was approaching Robin's room near the nurses' station when she noticed Elena hailing her from behind the counter.

"Hey, Candace, guess what?"

"What?" She smiled. Her friend was, as usual, radiating enthusiasm.

"You'll never believe how much money we've raised."

"What were we up to the last time you told me? Seventy-couple thousand, I think. And now it's even more?"

"We hit the hundred-thousand-dollar mark today."

"Wow!" Candace stopped in her tracks. "That's terrific, Elena."

"I know. The *Dispatch* ran the first one of those interviews with a former patient, and there's been a spike in giving since then. If we see an increase every time Valera puts another of those interviews in the paper, I can't imagine how much we might make in donations."

"Donations for what?"

Candace and Elena both turned. Robin stood in the doorway of her room. "Sorry," she said. "I overheard you talking, and I'm just bored enough to be rude."

Candace laughed. "You're not being rude. We weren't exactly having a private conversation."

Elena said, "We were talking about the donations we are receiving for the Wall of Hope campaign the hospital is running. Are you familiar with it?"

Robin nodded, putting both hands up to massage her back. "Just what I've seen in the paper. Although I didn't see the interview you mentioned."

"You were a little preoccupied yesterday," Candace reminded her.

"I guess I was." She looked at Candace. "I did see the article with the picture of you. You donated a brick in memory of your husband. And, oh! You were in it too." Robin turned to Elena. "But I don't remember who your brick was for."

"It's in memory of my parents," Elena said.

"That's so nice." Robin's voice was sincere. She looked over her shoulder. "Andrew's going home soon to get the mail, so he'll be bringing the papers in too. I'll read the article then."

Dr. Carpenter had taken Robin off the drug designed to hold off contractions late on Saturday. The night and the following morning had come and gone uneventfully, as Candace learned when she arrived at three on Sunday. She had switched shifts with another nurse who needed the evening free. "Are you still here?" she teased, as she stuck her head into Robin's room to say hello.

Robin grinned. "You can't get rid of me."

"So Dr. Carpenter's satisfied everything's going fine?"

The young woman slipped out of the bed, stepping into her slippers. "She told me it could be anytime, or it could be days yet. Weeks even. She said she's seen it happen infrequently, but she's had women whose labor was stopped who didn't go into labor until their babies were full-term, and—*oh!*"

Candace began to laugh. "That's not going to happen to you."

Robin's water had broken in a huge gush of fluid that splashed across the floor. She was looking down, mouth open as if she was stunned. Then she said, "Darn. I really loved these slippers."

Candace laughed even harder. "Come on, let's get you into bed, and I'll call the doctor. You'll be holding that baby in your arms anytime now!"

"That would be nice," Robin said. "Can I just skip the next couple of hours?"

"Every woman on the planet wishes it worked that way," Candace said dryly. Then she looked around as something occurred to her. "Where's Andrew?"

"He's at home catching up on some things," Robin said. "I told him I'd call if I got discharged today."

"Better call him right now," Candace advised. "Contractions usually increase in length and severity after your water breaks."

Robin looked a bit shaken as she sucked in her breath. "I'm having one right now." Then her shoulders relaxed, and she smiled. "That wasn't too bad."

According to her records, Robin had an epidural that prevented her from feeling the end stages of labor pain the last time, as well as a mild sedative to help keep her calm during what had been a terrible trauma. *Oh, honey,* Candace thought. *Just wait.* But, ever the diplomat, she merely said, "Let me get a wheelchair. We need to move you down to one of the birthing suites and get you on a fetal monitor."

"A wheelchair! I can walk," Robin assured her.

"Probably," said Candace, "but for the sake of our liability premiums, it's a rule that all patients must be moved in a seated or reclining position, unless specifically noted." She delivered the line in a singsong tone that indicated she was reciting something very familiar.

Robin rolled her eyes and laughed. "Sheesh. Okay then, find me a chair. I'm ready to have this baby, even if it is a little early. I just want to hold him or her in my arms."

It didn't take long at all to move Robin into a birthing suite and help her don one of the maternity nighties she had brought along. At Hope Haven, laboring mothers were encouraged to bring along their own clothing when it conformed to hospital standards. It was part of the birthing suite experience to make the laboring woman feel more at home.

By that time, Andrew had arrived in a frantic rush. "Am I late? Is it time?"

"It's not time," Candace said, pushing him into a chair. "Take a deep breath. You're going to be here for a while."

Chapter Twenty-Three

ROBIN'S LABOR PROGRESSED FAIRLY QUICKLY. Although her first child had not lived, her body had been through the labor and delivery process before; and second labors often went faster. Candace stayed throughout the evening. Dr. Carpenter checked in a couple of times, pronouncing that labor was progressing nicely as Robin dilated steadily.

"You're doing great," the doctor told Robin. "Keep up the good work."

Robin grimaced as another contraction gripped her. "Do I have a choice? It's not like I can take a break!"

Andrew laughed, and Candace laid an understanding hand on Robin's. "It can be a little scary, can't it? I felt as if I was just along for the ride, as if my body had taken over and knew exactly what needed to happen, and my participation was definitely optional."

Robin nodded, as Andrew coached her to breathe. "Exactly. This is going to happen whether I want it to or not." Her voice quavered. "But I do want it to."

At 7:45, Robin announced she was hungry for lemon sherbet. Candace smiled sympathetically as she shook her head. "Trust me," she said, "it would be a really bad idea to put anything in your stomach right now."

Robin frowned. "But I really, really am dying for it. I can almost taste it!"

"Almost will have to do," Andrew told her.

Robin turned and glared at her husband. "Some help you are!"

"Oh, good," Candace quickly intervened. "You're starting into transition."

"How do you know without examining me?" The words had deflected Robin's ire.

"Because a deteriorating attitude often is a strong indicator of it," Candace told her, trying to be tactful. "Let me call Dr. Carpenter."

Robin groaned as an especially strong contraction hit. "Oh, that hu-u-urts."

"I know," Candace soothed. "Your cervix is dilating the rest of the way now. Each contraction is a good sign that you're getting close to being able to push that baby out."

Dr. Carpenter arrived quickly. After examining Robin, she gently lowered the sheet and smiled at the young mother. "You're almost there. This is going fast."

"Good." Robin was puffing and panting. Minutes later, she announced, "I have to push!"

"Wait! Don't push." Candace ran to the door. Dr. Carpenter was standing in the hallway, and she returned immediately. Sitting down on a low stool at the foot of the bed, she examined Robin, then said with a great deal of satisfaction. "Go ahead and push, Mrs. Overing. Your baby's ready to join your family!"

With Andrew's encouragement, Robin steadily pushed the baby down and out of the birth canal throughout the next hour. From his position by the head of Robin's bed, Andrew managed to take movies of the momentous occasion with one hand. The other was being mangled by his wife as she brought their child into the world. Finally, with one final effort, the infant slid into the doctor's hands.

Robin immediately said, "Is—"

But as the sounds of furious squalling filled the air, her question was answered. Tears began to roll down her face, as she turned to Andrew. "We have a baby!"

The young husband was crying too. "We do," he said, leaning over to kiss his wife.

"It's a girl," Candace told them. The child weighed five and a half pounds, which the doctor proclaimed was "a pretty good weight for an early bird."

The baby was pink and healthy, and she continued screaming for all she was worth, prompting the neonatologist who had been called to say, "You could have saved me a trip. There's nothing wrong with this one!"

"Oh, she has a head full of dark hair," Candace said as she tugged a tiny pink-and-white striped knit cap down over the baby's head. Expertly, she swaddled the infant, and then brought her over to lay her in Robin's arms. "Here you go."

Andrew leaned over, wrapping an arm around his wife's shoulders. He looked up at Candace, and there were tears in his eyes. "Thank you," he said. "Thank you for all your guidance. It's been a difficult couple of months."

Candace patted his shoulder. "The worst is behind you." She chuckled, deliberately seeking to lighten the moment. "Unless you count all the sleepless nights you're about to have."

Andrew laughed.

Robin smiled. Then she turned her head and gave Andrew a meaningful look.

Her husband handed the video camera to Riley Hohmann, who also was in the room. "Could you . . . ?"

"Sure thing." Riley took the camera. "I do this all the time."

Andrew turned back to Candace and cleared his throat. "We have a special surprise for you."

Candace was bewildered. "What? You're supposed to be *getting* gifts, not giving them!"

"You'll like this one," Robin promised. She held the baby up, and Candace automatically took the little bundle, smiling down into the tiny, wrinkled face as she patted and rocked gently, barely realizing she was making the motions.

"Candace Crenshaw," Robin said, "meet Anna Candace Overing."

Anna Candace—Candace couldn't absorb it. "You're—you're naming her after me?" she whispered incredulously. Tears rose and her throat swelled; she knew she was going to cry.

Andrew rose and placed his free arm around her, still holding Robin's hand with the other as he looked down at their new baby. "We couldn't think of anyone whom we'd rather she grew up to be like," he said.

Robin was kept in the hospital so that she could begin her chemotherapy treatments the very next day. It had been her compromise with the oncologist, who had wanted her to start them immediately after the surgery, assuring her that chemo during the third trimester had been shown to be safe. Robin had hoped to put it off until she had breast-fed for several months, but she finally let go of that dream.

Now that she was able to hold little Anna in her arms, her first priority was ensuring her own good health so that she would have many years with her daughter.

Candace stopped in to visit with her for a few minutes before she began her treatments.

"Candace, I've made a decision," Robin said.

"Oh? About what?"

Robin smiled. "I would like to volunteer to be interviewed for one of your articles. That is, if you still are looking for people. I owe this hospital and all of you so very much—"

"You know you don't 'owe' us anything," Candace interrupted. "We just do our jobs."

"You do far more than your jobs," Robin replied. "And that's what I'd like to say. Hope Haven employs exceptional people . . . people like you. You have gone far above 'just' your job. You befriended me, you explained things in terms I could understand, you were honest with me, you nurtured my faith. . . .

"Oh, Candace, you can't know how deeply Andrew and I appreciate everything you've done. Speaking out in support of the hospital would be a small way to thank you and everyone here at Hope Haven." She looked around fondly. "What a wonderful place this is."

Candace couldn't agree more. "It is very special," she agreed. "I'll pass your message on to Elena. I'm sure someone will be in touch with you." She bent and gave the other woman a warm hug. "I will be praying for you during your chemo. Be sure to let me know how it's going."

A week after the birth of Robin's baby, Candace sat on a bench in the park watching her children play when she saw a familiar couple walking hand in hand along one of the park's walking trails near the edge of the playground. The man wore a baby carrier snuggled against his chest, and Candace could see two tiny legs dangling from it.

"Brooke?" Candace called. "Could you please watch your brother for a moment while I go talk to someone?"

"Where are you going?" Brooke asked, ever-cautious. She already was playing with Howie. The two children had been swinging for nearly half an hour, with Brooke occasionally taking time out to push her little brother.

"Right over there." Candace pointed to the couple.

"Okay."

Candace rose and walked toward the edge of the playground. "Robin!" she called. "Andrew! Hello."

"Hi, Candace." Robin beamed as she and her family turned and began to walk across the grass toward her. "How are you?"

"I'm good," Candace said, smiling. "How are you three doing?"

Andrew grinned. "We're great. Anna is already sleeping through the night, so we're not even the typically sleep-deprived new parents."

Candace laughed. "Lucky for you!"

"What are you doing here?" Robin asked. "Are your children here?"

"Right over there on the swings," Candace said.

"I'd love to meet them," Robin said, and by mutual accord, the three adults turned and headed for the swings.

"How's the chemo going?" Candace asked.

Robin shrugged her shoulders. "I haven't noticed any side effects yet, although it's still the early days. The doctor says different people tolerate it to varying degrees, so I'm hoping I'm one of the super-tolerant ones." She grinned.

Candace chuckled. "I hope so too." As they approached the swings, she said, "Brooke, Howie, these are my friends Mr. and Mrs. Overing and their new baby, Anna."

Brooke immediately slowed her swing and jumped off the seat. "Hi! Can I see your baby?"

In contrast, Howie gave them an indifferent wave and pumped his legs to make his swing go higher.

Andrew laughed. "Yeah. That's about how I felt about grown-ups and babies when I was his age."

Candace nodded wryly. "Mr. Manners, he's not."

Robin smiled and held out a hand as Brooke approached. "Hello, Brooke. It's nice to meet you." To Candace, she said, "She looks like you used to, although her coloring's different."

Brooke caught the reference and glanced at her mother questioningly. Candace said, "Robin was my neighbor when I was growing up. I used to babysit for her when she was a little younger than you."

"Wow!" Brooke received this news as if she'd just caught a glimpse of vital history, and both women laughed. "Way back in the day."

"Yeah," Robin said, still chuckling. "It was a long time ago." She indicated the grass at their feet. "If we sit down, would you like to hold the baby?"

Brooke's eyes rounded. "Oh yes," she said.

The four of them took a seat on the grass, and Andrew gently withdrew the baby from the sling. She was sleeping soundly, one little fist curled up near her mouth. Robin said, "She always sleeps like that. We expect her to start sucking her thumb any day."

Robin took the baby from her husband and carefully laid her in the cradle of Brooke's arms, adjusting them slightly. "There. You always want to make sure you support the baby's head until she's old enough to hold it up by herself."

"Okay." Brooke looked down at the infant in her arms, and Candace had to suppress a chuckle. Brooke looked as though she was afraid to move. "She's beautiful," the little girl said.

"Our baby has a very special name," Robin told her.

"What?" Brooke breathed.

"Anna Candace."

Brooke's eyes widened. "She's named after my mother?"

Robin nodded. "Yes. Your mother is a very special lady."

"She is?" Brooke sounded surprised that other people noticed this, and Candace grinned.

"Thanks, kiddo."

Brooke grinned back. "Aw, Mom, I didn't mean it like *that*." She turned to Robin. "Why is my mom special to you?"

Robin heaved a sigh. "I was sick when I was expecting Anna. For a while, I was even afraid I might not live."

Brooke's eyes grew so large they eclipsed the rest of her small face.

"But your mother," Robin went on, "your mother would not let me think negative thoughts. She even went to my doctor's appointments with me and explained some of the scary medical stuff."

Brooke smiled. "She's good at that." She looked down at the baby in her arms. "What would have happened to your baby if you died?"

Robin looked a little taken aback.

"Brooke," Candace began. "That's a very personal question—"

"But it's a good one, and I don't mind answering." Robin's gaze met Candace's over the little girl's head. "I was worried," she said, "because I would have hated to leave her when she needed me. But even if I did have to leave her, I knew she would be okay, because she had her daddy and grandparents to help."

"My father died," Brooke told her.

"I know," Robin said softly. "That must hurt a lot.

Candace bit her lip, afraid that if she tried to speak, she might sob. Without even realizing it, Robin was addressing Brooke's deepest sorrow.

Robin went on. "I thought about it a lot when I was sick, and you know what I think?"

Brooke looked up at her. Candace noticed she was running one index finger very lightly over the baby's soft fuzzy hair.

Robin said, "I think that one of the reasons God gives us mothers and fathers and grandmothers and grandfathers and other family members too—"

"Like my Aunt Susan?" Brooke was referring to Candace's elder sister.

"Like your aunt." Robin didn't miss a beat. "The reason God gives us all those people is so that when something bad and sad happens to someone we love, there are other people we love around to help us and care for us." She reached out and gently wiggled the baby's tiny toes, and they all laughed when Anna screwed up her little face momentarily in response and drew her leg away.

They were all silent for a few moments. Candace could almost see the wheels turning in Brooke's head, as she considered the things Robin had said.

Finally, the little girl broke the silence. "Maybe someday when I'm older, I could babysit for you," Brooke said in a very soft voice.

"I think that's a great idea," Robin said immediately. "How old are you?"

"Eleven." She looked up, her blue eyes wide and hopeful.

"*Hmm*," Robin turned to Andrew. "You know, honey, I think an eleven-year-old could be a very good mother's helper. You know, she could hold Anna while I fold laundry and do a little cleaning, and she could give her a bottle—"

"And I could push her stroller if we went to the park," Brooke offered.

Robin looked at Candace. "What would you say if I borrowed your daughter every once in a while, Candace? Do you think she would do a good job?"

"I think she would do an excellent job," Candace responded, trying to steady her trembling lips.

"Me too," Robin said. "She's your daughter, and I know what a good babysitter you were. You can teach Brooke everything you know."

Candace found it easier to smile this time, and her heart felt a little lighter than it had in a long, long time. "I'd be glad to."

The following week, Candace, James, Elena and Anabelle planned to gather in the courtyard for lunch on Thursday. It was significantly warmer and more humid than the day they first had gotten together; but it was so pleasant to be outside that no one minded.

Summer was progressing, and the baby cardinals had flown from the tree. This time next year, Candace thought, this area would have gotten a face-lift with the Wall of Hope, a paved courtyard and some new, lovely landscaping. She couldn't wait to see it!

Anabelle's eyes were shining, and she looked especially happy.

"Something must be going right in your life," Candace commented. "Spill."

Anabelle laughed as she did a spontaneous little victory dance. "I just got a phone call from Kirstie. She invited me to go shopping with her on Saturday." She cleared her throat. "I've been trying really hard not to be overbearing and intrusive."

"Sounds like it's working," James said. He grinned at her. "It's a whole new way of life."

Anabelle shook a mock-fist at him. "Smarty pants."

Elena was the last to arrive. She was grinning from ear to ear, her wide smile gleaming in the bright sun.

"Goodness gracious!" Anabelle said. "Don't you look like . . . " She paused for a moment. "Well, like the cat who swallowed the canary."

"There's a reason people use that cliché," James told her. "You can picture the type of smile immediately." He turned to Elena. "What's going on?"

"You'll never believe it." Elena dropped onto the picnic bench, fanning herself dramatically. "I'm in shock."

"Not too much shock to tell us why, I hope," Candace said.

Elena sat up straight. She looked around the group, milking every moment of suspense. "Drumroll, puh-leeeze!"

James obligingly began a rapid finger tap against the edge of the table.

"The hospital," Elena announced, "has received a two-million-dollar donation."

Candace was sure she hadn't heard that correctly. "*How much?*"

"Two million," Elena repeated. "That's one hundred thousand *times twenty*. I can't even imagine it."

Anabelle shook her head in wonder. "Are you sure? That's an awful lot of money."

"I'm sure. I saw the check." She grinned. "But only for a minute, because Zane was heading straight for the bank. He was terrified to have a check that big in his hands."

"Where did the money come from?" Candace still couldn't believe it. Who on earth would donate that large a sum? For that matter, who could?

Elena said, "Remember when Dr. Weller treated the little boy who blew off two of his fingers and nearly lost an eye in that fireworks accident last summer?"

"Yes." Anabelle shuddered. "That was really difficult."

Elena continued, "Dr. Weller gave him excellent emergency care. He also got a helicopter in quickly to take the child to Children's Memorial in Chicago, and he personally went along."

James chimed in, "The board reprimanded him for not following established protocol for flight transfers, but if he hadn't skipped protocol, that child might have lost his eye."

"What does this have to do with the donation?" Candace steered them back to the original topic.

"The grandparents are quite wealthy. They were horrified when they heard Hope Haven might have to close. That family lived the experience we've all talked about—if this hospital hadn't been here, that child's outcome might have been very different. They feel very strongly about keeping our doors open."

"Two million dollars," James said slowly. "But even that won't last very long."

"Zane told me this morning that we're very close to raising enough money to keep the hospital open for at least the next year."

"That *is* excellent news," Candace said. "I've been wondering whether I'm foolish not to be looking for other work. But that is a sign that I am meant to stay here."

"There is one catch, though," Elena admitted. "They stipulated that the money go into a trust or endowment that would supply interest income. So we really won't be getting two million to spend."

"Still," Candace said, "it's quite a gift."

"Especially for one single brick!" Elena said with a grin. "I would have given them a dozen, but one is all they want."

"How did your meeting with Cam go this morning?" Anabelle asked.

"The campaign is going unbelievably well. We have enough bricks now to build an entire wall about waist-high around the courtyard. That's what we met to talk about. Cam thinks we should use additional donations to pave the courtyard with engraved bricks as well."

"That's a great idea." Anabelle gave it her seal of approval in the form of a short burst of clapping.

"Your husband is a genius," Elena told her. "No wonder your property is so beautiful all year-round. He's got an entire plan in his head for landscaping this area." She reached down and picked up a cardboard tube, opening the end and sliding out a large sheet of paper. "Here's the plan for the courtyard. Wanna see?"

"Of course we want to see," Candace said. She held one end of the rolled paper as Elena smoothed it across the picnic table.

James moved to hold down the other end, freeing Elena to point to various areas. "As I told you, the wall itself will be three feet high. Cam has worked built-in planters into the design here, here, and here; and these spaces in the middle are for two ornamental trees. It's about twice the size this little spot is right now."

Candace was dazzled by the project. Cam's careful drawings brought it into focus, and she could practically see the finished product. "This is going to be stunning!"

"I know." Elena took the drawings and rerolled them. "I can't wait until we get started."

All three women turned to regard James.

"Have you made a decision yet?" Elena asked him.

James wouldn't look at any of them. "I have," he said quietly.

There was a moment of silence fraught with tension. Candace tried to imagine how their little group would change without James, whom it appeared was planning to—

"I turned down the job at Children's. I'm staying."

"James, that's *wonderful*." Anabelle was beaming as Elena leapt up and gave him a huge hug.

"I'm so happy to hear that." Candace's heart felt so light she couldn't stop smiling. "What made you decide to stay?"

James shrugged. "It was a number of things." He looked at each of them. "You," he said to Elena, "are working so hard on fund-raising to keep Hope Haven open. And you." He pointed at Anabelle. "You impressed on me how much the four of us need each other's support. All of us are stronger because of this little group."

Finally he looked at Candace. "You gave me faith too," he told her with a smile. "You and I have similar situations in that we both support families on one income. If you are willing to place your faith in this place staying open, how can I do any less?"

Candace sent him a gentle smile. "I continue to have faith that Hope Haven will get through this financial crunch."

"I'm awfully glad you're planning to stay," Anabelle said. "I have to thank all of you for your hand-holding while I adjust to my empty nest. Our little group just wouldn't be the same without you, James." Then the older woman reached down beside her and lifted a large canvas bag into her lap. "I brought a little something for each of you," she told them. "I thought it was time to celebrate our friendship."

She shook the bag upside down on the table, and several T-shirts in a lovely shade of sky blue tumbled out. Picking them up and checking the sizes, she distributed one to Elena, to James and to Candace, picking up the last one for herself. Each shirt had the recipient's name and "Hope Haven Hospital" on the left front pocket area. "Look at the back," Anabelle urged.

"Oh, this is great!" Elena crowed. "Thank you, Anabelle."

James read the script on the back aloud. It was Romans 15:13. "'May the God of hope fill you with all joy and peace in believing, so that by the power of the Holy Spirit you may abound in hope.'" He looked up, grinning. "That's a good reminder for me, isn't it?"

"It's good for all of us," Anabelle said. "I chose the color because it reminded me of the color of the summer sky, and summer is when we really got to know each other."

"This is beautiful," Candace told Anabelle. "Thank you. I'll wear it with pleasure and think of you every time I put it on."

Anabelle's eyes shone; she was clearly moved by the reception of her gifts.

Candace glanced at her watch. She had a lady in labor upstairs, and she needed to get back. "I have to run," she said, "but could we share a prayer before I do?"

"Great idea," Elena said.

They all joined hands. Elena opened, then Anabelle and James spoke.

When it was Candace's turn, she prayed with a heartfelt fervor inspired by the three believers around the circle. After a brief pause, she concluded with: "And Lord, thank You for the gift of these new and precious friendships, the support we offer one another and the joy that we share in our hearts. Bless us each one. Amen."

As she looked around at the smiling, chattering group of people about whom she had come to care so much, she felt that somehow, some way, she was beginning a new chapter in her life—a chapter filled with friends, family and the faith that right here at Hope Haven Hospital was where she was meant to be.

About the Author

Award-winning author Anne Marie Rodgers has published more than forty novels since 1992, several of which have been best sellers. Her work for Guideposts includes stories in the series Tales from Grace Chapel Inn and Mystery and the Minister's Wife.

Anne Marie has been involved in animal rescue and foster-care efforts for many years. After Hurricane Katrina, she volunteered at the Humane Society of Louisiana, saving animals left behind during evacuation efforts. She also has raised guide dog puppies. Anne Marie currently volunteers at a wildlife rehabilitation facility near her home in State College, Pennsylvania, where she cares for orphaned and injured animals, which are released into the wild after their health is restored. The experience has allowed her to get up close and personal with bobcats, fishers, and bald and golden eagles, along with many other more common species.

In addition to her work with animals, Anne Marie enjoys a variety of needle arts and sings with her church choir.

Read on for a sneak peek of the next exciting and heartfelt book in *Stories from Hope Haven*.

It's available through Guideposts' direct mail program by calling Customer Service at (800) 932-2145.

Chasing THE *Wind*
by
Patricia H. Rushford

OR SOME FOLKS, MONDAY MORNINGS WERE A drag, having to get up early and trudge to work after a restful or fun-filled weekend. To Anabelle, morning was a gift. Though she enjoyed her days off, she loved her job in the Cardiac Care Unit at Hope Haven Hospital. She also loved new beginnings and mornings were just that: a time to reflect and aim for new opportunities.

Anabelle yawned and did a few stretches before heading for the shower. After drying her short, easy to style hair, she dressed in navy slacks and a pastel floral top. Makeup was a matter of dashing a little mascara on her lashes and blush on her cheeks—and lately, drawing pencil lines on her vanishing eyebrows.

She grabbed one of half a dozen lab coats that hung in her closet, made sure she had her glasses and name badge and headed out of the bedroom.

Cameron was still sleeping and probably would be until seven when he'd have his coffee, read the paper and go to the gym for a workout. Not that he needed a gym. Their small farm kept him busy enough. The property included two pastures and a small barn, which housed a number of cats and a palomino gelding named Rusty, owned by Heather Jones, the darling twelve-year-old neighbor girl. The Joneses paid them thirty dollars a month to keep Rusty in their pasture since they had no land other than their small lot.

She smiled not feeling the least bit resentful of Cam's retirement. With the amount of time he spent puttering around the farm and his shop and helping their son Evan out with his landscaping business, he was busier now than when he'd worked full time. But he seemed happy and that's what counted.

Anabelle poured coffee from the full carafe on the coffeemaker. She enjoyed being able to set the timer the night before and having the coffee perfectly brewed when she was ready for it.

How spoiled they were getting. She smiled and set the carafe back, knowing it would stay warm for Cameron. It hadn't been that many years ago when she'd shuffled out to the kitchen first thing in the morning all blurry-eyed to put the coffee on. Back then they'd had few choices and always bought Folgers. Now she preferred the special roasts and usually ground them herself.

Taking her Kinkade design cup to one of her two favorite spots in the wide living room, Anabelle set it on the end table and opened the vertical blinds to the sliding patio door. She pulled open the door and breathed in the fresh damp air. Her plants had weathered the rain just fine.

After closing the door, she sank into the cushioned rocking chair that had once been her mother's. Placing her feet on the ottoman, she paused to enjoy a patch of sunshine as it dappled the trees in the private backyard and turned last night's rain into crystal droplets. Moments later clouds blotted out the patch of blue sky.

Summer was coming to an end. Soon the leaves would be turning. The vine maple had already begun wearing its fall regalia. She still had some dahlias along with several large hydrangeas blooming. The leggy geraniums would need cutting back soon and she needed to deadhead the roses. Maybe she'd have time after work today—if the weather cooperated.

Anabelle slipped on her reading glasses and dipped into her basket of books and magazines. This year she'd chosen to use Oswald Chambers' *My Utmost for His Highest* as her daily devotional. Starting the day in thoughtful introspection and prayer always seemed to improve her perspective on life no matter what lay ahead.

Today, Anabelle had a hard time staying focused. Her mind kept going back-and-forth, from reading about prayer life to thinking about Drew Hamilton. She finally gave up reading and spent the next few moments praying specifically for the good doctor whose wife Genevieve was worried about his health.

After fishing a package of salmon out of the freezer for dinner, Anabelle poured a glass of orange juice and ate a quick granola and yogurt breakfast. At six thirty, she backed her new silver Ford Fusion out of the garage and headed into the rain.

Wipers swished at the sheets of water but did little good. She smiled at the irony. With all the innovations made on automobiles lately, it seemed someone could invent a better way of clearing the window in a downpour.

Her new sedan got around forty miles per gallon and could go about seven hundred miles before needing a fill-up. The dashboard with all its buttons and displays looked like the panel of a 747. She still didn't know what half of them were for.

Anabelle maneuvered the car along the familiar road, barely able to see the bulky shapes of cars and trucks. The two and a half miles to Hope Haven took twice as long to navigate as it normally did. Finally the hospital loomed ahead of her. By rote, she eased into her usual spot in the staff parking lot. Retrieving her floral umbrella with a Monet garden scene from the backseat pocket, Anabelle waited for a few moments in hopes the rain would subside. No such luck. If she waited much longer, she'd be late. And Anabelle Scott was *never* late.

She opened her umbrella and made a dash for the door. She held the door open for several other staff members including Elena Rodriguez, her good friend who worked in Intensive Care.

"Thank you!" Elena sounded winded. "I forgot to grab my umbrella this morning. Too much else on my mind, I guess." Elena shook the rain from her long dark hair. "But what's a little rain? I'm certainly not going to melt." She laughed. "Although for a few minutes there, I was afraid I might wash away."

"You're in a good mood." Anabelle closed her umbrella and shook off some of the water.

Elena's dark features brightened even more. "I am. Isabel is turning five in two weeks and I am going to throw her a big party."

"That sounds delightful. I must say, I envy you having that darling little girl around." Anabelle pressed the elevator button and the doors swished open.

"I know you do." Elena gave her an empathetic smile. It wasn't the first time Anabelle had brooded over not having a grandchild of her own. "You are always welcome to share Isabel with me—especially when I need a babysitter."

"You are too kind." Anabelle chuckled.

"In fact, Isabel told me to be sure to invite Auntie *Amabelle* first. You are her favorite person since you made her that adorable princess quilt."

"Well, you tell her I'm honored." Having her quilts used and loved by those who received them gave Anabelle as much joy as making them.

The women hurried to their lockers where Anabelle removed her rain jacket and umbrella. She adjusted the long chain that held her reading glasses and tucked the glasses into the upper pocket of her lab coat. Pausing at Elena's locker, she asked, "Want to plan on lunch around noon?"

"I'll do my best." Elena pulled her long dark hair into a ponytail and twisted it into a scruffy bun. She was wearing her *Finding Nemo* scrubs. Elena, being a talented seamstress, made many of her own clothes. "You know how crazy Intensive Care can get."

"Cardiac Care as well. Let us hope for an uneventful day."

"Right. And what dream world are you living in?" She laughed at the idea.

"We can always think positive." Walking away, Anabelle had no illusions of a quiet day in CCU. They had at least one patient going to surgery with more likely to come as patients received diagnoses.

"See you later," Elena called after her.

Anabelle took the stairs to the second floor and turned right to go into the Cardiac Care Unit. She stepped inside her office and left the door open to air the small space out. The stacks of files and notes on her desk told her the weekend must have been hectic.

Anabelle pulled out her glasses and scanned the weekend happenings to bring herself up to date. They'd admitted a couple of patients who were sent home on Sunday. Mr. Blake had been admitted the day before in preparation for his surgery this morning, as well as Olga Pederson, a woman admitted at five this morning. *Age 83—atrial fibrillation.*

Anabelle paused to check the schedule for the day's surgeries. Though she worked in Cardiac Care, she liked to keep up on other areas as well. This morning, however, she had a specific reason. Dr. Hamilton would be doing the open-heart surgery on Mr. Blake at 8:00 AM, which meant he probably wouldn't be out of surgery until around one. She'd try to talk with him then about his wife's concerns. Genna had confided in Anabelle at their quilting club meeting that her husband was overworking himself and she had asked Anabelle to keep an eye on him.

Tucking her concern for him toward the back of her mind, Anabelle took off her glasses, slipped them into her pocket, then grabbed her clipboard and headed to the unit. She checked her watch and inhaled a deep breath. Just in time for report. There, she, the day nurses and the aides would hear details about each patient and formulate care plans for the rest of their shifts.

In his rush to get to work, James Bell forgot to take a jacket, and by the time he arrived at the hospital, the rain was coming down in sheets. In the race from his car to the staff entrance, the rain soaked through everything. A large puddle remained in the elevator as he stepped out onto the third floor where he then slogged to his locker.

Like many of the nurses who wore scrubs, James usually changed at the hospital. He preferred wearing the hospital-provided blue or green, which saved Fern and him from having to do even more laundry than they already had. He removed his shoes and set them in the bottom of his locker while pulling out his white clogs. He hung his damp jeans on a hook to dry and pulled a fresh pair of scrubs off the linen cart.

James barely made it in time for report. Susan Mills, head nurse for the unit, smiled up at him. "Rough morning?"

He grinned and wiped a hand over his wet hair. "I'm good. Dr. Hamilton called me last night to assist with his open-heart this morning."

James entered the General Surgery Suite which was situated next to Day Surgery on the third floor, and went straight to the sinks. He performed the presurgical washing ritual they always did. James stood next to Dr. Hamilton and sensed that something was off. Moisture beaded on the older man's forehead and he looked uncomfortable. "Are you feeling all right, sir?"

"I'm fine." He took in a sharp breath. "A little heartburn is all. I should know better than to eat sausage for breakfast."

The cardiac surgeon, Harriet Hildebrand—Dr. Hildie to her patients and much of the staff—arrived and began talking with Dr. Hamilton about their patient, Dillon Blake. James completed his scrub, shoved his arms into the gown the operating room nurse held out to him and turned so she could tie it behind his back. He donned gloves and headed into the sterile area.

One nurse was assigned to stand watch to keep the area sterile. Another laid out instruments on the trays, and the anesthesiologist sat at the patient's head watching the monitor. The patient murmured something unintelligible as a nurse told him he'd be asleep in less than a minute, which he was. The tray holding the heart-lung machine, which would support the patient's circulation during the surgery, sat at the ready. Even though the surgery was commonly done, James couldn't help feeling anxious.

The doctors approached the patient and the procedure began. Within minutes the man's chest had been opened and clamped. James had seen the inside of the chest cavity many times, but seeing someone's heart beat was nothing short of a miracle. He prayed the surgery would go well and that the heart valve would be repaired.

James watched intently, handing off instruments as Dr. Hamilton asked for them, anticipating his every move. The heart-lung machine took over the work of the patient's heart so that repairs could be made. Everything was running very smoothly.

Then, very suddenly, Dr. Hamilton moaned and began to sway. The instrument he was holding clattered to the floor.

"Oh no!" someone shouted.

"He's going down!" James' adrenaline kicked into high gear. He grabbed Dr. Hamilton under the arms and pulled him back away from the patient and toward the door.

In the ensuing chaos, Dr. Hildebrand stepped in and seamlessly took her colleague's place. She quickly reordered the room and the OR staff continued on as if nothing had happened.

But something *had* happened. James paid little attention to the surgical team now. He had taken one look at the doctor's ashen face and sweating brow, put his ear to the doctor's chest and began shouting orders.

"Call a code blue."

James immediately started chest compressions as a respiratory therapist tipped Dr. Hamilton's head back to establish an airway and attach valve mask resuscitator.

"Code blue surgery. Code blue surgery."

The operator's loud steady voice repeated the order again and again over the hospital's PA system. Within seconds the emergency response team appeared. While James continued the compressions, four members of the team lifted Dr. Hamilton onto a stretcher. James rose with the stretcher and ran with them as they moved him from the operating arena to the Day Surgery Unit.

James kept up the compressions, then stepped back when the paddles appeared and one of the nurses yelled, "Clear!"

Someone had already hooked the doctor up to a portable heart monitor. The first jolt with the paddles produced no change in his weak heart rate. A second zap along with the epinephrine got the heart beating on its own. Dr. Hamilton's heart transitioned into a normal sinus rhythm.

James felt like he'd just run a marathon. He sat for a moment while the team took Dr. Hamilton into one of the Day Surgery cubicles and hooked him up to the necessary monitors.

Since Dr. Hildebrand was still in surgery, James took it upon himself to call Dr. Hamilton's wife at their home. After several rings, he heard the voice mail greeting and began to speak. "Mrs. Hamilton, this is James Bell at the hospital. It's your husband, ma'am. We need you to come to the hospital as soon as possible."

A Note from the Editors

Guideposts, a nonprofit organization, touches millions of lives every day through products and services that inspire, encourage and uplift. Our magazines, books, prayer network and outreach programs help people connect their faith-filled values to their daily lives.

Your purchase of *Stories from Hope Haven* does make a difference! To comfort hospitalized children, Guideposts Outreach has created Comfort Kits for free distribution. A hospital can be a very scary place for sick children. With all the hustle and bustle going on around them, the strange surroundings, and the pain they're experiencing, is it any wonder kids need a little relief?

Inside each easy-to-carry Comfort Kit is a prayer card, a journal, a pack of crayons, an "I'm Special" wristband to wear alongside the hospital-issued one and a plush golden star pillow to cuddle. It's a welcome gift and has a powerful effect in helping to soothe a child's fears.

To learn more about our many nonprofit outreach programs, please visit www.guidepostsfoundation.org.